Debbie Johnson is an award-winning author who lives and works in Liverpool, where she divides her time between writing, caring for a small tribe of humans and animals, and not doing the housework. She writes feel-good emotional women's fiction, and has sold more than a million books worldwide. She is published globally, and has had two books optioned for film and TV.

facebook.com/debbiejohnsonauthor
x.com/debbiemjohnson

Also by Debbie Johnson

The Comfort Food Café series

Summer at the Comfort Food Café

Christmas at the Comfort Food Café

Coming Home to the Comfort Food Café

Sunshine at the Comfort Food Café

A Gift from the Comfort Food Café

A Wedding at the Comfort Food Café

Standalones

Cold Feet at Christmas

Pippa's Cornish Dram

Never Kiss a Man in a Christmas Jumper

The Birthday That Changed Everything

The A-Z of Everything

THE COMFORT FOOD CAFÉ

DEBBIE JOHNSON

One More Chapter
a division of HarperCollins*Publishers* Ltd
1 London Bridge Street
London SE1 9GF
www.harpercollins.co.uk
HarperCollins*Publishers*
Macken House, 39/40 Mayor Street Upper,
Dublin 1, D01 C9W8

This paperback edition 2024
1
First published in Great Britain in ebook format
by HarperCollins*Publishers* 2024

A catalogue record of this book is available from the British Library

ISBN: 978-0-00-868545-4

Printed and bound in the UK using 100% Renewable Electricity
by CPI Group (UK) Ltd

This one is for my wonderful Facebook community – thank you for all your support!

STAFF WANTED - MUST BE COMFORTING!

We are looking for a hard-working and enthusiastic person to join the team at our busy seaside café on the glorious south coast. To put it into food terms, the main ingredients in this recipe are: friendliness, empathy, the ability to both work under pressure and to sit around eating cake, and basic cooking skills (though we won't turn our nose up at advanced cooking skills!). Absolutely essential ingredients are a robust sense of humour, being a good listener, and having a genuine interest in human beings – because at our café, you're just as likely to be listening to somebody's life story as serving them lunch. If you have catering experience, great – but it's not vital. More important is your experience of life. Pay is average, but the job comes with free muffins, and a place in a bustling and supportive community in a beautiful part of the world. The role will initially be offered on a trial of three months to see if we're a good fit, and we can help you with accommodation if you're not local. Family, pets, and personal quirks are all very welcome. If you're interested, send us your heart and soul in email form, telling us why you think you're right for the job.

Posted by Laura Hunter-Walker, manager of the Comfort Food Café

Chapter One

Dear Laura,

First of all, I have to be honest: I'm writing this on behalf of my mum, Maxine (though everyone calls her Max). She has no clue I'm sending this email, and she'd probably kill me if she did, but I'm willing to risk death to do this, because something about your job advert made me think it was perfect for her. You know when something just makes you tingle because it's so right, like all your spider senses have been set off, but in a good way?

I was considering coming up with a dramatic back story to catch your eye—like our father is a gambling addict and lost our family home in a high-stakes poker game at a casino in Montenegro, or Mum has just come out of a decade-long coma after a freak unicycle accident. Something with oomph that would make her stand out from the crowd.

In the end I decided that would be a fib too far. I'm

already being shady, sneaking around behind her back, without lying about her as though she's not interesting enough in real life. I think that's already one of her problems: she doesn't think she's interesting anymore, and it won't help if her own daughter fictionalises her as well. She's had a few years of Totally Crap Things happen, and now she seems to have deflated. She's a bit like one of those squashed helium balloons that got stuck on a bush, and it makes me really sad for her.

The other day, we were watching *Dracula*—you know that old version with Keanu Reeves and Gary Oldman in it? Though she told me off for calling it the 'old version', because apparently 1992 was only five years ago in her head... Anyway, I'm sure you know the one. She said, after it finished, that if she was in a story like that, she wouldn't be Dracula, or Van Helsing, or Mina, or one of the glamorous vampire chicks. She wouldn't even be Renfield, she said—she'd maybe be in with a chance at being the servant who empties Renfield's slop bucket at the asylum. That's how much she sees herself as a background character, and I absolutely hate it. Everyone should be the star of their own story, shouldn't they—or at least the co-star?

That all sounds a bit depressing, I know, but I wanted to explain why I'm doing this. My mum needs a change, badly. She needs to get away from her life and make a fresh start, somewhere new, where she can stop seeing herself as dull and unimportant. She needs to feel useful, not like Renfield's slop bucket slave. At the moment she's forgotten all the good things about herself, like how kind she is, how funny she is, how she's the type of person who keeps a pocketful of pound coins every time she goes into town to give to homeless people. How she always stops and chats to them when everyone else tries to walk as far away as they can.

How she's always the one who gives up her seat on the bus, or helps a mum carry a buggy up the stairs, or offers to pay for someone's shopping if they've forgotten their purse. This stuff used to make me roll my eyes and feel embarrassed when I was younger, but now I see these little things for what they are: the signs that my mum, my lovely mum, is a really decent person who deserves better than what life has given her recently.

I'm nearly nineteen now, and all my friends still think she's the best and wish she'd adopt them. Everyone always hung out at our house—she was the mum who'd always give us lifts, or provide pizza, and bring the mattresses downstairs so we could have a movie night sleepover in the living room. The 'treat box' was never empty, and she always had a smile on her face. She rarely lost her rag, even when someone had puked Malibu and Coke on the dog (true story). She'd just pull a face and say 'well, we've all been there…'

Stuff like this should be more important, shouldn't it? It should get more respect in the world. I mean, she's never been famous or had a high-flying career, but she's so kind and brilliant and nice, and I think that makes her extraordinary.

If you're wondering why she's going through such a low spell in her life, it's not one big dramatic thing. It's like a cavalcade of crap, a snowball of shit that's built up and up until it's basically squashed her (excuse my language but they're the mildest words I can use). I'll tell you about it, but this isn't in order—it all kind of smushed together anyway.

Her mum, my nana, died about a year and a half ago. It wasn't a tragedy—she was in her late seventies—but Mum had looked after her for years after her dad passed away. So she didn't just lose her mum, which would have been bad enough—I think she lost a bit of her purpose as well. She'd been caring for her for so long and suddenly she was gone, and that left a big nana-shaped hole in her heart and her life.

Then a while ago, she got made redundant from her job in a supermarket. I know it doesn't sound exciting, and honestly, when I was younger, I was a bit embarrassed when she used to turn up at school in her uniform (yes, I seemed to spend a lot of time being embarrassed; I think this is a normal girl thing). I suppose I wanted my mum to be more exotic, like a movie star or a footballer's wife or even just someone who worked in an office and wore high heels.

Thing is, she loved her job—loved all her regulars, and chatting to everyone who popped in, and telling me tales about the 90-year-old man who bought flowers for his wife every Friday, and the woman who was addicted to wine gums but hated the green ones. She used to say all of human life was there, and most of it fancied a four-pack of Carlsberg and a giant bag of Wotsits. She really enjoyed it, especially the old people who used to come in for 'their bits'; she said she could tell sometimes she was the only person they spoke to all day.

Then that thing happened where the supermarket brought in self-service tills instead, and swapped the humans for machines. I mean, I suppose we're all used to that now, but I never use them on principle, because I've seen the other side. Not just my mum losing her job, but my mum getting upset at the thought of all those old people struggling to scan their ready meals for one and trying to chat to a screen. I'd never even thought about the human side of it all before, just thought they were convenient, and if I'm honest, I was glad I didn't have to stand in a queue behind those old dears and their endless chat to the people on the tills. I'm a bit ashamed of that now.

So, she lost her mum and lost her job, and also my older brother Ben went off to uni in Manchester. This was a bonus for me, because he's an absolute arse and we get on about as well as Will Smith and Chris Rock at the Oscars. For some weird reason, though, she actually likes having him around, and when he left she was really sad. I caught her once sitting on his bed and crying, clutching a pile of dirty socks and soggy towels he'd left on the floor. I don't understand why she misses him—I mean, it's not like it was me who left, the far superior child!—but she does. Must be a mum thing.

This was all bad enough, but even worse was my dad—

or as he's also known, The Biggest Twat in the Universe—walking out on her. People, even Mum, keep telling me this is a 'complicated' subject. That marriages are complicated, life is complicated, relationships are complicated. They say this like it excuses literally any kind of behaviour. I know I'm only eighteen and three-quarters, and therefore have less life experience than a garlic naan, but I still think that's bullshit. Like, can you imagine this excuse being used anywhere else? 'Yes, m'lord, my client was indeed found covered in blood, carrying the murder weapon, and wearing a T-shirt that said "Guilty as Charged!" on the front, but in his defence, it was *complicated*.'

In this case, it wasn't that complicated. My dad left my mum—left us all, let's be blunt—and moved in with a woman he'd been seeing behind her back for almost two years. So basically, while she was still looking after, and then grieving for, Nana, and saying goodbye to Ben, and getting shafted by self-service machines, he was sneaking around like love's middle-aged dream with a woman who runs a cocktail bar in town. That was about ten months ago now, and she's still reeling.

He's tried to dodge all of the responsibility for this, to the point where he seems to be blaming everything, from my mum to Guinness to global warming, for the choices he's made. Anything other than admit he's in the wrong. He's taken the things that make my mum special, and used them against her: she was too wrapped up in worrying about the kids, too concerned with other people, too busy caring for Nana. Too preoccupied to pay him enough attention.

Basically he's a giant baby, and doesn't even see how self-obsessed he is. At one point he even muttered the immortal words 'Well, you can't deny you've let yourself go a bit, can you?' Unfortunately for him, I was outside the room and overheard this gem, then walked in and slapped him across the face. He was horrified; Mum was horrified; I suppose even I was. But using the Rule of Grown-Up Life, I can just say 'Well, it's complicated', and get away with it, can't I?

I mean, it *is* complicated. I miss my dad but I also despise him. I love him but I also have no respect for him. Because of him leaving, we had to sell the house I grew up in, and now live in a much smaller place. Our whole lives have been tipped upside down, especially Mum's. She's made the best of it, but the best isn't exactly awesome.

So now he's run off, and Ben's away, and I'm at home seeing her very quietly and very slowly fall apart. She's even doing that in a kind way, as though she doesn't want to inconvenience anyone, and she probably thinks she's fooled me. Anyone who didn't know her as well as I do would think she was fine.

She's one of those people who always says good morning to random strangers, and knows everyone's life story on the dog-walking route, and always has a smile ready. On the surface, she's Little Miss Sunshine—but I know better. I hear her crying in her bedroom late at night, and see her looking at her own body as though she can't believe it's hers. She stays cheerful until she thinks I've left the house, and then sinks into blank-faced misery. I know this because I forgot my headphones once, and came back in without her knowing. It was horrible and I snuck straight back out because I knew she'd be upset if she knew I'd seen her.

She's doing her best to put on a good front, but her confidence has gone. It's one of the reasons she hasn't applied for a new job yet, and is living off her redundancy. It's like she can't see her own value anymore. She's still a great mum. She forgets her own issues as soon as I have one, and sometimes I even make them up to give her something to fix. But I can tell she's completely grey inside, when she used to be rainbow, if that makes sense. It's like she's become the Invisible Woman, and I want her to be seen again. I want her to see herself again.

I know I've gone on a bit—you did say 'heart and soul' to be fair—and some of this has been a bit heavy, and probably all of it is inappropriate. So I also wanted to tell you some of the positives, which might even be relevant. Well, the empathy bit and the good listener bit are definitely covered—those are her defining characteristics. Dad used to wind her up and call her the 'empathy sponge', because she got so involved in the way other people might feel—except he saw it as a bad thing, obviously, because he was like an empathy void instead.

She's a good cook; she's raised a family, and we always ate well. She can bake, and do a mean Sunday roast, and seems to enjoy feeding people. I love cooking too, and sometimes there's a scuffle in the kitchen about who gets to make dinner—so you might even get a BOGOF deal.

My mum is really hard-working, and one of those irritating people who lives that whole 'if a job's worth doing it's worth doing right' ethos. And she's really good at making a home. I don't know how to describe this—she just has a knack for it. She's always up a ladder doing the decorating, and she loved giving our rooms a new look, and her idea of heaven would be taking a blank canvas house and making it into a home.

When we moved into the new house, it was pretty grim. It belonged to an older man and it hadn't been painted since about 1902. Everything was really ugly and grimy and it felt like the place where hope comes to die. She got to work straight away and transformed it—and within a month it didn't feel like that. It didn't feel like somewhere crap we'd been forced into because of Dad's roving penis. It felt like our home, where we'd always lived, clean and fresh and comfy. Not sure that's any use in a café, but it's a really nice thing about her, and something she genuinely loses herself in.

Anyway. That's that, I suppose. Except, full disclosure, it's probably not just her who needs a fresh start. It's me as well. Everything that's gone on has affected me too, plus I split up with my boyfriend and messed up my A-levels. Maybe they were all connected, I don't know, but everything seems to have gone massively wrong. I didn't feel ready to leave Mum and go to uni anyway, and I wasn't even sure what I wanted to do, but it's never nice to fail at things, is it? I might do resits at some point, and my school said they can set me up with some online courses as well, so all is not lost—I could rediscover my inner genius in Dorset! I just know that maybe a change of scenery will be good for both of us, away from the past, and everything that reminds us of all that stuff that's gone massively wrong.

So, that's it, Laura. If you have any questions—like 'who is this crazy person?'—then feel free to ask! Even if I never hear from you, it felt weirdly good to get all of this written down. Cathartic, to use a fancy English A-level word.

Sophie Connolly xxx

Chapter Two

My name is Maxine Connolly and I am officially Not a Morning Person.

I used to be, back in the mists of time, when I had an early shift at the shop, or when I needed to get round to my mum's to sort her out for the day. And, even further back, when there were school runs to do—but that's so long ago it feels like a dream sequence now.

I kind of miss the school run era. It felt like a grind of logistics and assemblies and ironing back then, but now I see how magical it was. It didn't seem like it at the time, but having young kids was way easier in some ways than having grown-up ones. When they're little, you can control their world, keep them safe, make them happy. You always know where they are and who they're with, and jumping in a muddy puddle or eating a chocolate Hob Nob can distract them from their woes.

When they're older, when they're teenagers, all that

changes. You stop worrying about broken limbs and start worrying about broken hearts. They start lying to you, and they have friends you don't know, and they drink vodka in the park instead of asking you to watch them go down the slide.

The other thing they do, apparently, is apply for jobs you don't want on your behalf, without asking your permission. Or maybe that's just specific to my teenager.

Sophie takes advantage of the fact that I am no longer a morning person to slip that one in, super-casual, leaning against the kitchen counter still wearing her tiger-print onesie. She does it while I'm still staggering around the kitchen in my dressing gown, my eyes glued together with sleep and desperate for coffee to bring me back to life. I mean, what kind of evil genius tells someone about a major life change before they've even had their coffee? I've let our dog, Gary, out for a wee, and that's about as much as I'm capable of.

'Mum,' she says, looking all awake and young and annoying, 'we're moving to Dorset for a few months, all right? I found you a job. I've had enough of you lazing around the place while I bring home the bacon…'

Sophie has a part-time job in an amusement arcade, where she gives people plastic cups full of coins and makes sure nobody sneaks in with a screwdriver to steal the takings. It's that kind of place. She only does Saturdays, and what she earns she spends on herself, usually via the medium of 'vintage' clothes off the internet or old-school video games for her PlayStation.

'You don't bring home the bacon!' I bleat, waiting for the kettle to boil and then realising I haven't switched it on.

'Sometimes I do. Like the other week, you sent me out specifically to the shop to buy bacon, because you wanted to do a fry-up. So, technically speaking, I brought home the bacon, didn't I?'

'Technically speaking, you're being an arse this morning. I haven't even had my coffee. Why are you expecting my brain to function?'

'I never expect your brain to function,' she replies, deadpan. 'I've given up all hope. I'm not even a hundred per cent sure you've got a brain at all. But what you do have is a super-duper, totally awesome daughter. Who has found you a job.'

I've managed to combine coffee granules and hot water by this stage, but I'm still confused. I mean, I know I'll have go back to work eventually, but at the moment it's a vague concept, lurking on a distant horizon. A bit like the diet that you always plan to start tomorrow—the one that feels okay in theory, as long as you don't actually have to open a packet of Ryvita and stock up on zero fat cottage cheese.

'I don't need a job yet,' I mumble, blinking my eyes in the hopes that everything will stop looking blurry.

'Yeah, you do, Mum. I'm not talking about paying the gas bill here; I'm talking about the fact that you've become a recluse. All you do these days is sit around watching telly, and it's not a good look. I think it's time you removed your head from your own backside.'

'Charming. Parenthood is so rewarding,' I reply, rooting in the bread bin so I can make some toast.

She has a delightful way of expressing herself, my darling child, but she does have a teeny-tiny speck of a point as well. I don't actually want any toast, but it gives me something to do to mask the fact that her words have stung me. That she might be right.

Financially, there is no burning need for me to go back to work. I have enough money for us to live on for a little while longer, because of my redundancy package and because we've sold our four-bedroomed detached for a really good profit. We'd almost had the mortgage paid off, and Ben was away at uni, so it made sense. Even after setting aside a bit for the kids and splitting the rest with Richie, my ex, there was enough for me to invest in a run-down terrace that needed 'cosmetic improvement throughout'.

It made sense, but I hated selling our house. I hated showing bright young couples around, trying not to point out the flaws: the garden that floods every winter, the damp patch in the extension, the one tile missing from the roof. I wasn't ready to give up on it or, I suppose, my marriage. I wasn't ready to leave all those memories behind.

The good ones outweighed the bad ones, even after the last couple of years. It was still the house where we brought Ben and Sophie home from the hospital, small and wrinkled in their baby carriers. Still the house where we'd had happy Christmases and birthdays, and endless family film nights and takeaways and rows and cuddles. Still *our* house, and so much more than bricks and mortar.

But Richie didn't seem to agree with me on that—he'd either erased those memories or they weren't as happy as I thought—and it sold way too quickly. All that shared experience, all those years building a life together, were dismantled and packed into moving vans in the space of a day. I still walk past it sometimes, see the new family that's living there. It always makes me cry, and I really must stop doing it. It's that kind of behaviour that makes me think Sophie might have a teeny-tiny speck of a point.

So money-wise, I could survive a bit longer being an unemployed layabout, but work isn't just about money, is it? Not for me, anyway. Mentally, I probably need to get back out into the world, to start interacting with the land of the living again. Every day I stay at home, every day I spend watching TV and avoiding real life, it gets harder to escape the clutches of my sofa.

I'm a sociable person, always have been. I like people. I find them endlessly fascinating. I have been known to stay on a bus way past my stop just to carry on an interesting conversation, and I never met a life story yet that I didn't have questions about. Sophie says I'm just nosy, but I prefer the word 'engaged'.

These days, though, I'm neither, and I know it's upsetting her. I know I used to embarrass her when she was a kid, being on first name terms with her teachers and stopping to chat to random strangers on the street, but bizarrely, now I've stopped she seems to miss it. I hate the fact that my daughter is worried about me, at a time in her life when she should be completely carefree.

It's because of that that I actually listen to her when she carries on talking about my 'new job'. All my instincts are screaming at me to tell her to shut up, to leave me alone. Maybe give her some kind of 'I'm-the-grown-up-here' speech, or at the very least skulk off with my coffee. Instead, I just stare at her some more, and wait for her to proceed. I know she will—Sophie is incapable of staying quiet for more than five minutes unless she has a games controller in her hand.

'So,' she says, twisting her long dark hair around her fingers, a sure sign she's actually a bit nervous, 'you'll be working in a café, in Dorset. On a hill. I didn't even know where Dorset was to be fair, but it's the seaside, and you know I love the seaside.'

'Right. Well, what will I allegedly be doing, in this café, on a hill, at the seaside?'

'Cooking and, like, talking to people.'

'Talking to people?'

'Yeah. That's kind of part of the job description, and why I thought you'd be good at it. It's called the Comfort Food Café, and it looks gorgeous. They have an Instagram account you could look at. Lovely cakes and dogs and views of the beach. And men, actually—all the men on the pics are really hot. Maybe they hired models? Who knows? Anyway. That's where your new job is.'

'I see,' I say, leaning back against the counter, feeling an ache in my back from yet another restless night's sleep.

'And did they headhunt me? Narrow me down from a list of candidates passed on to them from NASA? Find me after an extensive search of boring loser chicks in the UK?'

'You're not boring, and you're not a loser—but you are really irritating! I applied for you, and obviously I did an extremely good job of it.'

'Did you pretend to be me when you filled in the form?' I ask, feeling horrified. I dread to think what she put down as my hobbies and interests—naked bungy jumping, cage fighting, sex clubs. I wouldn't put it past her. She once told her sixth-form English teacher that her dad and I had split up because I decided to be a bride of Christ, change my name to Maria von Trapp and move to a convent in Austria. The teacher knew us too well to believe her, but apparently she shared this revelation with the earnest delivery of an MP swearing they had no idea a party during lockdown was breaking the rules.

'No, there wasn't a form,' she says, stealing my toast as soon as it pops up and slathering it with butter. 'It was all a bit weird really. I had to send them an email, and pour heart and soul into it. And before you ask, no, I didn't tell any huge lies—not even a small one, Mum! I can show it to you if you like, but I'd rather not. I'm actually nice about you in it, and it might fracture our fun Spongebob versus Squidward vibe.'

We pause at that point, and both of us say, at exactly the same time: 'I'm Spongebob!' I mean, nobody wants to be Squidward, do they?

I am curious about what she's said about me, of course,

but something about the set of her face puts me off insisting she tells me. I'm guessing she put a lot more heart and soul into her email than she's currently comfortable sharing with me.

Again, I'm aware of how hard things have been for her as well recently: her dad leaving, the move, the split with Jack, bombing her A-levels, Ben being away (much as she pretends to hate him, I know she misses the constant combat). Even as she explains her insane plan, she looks nervous, jittery, and maybe underneath that even a bit sad. I can tell that she desperately wants me to listen, to believe, to at least give it all a chance. She's trying so hard to come off as a confident grown-up that she seems even more like a little girl, which always melts me.

Maybe, I think, as I sip scalding hot coffee and watch her perform her obviously rehearsed big sell, I've underestimated how bad things have been for her. Or maybe I've underestimated how much she's noticed about me. Us mums like to think we're superheroes, don't we? Putting on a brave face, always convincing our kids that everything is fine. Like that scene in *Titanic* when the mum puts her babies to sleep and reads them a bedtime story, even as the ship sinks.

It's a lot easier when they're little, when they believe every word that comes out of your fibbing mouth. They even believe that a magical fat man in a red suit climbs down every chimney in the world with sacks full of toys. That's probably the first whopper we tell our kids, and we carry on doing it.

But if Sophie thinks I'm so down I need a pick-me-up in the form of a relocation package and a new career, I've obviously not done that good a job of hiding quite how low I've sunk. That makes me cringe inside, but it also makes me listen.

'Why,' I eventually ask, 'were you looking for jobs for me in Dorset anyway? It's hours away!'

'I know. And to start with, I wasn't looking for jobs for you; I was looking for me. Just browsing. Then I accidentally got sucked into one of those internet rabbit holes, you know? Where you keep clicking buttons and your brain keeps expanding to take in all the new crap you've just discovered?'

'I am familiar with that, yes. But Dorset?'

'I thought it was Cornwall, not gonna lie. And I know you like Cornwall. And I decided you should get a job and this one seemed just about random enough and weird enough that it might work. I was kind of surprised when it did. Anyway. None of that matters now. You've got a video call with Laura, the manager, at ten this morning—so for God's sake, go and wash your hair, will you? I've sent you her number.'

That shocks me out of my stupor, and a glance at the big round clock on the wall tells me it's already twenty past nine. Shit. This is real. This is happening. I realise I'm doing a goldfish impression, and she says: 'You will do it, won't you, Mum? You'll at least talk to her? For me?'

I narrow my eyes at her, knowing I'm being manipulated but helpless to resist. She even gives me a cheeky wink, waving her pilfered toast in the air as she sashays out of the kitchen, telling me she has a hot date with *Sonic the Hedgehog*.

I finish my coffee and consider making some more toast, but realise that I have no appetite. I also have no energy, and even less desire whatsoever to have a video call with a strange woman who is expecting to be my boss.

Having no energy isn't a new feeling for me at the moment. It hasn't been for a long time. Some of it left me when my mum died, and I still miss her every single day. She had COPD and her last few years were tough. She was housebound, and the only joy she had in life was from me and the kids visiting her. It was a lot of pressure, but I loved her so much I never minded. After we lost her, I was suddenly rich in time, but poor in motivation.

Since then, life hasn't exactly been a roller coaster ride of fun, and everything that has happened has chipped away at me. If I was a statue and not a human being, I'd just be a skinny little spike of marble by now.

I hear woofing from outside, and realise that Gary is still out there, the poor thing. I open the door and he rushes in, a flurry of fur and wagging tail, his little black face seeming to smile up at me. He's a rescue from Hungary, and nobody can figure out what he's made of, even the vet. A dash of dachshund, a splash of spaniel, a lashing of lurcher. He has short legs, but the broad rib cage of a running dog, and he can sprint like the wind.

He jumps up and licks my bare kneecaps, and I scratch his ears. He's such a misfit, such an ugly little thing with his mismatched limbs and his weird bow-legged shape, but he's endearingly full of love.

'What do you reckon, Gaz?' I say, kneeling down so he can give me a kiss. 'Should we go for it, or should I tell this Laura lady that it's all been a terrible misunderstanding?'

Gary ignores me, and licks his own bum. Sage advice.

I feed him, then make my way upstairs. I might as well have a shower anyway, because that's generally a win in life. If nothing else, this video call makes me wash and blow dry my hair and put a little bit of slap on. It's been a while, and I have to admit a touch of tinted moisturiser does pick me up.

By the time ten o'clock rolls around I'm sitting on the bed, looking spruced but feeling nervous. This is insane, I tell myself. I can't move to Dorset and work in a café; the whole idea is madness. I will be polite, and talk to Laura, and explain that this has all been a mistake. That Sophie over-stepped, that she'll have to find somebody else. I'm sure it won't be a problem. And also, I mean, what kind of person offers someone a job without even interviewing them anyway? This is a whole new level of chaos, even by my standards.

I dial the number Sophie has sent me, and when it's picked up, I am extremely surprised to be confronted by two small girls rather than a café manager. They can't be more than four or five, and are giggling and holding their hands over their mouths as they stare at me. Both of them have masses of curly brown hair, and they are absolutely identical apart from their clothes. One is in a hot-pink Barbie T-shirt, and the other is wearing a Spiderman top.

'Hello?' I say tentatively, wondering if I'm somehow being pranked. 'Is Laura there?'

'She's having a poo!' announces one of the girls, giggling even harder.

'A reallllly big one! Super-smelly!' the other adds, holding her nose, and the two of them dissolve into hilarity. I hear a big woof in the background, and Gary's ears prick up in response. He's as confused as I am.

There's a sudden blur as the phone is clearly grabbed, and a harassed-looking woman appears on my screen. It doesn't take a big leap to see that she is the twins' mum, as she shares the curly hair. It's twisted up into a messy bun, framing a round but pretty face.

'I was *not* having a poo!' she declares wholeheartedly, shooing the girls away. 'I was stopping our Labrador from eating a bag of Haribo Tangfastic! Please, please, please say you believe me. This is not the first impression I wanted to make!'

I have to laugh at her sheer exasperation, and reply: 'I have a dog who steals food too. And hey, even if you were having a poo, so what? We all have poos, don't we?'

'Wise words, Max— Wait, are you Max?'

'I am. And you must be Laura. I assume the terrible twosome belong to you?'

She grimaces, but you can see she is amused by their antics. My kids were born a year apart from each other, which was close enough for carnage. I can't imagine having two at the same time.

'For my sins, yes—Ruby and Rose. A little late-in-life blessing from the universe. I also have Lizzie, who's just turned 23, and Nate, who's almost 21. Long story, to be shared over a bucket of Prosecco and a barrel of cheese. Hopefully we'll be able to do that when you get here.'

I am silent at this point, biting my lip and suddenly out of words. This is the perfect time for me to say no. To explain that I am not coming. Except … well, a bucket of Prosecco and a barrel of cheese don't sound bad, do they?

'Are you okay? Has the screen frozen, or is that the look of a woman wondering if she's just teleported into Willy Wonka's chocolate factory? Are you seeing Oompa-Loompas? Is everything feeling a bit weird and psychedelic?'

'Umm … yeah, a bit. I mean, to be honest, Laura, I found out about all of this less than an hour ago. One minute I'm on a coffee hunt, expecting an exciting day of watching Netflix, and the next my daughter informs me we're about to move to Dorset. I haven't even had time to look at the café, never mind formulate a response that makes me look like the kind of person you'd want to give a job to. Which I'm probably not, by the way.'

'Yes, you are!' she says firmly, nodding so enthusiastically that her bun collapses, 'I can already tell. I'm sorry if this has been an ambush—my kids used to do stuff like that to me as well. It was like living in a fun house, never knowing when the floor was going to tilt and tip me on my arse. So, just to give you a little reassurance, if this seems crazy, then it is. Crazy is kind of the default setting here.'

'You don't have to be mad to work here, but it helps?'

'Yes. The company motto. Look, I understand why you're confused. But when Sophie's email arrived, I just knew you were the same as me. Or the old me, anyway.'

My nosiness—no, I mean 'engagement'—kicks in, and I have to ask: 'What do you mean?'

'Well, ages ago, Max, I was in a bad place. My husband had died a few years earlier, and I was on my own. Lizzie and Nate were fourteen and twelve. I didn't know where to turn, and I was grieving, and we were all a mess.'

I can hear the twang of pain in her voice, and I can tell that her husband might be gone, but he's not forgotten. My empathy sponge is immediately activated, and I say: 'Gosh, I'm so sorry. That must have been awful for you, Laura.'

'Yes, it was, no use sugar-coating it. It was the lowest I've ever been in my life. You know those points where you have no confidence, no self-belief, no direction? Where you feel like you're a crap mum and a crap human being and you can't even remember a time when you had any control at all over your own destiny?'

I nod, and suddenly wish I'd insisted that Sophie showed me what she'd said about me to this woman. That description is so close to how I've been feeling for so long now that it doesn't seem like a coincidence.

'Well, when I was at that point,' Laura continues, 'I saw

a job advert, very like the one that Sophie responded to. In fact I stole some of the wording from the original, because nothing here has changed. I'm going to risk sounding like a complete flake here, but this place—the Comfort Food Café —isn't like anywhere else. It's special. It's a place people can come when they need something, even if they don't know what it is yet, even if it's just a safe spot to slow down and have a rest.'

'It sounds like a cross between a health spa and a rescue centre.'

'Exactly!' she replies, laughing. 'See, you already get it! We collect strays, and we look after them, and I don't want that to put you off or make it sound like you're a dog or anything, because I was the stray myself at one point. Everyone here has a story to share, and from what I hear about you, you're a big fan of listening to people's stories.'

'Did Sophie tell you I was really nosy?' I ask, grinning.

'No. She told me you were hard-working, and funny, and kind, and caring.'

This is so unexpected, and so utterly lovely, that I feel tears stinging the back of my eyes. I am embarrassed, and hope she can't tell I'm on the verge of blubbing.

'Oh. Right. Well, that was nice of her. She usually says I'm annoying.'

'Well, she's a teenage girl. You're not doing your job properly unless you're annoying her. Anyway. All of those qualities are exactly what we're looking for here, for this job. One of our staff—Willow, you'll meet her when you get here—is taking off to do some travelling, and I've just got a feeling that you're going to be the perfect person to replace her.'

'But why?' I ask, genuinely confused. 'You don't even know me.'

'Psychic powers,' she says, tapping the side of her nose as though she's sharing something top secret. 'And instinct. I'm a big believer in instinct. We got a few responses to the ad, but yours—okay, Sophie's—stood out. I knew it was the one, and I'm afraid I can't give you any more scientific an answer than "just because". Plus, it's only a trial, isn't it? If you hate it here, or it doesn't work for any reason, then you can leave. We're not going to kidnap you and keep you in our secret underground dungeon.'

'Do you have a secret underground dungeon?'

'We have a cider cave, which feels a bit dungeon-y, but it's full of booze so it could be worse. Look, the point is, come and give it a go. Let's take a chance on each other. Bring Sophie, bring the little dog I can see sitting next to you. Bring all your hope and all your optimism and all your faith—plus maybe some wellies, 'cause it gets really muddy down here in autumn. What do you say, Max? Shall I get that bucket of Prosecco on ice for you?'

As she says this, a blur of black appears behind her, followed by Ruby and Rose running past in a flurry of curls. There is screaming and barking and the sound of furniture being knocked over.

Laura stares off screen, unfocused, then turns back to me.

'I've got to go,' she says, shaking her head. 'Midgebo has the Tangfastic again, and he'll be shitting rainbows if I don't get them off him. Just think about it, okay? That's all I ask!'

Chapter Three

'You do know this is a stupid idea, don't you?' I ask, as Sophie turns the key in the ignition. This simple act fills me with fear and dread. She only passed her test a few months ago and drives like she's auditioning for a role in one of the *Fast and Furious* films.

'Me behind the wheel, or going to Dorset?'

'Erm, do I have to choose? They both feel bloody terrifying!'

'That,' she says, screeching out from our parking spot without checking her mirrors, 'is because you're a big cowardy-custard, Mum. You're a jelly in human form. A spineless blob of a person, wearing an outfit that should be burnt at the stake for crimes against fashion.'

'Thanks for the pep talk,' I reply, glancing down at myself. 'And what's wrong with my outfit? It's comfortable, and it hides my jiggly bits!'

Truth be told, I don't have as many jiggly bits as I used

to. Turns out that your husband leaving you is a really effective way to slim down. I should probably write some kind of self-help manual: *Lose Your Man and Three Stone in One Easy Life Crisis*. I still *feel* jiggly, though, and that's what counts.

'Mum, you have massive boobs and a big arse, and a bit extra in between. You're just like Jessica Rabbit after she popped out a couple of kids and ate too many carrot cakes. The jiggly bits are hot. You know those music videos for R&B songs, where there's loads of really fit women twerking in a basement, or at a car wash or whatever?'

I nod, not unhappy with where this unexpectedly complimentary conversation is landing, and she replies: 'Well, if they made one of those with middle-aged women and cellulite, then you'd definitely be in with a chance!'

Right. Well. There you go. I'd give her a slap but she's driving, and I don't want to die. I might be middle-aged—is 43 middle-aged? I suppose it is—but I'm hoping for a few more years yet.

I gaze out of the window as she heads towards the motorway, watching the blur of houses and cars and buses rush past through rain-streaked glass. I stay silent for a moment, because every now and then, I remember that not so long ago, I wasn't quite as deeply committed to having 'a few more years'.

Don't get me wrong, I was never planning on harming myself; I was never quite at the stage where I could do that to the kids, and was always brutally aware of how much of a shadow that would cast over other people's lives. Not just

Sophie and Ben, but everyone who was touched by it, everyone who vaguely knew me, even the person who'd find me.

I remember reading an interview with the actress Kathy Burke where she talked about being so low because of menopause and illness that she'd considered taking her own life, but didn't want to traumatise anyone. In the end she came up with an ingenious plan involving a hotel suite and warning notes on the door, and even more importantly, obviously didn't put the ingenious plan into action. Maybe, like me, it was just something that she kept hidden in the back of her mind like a last resort, a fail-safe, the ultimate escape hatch if things really did get too dark.

I feel a flush of shame as I even admit these thoughts to myself, and then get annoyed about the fact that I'm ashamed. Wouldn't I be the first person to say there's no stigma to suffering with your mental health? Yes, I would … to other people. Funny how we judge ourselves more harshly than everyone else, isn't it?

Anyway, I decide, swiping my hand across the now steamed-up window, I don't feel like that anymore. Life hasn't suddenly changed—my mum hasn't come back to life, and Richie is still with the Other Woman—but I'm not unemployed, at least, thanks to my very rude daughter. She's currently singing along to a track by a singer called Peaches, which repeats the title line, 'F**k the Pain Away' over and over again. It's a super-catchy tune, but it's not an image any mother wants to associate with her teenaged offspring.

It's been just over a month since I had that first conversation with Laura, and it was followed by several more. I wasn't instantly sold, but she's persistent, I'll give her that. I think maybe she was projecting some of her past self onto me, and that made her even more determined to drag me out of my old life and into the new. The new, she assured me, was one filled with fun and friendship and cake. Laura seems incapable of having an entire conversation without reference to cake.

She'd filled me in on all her 'regulars', the familiar faces that make up the café's loyal clientele, and introduced me via the screen to Cherie Moon, the actual owner of the café. Cherie is an older lady, apparently in her early eighties, though she could get away with claiming younger. She has one of those timeless faces, lined and creased but so full of life that the vibrancy of her years overshadows the ageing process.

As far as Cherie was concerned, it was already a done deal that I'd be joining them.

'Laura says you're the one, my love,' she'd said, shaking her head resignedly. 'It's like the moonlight—you can't fight it. What's your comfort food anyway, so we can stock up?'

This, I've learnt, is one of the café's quirks: knowing everybody's personal comfort food, and always having it on hand. I've been told that's anything from chicken and mushroom Pot Noodles through to home-made jam roly-poly, and whatever I desire, it will be waiting for me.

'Erm … lobster thermidor?' I'd suggested, though

33

truthfully I have no idea what that even is—it just sounds posh.

'I'll swim out to sea and catch one for you myself, darling,' she'd responded, her laughter lines crinkling in a way that reminded me of my mum. She laughed a lot, my mother, even when her life was hard and painful. The only thing she loved more than having a good laugh was watching repeats of Inspector Morse, and making inappropriate comments about how 'rugged' John Thaw was in *The Sweeney*.

Thinking about my mum somehow triggered me into telling Cherie, 'Bakewell tart. My mum used to make it when I was little.'

'That we can do, my sweet,' she'd answered, tapping the side of her head. 'It's now noted in my mobile encyclopaedia. See you soon!'

Somehow, during the course of these bizarre long-distance interactions, my initial resistance was worn down. The more I spoke to them, the more I looked forward to our next call, the more it seemed to make sense. As our connection built, it started to feel like a perfectly rational decision to put my fate in the hands of these eccentric strangers. After every entertaining chat, it felt more logical: Sophie wanted to do it, and really, what did I have to lose?

Eventually, I realised that the answer to that question was 'not much'. It was a chance encounter with Richie and the Other Woman (real name Valerie) that pushed me past my tipping point. We accidentally bumped into each other in the Boots in town. She was buying expensive skin care products, and my basket contained some Gaviscon and a bumper pack of Imodium Instants—my humiliation was complete. Valerie is the kind of woman who gets her roots done every month, and factors the cost of shellac nails into her essentials budget. She's so glamorous she probably wears high-heeled socks.

It was one of those awkward encounters where everybody concerned probably wished they'd seen each other quicker, and managed to hide. After an excruciating few minutes of tense small talk, I'd exited stage left as fast as my decidedly unglamorous Skechers could carry me, my heart pounding and my stomach churning.

When he first left, the pain was raw and brutal and felt like it would never end. Now, it's like having grit in your eye: always there, but you know it's probably not going to kill you. Seeing him—seeing *them*—in the flesh, though? That's still agony, and makes me feel small and pointless and heartsore. Like I've got the tip of a screwdriver in my eye.

Richie and I were together for twenty-three years, and while it wasn't perfect, I was always content. I assumed he was too, which was a mistake. He'd been seeing her behind my back for a long time before I found out.

I think that's what hurt the most: not just that he left, but the mockery he made of our whole marriage. That he'd been seeing her, then coming home to me. It's not a fair comparison, is it? She was the foxy mistress who always had her fancy knickers on and was constantly ready to rumble in the bedroom. I was the chubby wife who asked him to put the bins out, last bought fancy knickers in 2009, and was usually way too tired to rumble in the bedroom. I didn't stand a chance.

After Boots-gate, I realised that there was always going to be a risk of these random encounters happening. We live in a suburb of Birmingham called Solihull, and it's a nice place, but it is always going to be the place where my past lives. The past that now has a new haircut and a hipster beard and wears skinny jeans.

I realised that I didn't want to walk around worried I'd end up with a screwdriver in my eye, and that I'd quite like to get rid of the grit as well. That I needed the change as much as Sophie kept telling me I did.

I drove up to Manchester to talk it over with Ben and take him out for a cheeky Nandos. He'd got a job there working as a night porter in a fancy hotel, and had only been home for weekends during the summer. I missed him, but was glad he was enjoying life up north.

When I told him about our escape plan, he told me it was mental, but 'maybe you need a bit of mental'. I had to discuss it with him—despite Sophie's claims that he was irrelevant—because it affected him too. Or at least it affected where he'd be bringing his dirty washing back to for the Christmas break. He basically told me to go for it, and by doing so, my last thread of an excuse officially disappeared.

Once I'd decided, it was all surprisingly straightforward. I spoke to a lettings agency about renting out the house for a few months, and was pleasantly surprised to find that it was a 'high demand property, exceptionally well presented throughout'—go me. That's a big change up from 'requires cosmetic improvement'. A short-term tenant will be moving in next week, on a three-month contract, which means that Sophie and I are free to roam to our heart's content.

It's still insane. It's still probably the single most reckless thing I've ever done in my life, but somehow, it might just work. And if it doesn't, at the end of the three months, I won't have lost anything at all.

Now our bags are packed, Sophie's said her goodbyes, and Gary is curled in a small ball on the backseat, next to my daughter's vital collection of games and devices. We're off to the Comfort Food Café, and a whole new life. Or at least a whole new three months.

Sophie bullies her way onto the motorway, and immediately zig-zags into the fast lane, where she hammers our poor Toyota for all she's worth.

'We've got hours to go yet,' she says, turning the music down. 'Let's play some games. I'll start. Who's your favourite Hun? Mine's Attila, and you can't have the same one!'

Chapter Four

L aura told us to go straight to the café, where we will be given a 'proper Comfort Food welcome'. This is a slightly terrifying prospect, but not as terrifying as my daughter's driving. I take over after an hour because my nerves are shredded.

They aren't much better by the time we wind our way into Dorset, because the weather is absolutely horrendous. It's late September and summer is already a distant memory.

'Is this a storm with a name?' Sophie asks, leaning forward and peering through the windscreen. The wipers are on full, but they're barely keeping up, and the wind is howling around the roof rack like it's trying to claw its way inside the car. Gary keeps letting out little yips that tell us he's keeping a close eye on the situation.

'I think it must be a storm with a name,' she decides. 'I

think maybe it's Storm Beelzebub. I wonder if the café will get blown off the cliff?'

'Probably,' I answer, 'because that's what happens when you give me a job.' I think it is a storm with a name, but I vaguely remember it was something girly from the seventies, like Storm Sandy or Storm Babs or whatever…

The motorway has been a grim experience, a constant flow of impatient traffic and spray from what seemed like every goods lorry ever manufactured in the Western hemisphere. It was a huge relief to escape onto the still-busy roads that led us through Glastonbury and Yeovil, and now we are making slow but steady progress through quiet country lines that are lined with dripping-wet hedgerows, surrounded by fields in every imaginable shade of green. Even with the hellish grey sky and the torrential downpour, I can see how pretty it is—like a vibrant patchwork quilt that's been draped over the landscape.

Every mile we cover seems to be taking us closer to the coast, and Sophie gets excited every time we catch a glimpse of it between the rolling hills. She's a child who grew up in the Midlands, and screams 'I can see the sea!' whenever it pops into her line of sight.

'What does it look like?' I ask, concentrating on obeying my first rule of driving, and in fact life: don't crash.

'Ummm … grey, to be honest. And big. And I suppose wet.'

'Wow. I can see why you got that grade 8 in your Geography GCSE.'

'I know, right? I should probably start my own YouTube channel: *Seeing the Sea with Sophie!* What do you think?'

'I think we're nearly there. According to the directions we should be coming up to the turning that takes us to Budbury.'

'That's a nice name, isn't it?' she asks enthusiastically. She seems insanely excited about all of this, and it makes me smile inside. 'Like, "buds"—new growth, change, optimism. All that good stuff. It's there! It's there, I see it! Next left!'

Sure enough, within a few minutes of a quick-fire indicate-and-turn, we are driving down a long and winding road that stretches like a ribbon through the village. I think the word 'village' might be overstretching, as there seems to be only one street. But it is a good street that possesses all of life's essentials.

I see a small butcher's shop and grocery, a community centre, a pharmacy, a florist and—hallelujah!—a pub called the Horse and Rider. Scattered between these are rows of small terraced houses, the type that were probably built as workers' cottages for fishermen and agricultural labourers, and now look quaint and pretty with their rough whitewashed stone exteriors.

I still don't know where exactly Sophie and I will be staying; Laura just said she had it sorted, and not to worry. I'm trying to go with the flow, but I am pretty tired now, and suddenly feeling a bit overwhelmed. It's been a tough journey, and now I'm about to meet a load of new people and begin a job I've never even done before. I'm not usually the kind of person who puts a lot of stock in signs and portents, but landing here in the middle of a monsoon doesn't exactly feel like a good start, either. If a seagull crashes into my windscreen, I'm turning around and going home.

I keep these thoughts to myself, as Sophie is wittering on incessantly about how lovely everything is, and wondering out loud if there's a games arcade, and planning to join the local jam-making society. I do a bit of a double-take at that one, and she says: 'This has got to be the kind of place that has a jam-making society, don't you think? I've always wanted to learn how to make jam. Then once I've mastered it, I'll start my own YouTube channel … *Make the Jam with Sophie!*'

I shake my head, and keep my eyes on the road as it curves and dips further down towards the coast. I think maybe she's a bit nervous too, and the verbal overflow is just her way of expressing it.

As Laura promised, there is a small car park ahead, and I manoeuvre the car into a space between a little Fiat 500 and a small van. It's painted white, and the side features the Comfort Food Café logo, its name made out of trailing red roses. Beneath, it bears the words: 'Making the world a better place, one cake at a time.'

Maybe, during the 2020 hellscape, the café, like many other businesses, started doing deliveries. Or maybe they always did. Or maybe I'm overthinking this, and it doesn't really matter anyway, other than as a way to distract myself from the fact that we are here. Amazing how fascinating the most mundane of things can become when you're trying to avoid something else, isn't it?

We both clamber out of the car, and I immediately brace myself against the wind. It's so strong it feels like it could sweep us away, and send us tumbling down towards the waves. A few random items are blowing around: a broken umbrella, a map that was probably once folded into a neat leaflet size, a beach ball... Definitely not beach ball weather, I think, as it gets carried away in a howling air current, bouncing and flying into the distance until it's a green and yellow speck.

I put Gary on his lead, and join Sophie at the side of the car park. My hair is whipping around my face, and the rain is ice cold against my skin, but I can still see how beautiful it is. A small, horseshoe-shaped bay, scattered with boulders and edged by red and gold cliffs that curve off into the distance. Today, the sea is wild and grey, topped with white surf that slings itself angrily against the sand—but in sunshine, on a milder day, it would be stunning.

'Where are the raincoats?' Sophie shouts over the gale, and I realise that we have made a basic packing error.

'Shit—they're in the roof box!' I say, looking at her in horror. This is not unpacking-the-roof-box weather.

'Never fear,' she says jauntily, obviously having taken on the role of She Who Will Not Be Deflated today. 'Back in a sec!'

She is going against the wind, her slender form bending into it and moving so slowly she looks like she's doing a mime. Gary leans into my legs, his tail tucked between his legs, obviously not keen. I'm ashamed to say I have no clue what the climate is like in Hungary, his home nation, but he loves the heat, our Gary. In summer, he goes and finds the nearest patch of sunlight and lies in it until he's had enough. Then he comes back inside panting, his smooth black coat shining and warm to the touch. Here, he just looks up at me with baleful amber eyes, as if he's blaming me for the rain.

Sophie runs back towards me—with the wind behind her this time so it now looks like she's being shoved by invisible hands—and passes me a black bin bag. It flaps around, and I'm momentarily confused until I see her tear a hole in the bottom and then pull it over her head.

'Ta-da!' she announces, grinning even though a raindrop is hanging off her nose. 'Insta-raincoats! I'm really good at making impromptu storm-wear. I think maybe I'll—'

'Let me guess? Start a YouTube channel about it?'

'Don't be stupid! I was going to say make some TikToks! Come on, it's up there, isn't it? This is shitty weather but it still looks gorgeous!'

She points up towards the building that I also recognise as the café. It's perched further along from where we are, looking a little precarious on the edge of the cliff. It's only half six, but due to Storm Linda—I remembered her name—the sky is already darkening, and the sun has been banished. The sky is made of black-streaked clouds that are hanging so low it's almost smothering, and the café is lit up brightly against the gloomy backdrop.

I put on my bin bag, and follow my daughter towards

the path that will lead us up—up to the café, and all those new people, and to physical evidence of the fact that I have clearly gone mad. I don't want to go, I realise. I'm actually so nervous my legs feel shaky. One of the especially lovely side effects of Richie's betrayal has been the complete evaporation of all my self-confidence. At some point, I think I must have started agreeing with him, and seeing myself as second-best. I hate that, and hope my time here will help me change it. If I can recreate myself for other people, maybe I'll get a new lease of life for me as well.

First, though, I have to tackle this path—or paths. I see as we cross the road that there are two. One has low-level steps in it, and the other is paved smooth, presumably for buggies and wheelchairs. Both of them are steep, but the paved one winds around the climb in a more meandering way. Gary decides on the steps, pulling me forwards behind Sophie.

There are various points where the path expands, with little fences to lean on as you gaze out at the view. And again, on a day unravaged by Linda, it would undoubtedly be gorgeous. Today, though, we just concentrate on heading up, our way lit by strings of fairy lights wavering in the wind.

When we reach the top, I see a wrought iron archway that we have to walk through. The top of the arch is decorated with metallic roses, painted in shades of red and green. The roses and the leaves are winding in and out of the words, WELCOME TO THE COMFORT FOOD CAFE. It is a beautiful touch, made with real craft and artistry, and I can imagine similar designs in different locations. I'd love to have a home big enough for its own version, and make a small vow to buy a Euromillions ticket before the next draw.

At the top of the path is a garden, sloping and steep, with wooden picnic tables and benches scattered around. It's a bit haphazard, and some of the tables look decidedly wonky, but the views out to sea would make the slippage risk worth it.

We make our way through the garden, past tubs and planters filled with flowers now flattened by the rain, and Gary pauses to lift his leg against a small metal post that seems to serve no purpose, until I see the little sign painted on the side that says, DOGS—PLEASE CHECK YOUR WEE-MAILS HERE!

Strings of lights are all around, swooping around the sides of the building, looping over the entrance to a small annexe that seems to be a book shop. Some of them are lifting and twisting in the wind, and I'm not sure how highly I rate their chances of staying attached.

The café itself is one storey high, apart from some windows built into the eaves, and is long and sprawling. It looks like it's grown organically along the side of the cliff, and its big windows are bright with light, casting a golden glow on the now apocalyptic world around it.

I stop for a moment, and bite my lip so hard I taste blood. It looks busy in there. I can see a lot of human bodies, and some canine, and although the wind is howling in my ears, I can still hear laughter and chatter and the background hum of music. It sounds suspiciously like 'A Whole New World' from *Aladdin*, being sung extremely badly by two female voices.

'You okay?' says Sophie, watching me as I watch the café. She reaches out, and pats the shoulder of my wet bin bag. I nod, even though I'm not. Time to be brave.

'Yeah, fine. And we're bound to create a good impression, dressed like literal bag ladies, aren't we?'

'It's recycling. Very hot topic in fashion these days. Come on, let's go in and see if they were right about the cake, shall we? Apart from anything else, Gary's doing that thing where he's so wet he looks like the love child of a seal and a rat.'

I glance down and see that she's right. His black fur is plastered to his body, and the whiskers on his long, narrow face are twitching. I give him a quick stroke and murmur some reassuring words. He's a lot better than when we first adopted him; back then he was scared of everything, including wires, crisp packets, and hairbrushes. He used to run out of the room in terror if we dared do anything threatening, like open a can of pop, and he hid from everyone he met. Things have improved a lot after four years with us, but he can still be nervy in crowds, and is especially shy around men. I've warned Laura about all of this, but she is sure he'll soon realise he is among friends.

I reach out to turn the handle, and as I do, a huge gust of wind blows the door wide open, so powerfully that it slams into the wall behind it. I'm left standing in the doorway in my dripping bin bag, and freeze in terror in case everyone turns and stares at me.

A few do, but most are concentrating on the performance. A little space has been cleared amid the tables and chairs, and two women are belting out Princess Jasmine's classic. They're in perfect harmony, both completely off-key. One has long red hair, and one has long pink hair, and they're both giving their all.

Gary sticks by my side as I make my way through, followed by Sophie. As I look around, trying to get my breath back, an old lady who looks like a garden gnome approaches me. She's very short, dressed entirely in beige, and has twinkling blue eyes almost completely swallowed by wrinkles. She could be anywhere between seventy and a hundred and ten.

'You must be Max!' she announces, helping me pull my bin bag off. 'It's so nice to finally meet you. I'm Laura!'

I pause with one arm free and the other still encased in black plastic, and stare at her in disbelief. This can't be Laura, surely? I mean, I know you don't always get an accurate impression of people on video calls, but...

'I've had a tough day,' she adds. 'Didn't have time to put my face on.'

She leaves me hanging for a few more seconds, mouth gaping open, before she cackles, loud and long. She claps her hands together in glee, and points at me.

'Got you there, didn't I? I'm not Laura at all, I'm Edie! Come on, come on, shut the door behind you—nobody invited Linda to this party!'

I realise that this is indeed a party, and that the room is pretty packed. It's deliciously warm and welcoming, especially compared to the conditions outside, and it smells divine. Like every kind of cake known to man—of sugar and spice and most definitely all things nice.

A very quick scan reveals all the usual café things: gingham tablecloths, small vases of flowers, a counter in front of a huge coffee machine, a fridge full of soft drinks, and a glass-fronted cooler for fresh food.

A slightly slower scan reveals a few more things, like lots of random posters and prints up on the walls. We've all got used to seeing KEEP CALM AND CARRY ON, but these are slightly odder. Like LIFE'S TOO SHORT FOR CELERY, which is most certainly true, and one that hangs by the serving counter that says, WE WILL ASSUME YOU WANT YOUR HOT CHOCOLATE WITH MARSHMALLOWS AND CREAM UNLESS YOU APPEAR TO BE DEAD.

One end of the room has a kind of lounging area with squishy sofas and beanbags, and a bookshelf crammed with board games and colouring pads and pens, as well as a huge assortment of paperbacks and maps. I'm so tired right now, the thought of lying down on one of those sofas, with a mug of the promised hot chocolate, is just about the most enticing thing I've ever imagined.

Edie gives us both an appraising look, and says: 'Good. You're both normal-sized humans. No need to worry about your heads. Tea, coffee, wine, mojito?'

I am momentarily confused, but soon realise what she means about our heads. The whole café is decorated with extremely weird items, and some of them are dangling from the ceiling. There's a mobile made from old seven-inch vinyl singles, and nets full of shells, and suspended on chains in one corner is a bright red one-man kayak. It's like the whole room has been set up like one of those baby play gyms, where they lie on a mat and reach up to touch the brightly-coloured objects hanging over their faces. Except, you know, for adults.

I love anything to do with interior design—I am a sad addict of any reality show that involves doing up a house or changing a room—and find the whole thing fascinating. None of it should work. None of it should make sense. And yet somehow it does—it looks quirky and odd and fabulous.

Sophie is looking around in wonder, and goes over to stroke a giant fossil that is perched on one of the shelves. It curls in on itself like a giant spiral, and is surrounded by smaller fossils of every size and shape and design. She always loved these when we used to take her to the museum, and she's already vowed to become the world's best fossil-hunter while we are here on the Jurassic Coast. Maybe she'll make a YouTube channel about it.

'That's an ammonite,' Edie pronounces proudly, as though she made it herself. 'One of the biggest found around here. It's 160 million years old, which means it's almost as old as me!'

Sophie smiles, and I can see that she is already half in love with Edie, as am I. Inevitably I suppose, she reminds me of my mum. It's the crinkled up laughter lines that do it.

I'm about to reply to her earlier question and ask for hot chocolate, when a big black Labrador comes surging towards us, bulling his way through people's legs, tail wagging so fast it's a blur. He's not the tallest Lab I've ever seen, but what he lacks in height he makes up for in girth. Midgebo, the famous Tangfastic thief.

Gary has been glued to the side of my leg up until this point, but he comes to life when he sees another dog. He loves other dogs, and I've always felt a bit guilty about him being by himself. I was looking at rescue centres for a pal for him when Richie dropped his bombshell, and it's never felt like the right time since.

The two woofers greet each other in the traditional way, with much sniffing of arses, and a few seconds later Midgebo is followed by Laura. The real Laura this time. She is exactly like she looked: round, pretty, her wild curls flying around her face. She's wearing a top with the words Mama Bear on them, over a picture of a polar bear and its cubs. I'm guessing Mothers' Day gift.

She smiles and gives me a big hug, even though I'm still half-wrapped in the bin bag. She immediately starts to pull it off me, and says: 'Come on over to the sofas. It's like a madhouse here tonight!'

'I noticed,' I say, as we all follow her. 'This isn't… This isn't for us, is it? I know you said you'd give us a proper welcome, but this is a lot.'

'Oh, no, don't worry, it's just serendipity! It's a kind of combo: goodbye to Willow, and hello to you. To be honest we don't need much of an excuse to throw a party around here. There's not much else to do, so we tend to make our own entertainment. Tonight, at Willow's request, it's Disney karaoke. That's her singing—looks like they're finishing, thank God—the one with the pink hair. The other one is her sister, Auburn. You'll meet her soon. Though she's the Budbury pharmacist, so hopefully you won't be seeing her professionally!'

As we settle down on the sofas, a new song starts— someone who actually has a half-decent voice doing 'We Don't Talk About Bruno'. I glance over and see a very petite ginger-haired woman holding the microphone.

'That's Zoe,' Laura says. 'She runs the bookshop, Comfort Reads, next door. She's very funny, in that waspish and sarcastic way that some people master, you know? Like, she'll say something hilarious but not even crack a smile herself? I don't know how she does that…'

Even as she speaks, Laura is smiling, and I'm guessing that's her default setting. She seems like such a happy person she could be a Disney character herself.

'I like your bin bag coats,' she says, watching as Midge and Gary frolic in the little space between the sofas. 'Ingenious.'

We've both now shed them, and Sophie replies: 'That was my idea, though to give Mum credit, it does stem from one of her very valuable life lessons: never leave home without a bin bag. She's right, too. Whenever me and my mates hung round in the park, I never had a wet bum, because I always had a bin bag to sit on.'

Wow, I think. I really am the world's best mother.

'What other life lessons did she teach you?' asks Laura, her head to one side. I'm dreading this one.

'Well,' says Sophie, grinning, 'there are a few, obviously, but the highlights would probably be as follows: never get separated from your mates on a night out. Always remember you're special. *Battleship* is a very underrated film. And, perhaps most importantly: don't be a dick.'

As she reels them off I have to laugh, because these are indeed very important things, and I recognise myself in them. I've clearly repeated them so often they've become part of Sophie's life bible.

'I love that last one!' exclaims Laura. 'Words to live by! But I'm ashamed to say I've never seen *Battleship*.'

'It's an action movie about an alien invasion, full of really hot men. And Rihanna's in it.'

'Sounds amazing. I'll have to check it out. Maybe we can have a movie night and watch it together? I do love a good movie night.'

That, I think, sounds so bloody nice. I also love a movie night, and it is one of the things I miss most from my old life. When all four of us lived together, we'd try and have one every Friday. We had a little ritual. We'd all put the names of films we wanted to watch in Richie's Aston Villa baseball cap, and do a draw to decide. Then I'd make popcorn in the microwave, and he'd go out to the takeaway place down the road to get us our tea—which was always called a 'shush kebab', because I'd be telling everyone to be quiet so we didn't miss any all-important dialogue.

After Ben went to uni, Richie left and we moved

house, everything felt more muted. I didn't want Sophie to feel like she had to stay in on a Friday night, so we abandoned the tradition. We still watched films together, but I don't think either of us felt capable of revisiting the way it was in the Time Before. I love the thought of watching a movie with Laura, and maybe creating a whole new tradition.

'Cake!' says a loud voice behind me, making itself heard over 'Bruno'. 'And hot chocolate to chase away that storm!'

In a cloud of tie-dyed kaftan, the woman I immediately recognise as Cherie Moon is among us. I hadn't realised, from my tiny phone screen, exactly how imposing she is. It's not just her height—though she's got to be nearing six foot; it's everything about her. She's solidly built, broad-shouldered, and has a fat plait of silvery-grey hair snaking down her shoulder. There's not a scrap of make-up on her face, but despite that she seems impossibly attractive. Like a walking, talking life goal.

She places a tray down on the table in front of us, and Laura immediately grabs hold of Midge's collar. Not a moment too soon, I realise, as he makes a desperate lunge for the cake that has magically appeared. Not just cake— Bakewell tart, two enormous slices, along with a little jug of pouring cream. Next to it are two big mugs complete with the promised marshmallows. I think I may have died and gone to heaven.

I see Sophie staring at Cherie in amazement, and bite back my laughter. Us city folk tend to think people in the countryside are all of a certain type, and here's Cherie, looking like she's time-travelled directly from a wild weekend at Woodstock to present us with baked goods.

'So,' she says, lowering herself carefully down onto the sofa, laughing as the other side poofs out from her weight. 'You're finally here! I think you two are going to have a ball. Don't be overwhelmed by tonight, you'll meet seven thousand people and they all come with partners or kids or dogs or back stories. You don't need to remember them all at once, and anyway, it's all written down in the files.'

'Files?' I repeat, scooping marshmallows off my drink with a long-stemmed spoon.

'Oh yes,' replies Laura, clapping her hands together. 'Cherie's files are amazing! On my first night here, she gave them to me for homework. Everything's in them, all the boring stuff like instructions on how to use the coffee machine, but also little background notes on our customers, and what their comfort foods are. Plus, a while ago, Willow did this thing for Tom—he's her husband now—when he first moved to Budbury. She wrote up a report on who everyone is and how they connect, and did it all like the houses in *Game of Thrones*—it's super-helpful!'

Sophie loves *Game of Thrones*, especially the books, and I see her perk up at this.

'I like that idea,' she says. 'Did you all have mottos and crests?'

'It wasn't quite that advanced, love,' Cherie replies, patting her hand. 'But maybe we've missed a trick and you can do that for us?'

'Maybe,' says Sophie, giving it some thought and

looking as serious as it's possible to be for a teenager who is unwittingly sporting a cream moustache. 'Once I know more about you all. I'll be collating my own files. Up here.'

She taps the side of her head as she says this, and it comes across as slightly more threatening than she intended. Cherie's eyes widen, and she replies: 'You do that, my love. I have nothing to hide, I swear!'

'Don't listen to her,' whispers Laura, leaning towards us. 'She's a cult leader!'

Cherie could, I decide, be a really good cult leader. She'd suck people in with her promises of cake and friendship, and they'd be trapped for life. At least that seems to be what happened to Laura.

As we chat 'Bruno' comes to an end, and there is a pause in the Disney karaoke.

'What are you doing?' Cherie asks, raising her eyebrows at us both. 'On the karaoke? It's compulsory, before you ask. Part of the job description. I did 'Colours of the Wind' from *Pocahontas*.'

She does look a bit like Pocahontas, now I come to think of it. Or maybe Pocahontas's grandma. Whatever she looks like, though, she's not getting me up on the karaoke. I used to enjoy it, and did a mean version of 'Hey Big Spender', but those days are gone.

'Sorry, Cherie,' I say, putting down my mug, 'but there's not enough Bakewell tart in the world to persuade me that's a good idea.'

Cherie looks as though she's about to argue, but Sophie

stands up, and announces: 'I'll do it! Watch and learn, mother, watch and learn…'

She strides over to the karaoke table, which is being run by a tall blond bloke who looks like a surfer, and chats to him. I stare in amazement as she takes the microphone, and stands there in front of a roomful of people she's never met. Wow. Such confidence, such poise, such … terrible singing. Sophie has many gifts, but pitch is not one of them.

Luckily, she's chosen 'You're Welcome' from *Moana*, and most of it is spoken rather than sung. She launches straight in, leaping around and flexing imaginary muscles as she sings Dwayne Johnson's part. It's a fabulous song, and a fabulous performance, and I shake my head in a strange mix of surprise and pride.

As she heads into the rap section in the middle, nailing every word, the 'Whole New World' singer with the pink hair walks over and joins us. She's wiping sweat from her face as she crashes down next to me, stretching long legs in front of her. She's wearing Doc Marten boots spray-painted in silver, and neon-green fishnet tights. It's a striking look, but as she has the build of a supermodel, she carries it well.

'Superb choice,' she says, nodding her head towards Sophie. 'One of my favourites. It's impossible to feel anything other than happy when you're listening to this. I'm Willow, by the way, and you must be my replacement!'

'Um, yes. I'm sorry?'

'No need to be sorry. I'm off travelling the world with my sexy husband and our faithful hound, Rick Grimes. He has his pet passport and tomorrow, we're getting a ferry to

France! I've never even been abroad before, and much as I'll miss this place, I'm so excited.'

I try to engage with the conversation, but my mind is stuck on the fact that they have a dog named after a character from the *Walking Dead*. Mine is called Gary, which is an odd name for a dog, but he's a rescue and was called that when we got him. That's my excuse and I'm sticking to it.

Also, I think, catching up with the rest of what she said, she's never been abroad before? She looks to be in her late twenties or early thirties, and it's unusual for someone of that age to have not even gone on a package holiday. I'm sure there's a story there, and wonder if the files Cherie mentioned will fill me in.

'That sounds fantastic,' I reply. 'Where are you going after France?'

'I don't know!' she says, eyes wide and shining. 'Isn't that brilliant? There's no schedule, no timetable, no plan. I absolutely love it. Maybe we'll drive through Spain, and on to Morocco. Maybe we'll go to Italy. Maybe we'll just spend a year in Provence. Who knows? Anything could happen!'

She seems quite giddy with all of this, and I see Laura and Cherie exchange a look. I'm not sure what the look is, part amused, part sad maybe? I can't decipher it, so I just smile and agree, and we carry on watching Sophie.

I realise, as she reaches the end, that I'm feeling more relaxed and comfortable than I have in a very long time. Something about the company of these women—these strange, welcoming women—has allowed me to unclench. I don't really know them, and they don't really know me, but the whole experience feels warm and safe and pleasant. Nobody is judging me; nobody is weighing me up and finding me lacking. Nobody is looking down at me.

I have fine company, and Gary has a friend, and I am eating home-made Bakewell tart in a café on the coast. This morning, I was a frazzled middle-aged woman defined by what I'd lost—my mum, my husband, my job, my home. Now, I feel like … well, I don't know what I feel like yet, but it's none of those things. For the first time in years, my life has potential. I don't quite trust this feeling one hundred per cent, but I want to—I want to be like these ladies. I want to be part of their world. I want this to work.

I stare over at Sophie, and she looks directly back at me, holding the microphone close to her face. She gives me a cheeky wink, points in my direction, and sings, 'You're welcome!'

Chapter Five

The party winds down at about nine, which I'm told is considered a late night by Budbury standards. I see Sophie do a double-take at that, and wonder how she's going to settle here once the novelty wears off. She's used to the bright lights of Birmingham, and to be honest, even our little suburb has plenty of bars and late-night hang-outs. This will, in the words of Jasmine, be a whole new world for her.

I've met about a million people, and they have all been lovely and incredibly welcoming. I'm worried that I won't remember anybody's name, never mind their comfort foods, and am glad that the café is closed tomorrow—and every Monday—so I can do my homework.

We wave people goodbye, and they head off in different directions, some to the car park, some to the village, others across the fields. All of them buffeted and battered by the wind, which shows no sign of letting up. Sophie tells us we can expect gusts of up to 90mph, and there are already a few casualties outside: one of the picnic tables has been upended, and a strand of the fairy lights has been dislodged, now snaking its bright trail across the grass, twisting and winding in the air.

Laura's daughters and Midge have gone home with her husband, Matt, and Sophie and I stay back with her and Cherie to help with the tidying. It's only a light clear; apparently the day after a party everyone reassembles to do the big stuff, and the café gets a deep clean. Tonight, we mainly walk around with bin bags, throwing in paper plates and uneaten cake.

Once we're done, Cherie announces that she's off to bed, hoping to dream of all things Disney.

'Especially the Beast,' she adds saucily. 'I always thought he was strangely sexy… Anyway, goodnight, my loves. Max, Sophie, I'll see you tomorrow or on Monday, either is fine. I think you're going to fit right in here. You're just mad enough.'

She gives us hugs that are so good, so comforting, that I suspect I have now been ruined for hugs forever. Nothing will ever come close to being clasped deep into Cherie's tie-dye kaftan.

'Just mad enough,' repeats Sophie, grinning. 'I like that. I might get a T-shirt made.'

She yawns, and covers her face with her hand as though she's embarrassed—a mere nineteen-year-old whipper-snapper, already tired out. It's contagious, and I immediately join in as I watch Cherie retreat through the café's kitchen. Apparently she has a little flat upstairs, full of vinyl classics, rock memorabilia and booze. It sounds like quite a party, Cherie's flat.

'Come on then,' says Laura, passing us two fresh bin bags for coats and buttoning up her parka. 'We better make a run for it!'

Apparently we are going to be staying in a cottage called Hyacinth House, at the Rockery, a holiday complex also owned by Cherie. Because we're here on a three-month trial, Cherie is insistent that we don't pay any rent, which seems extremely generous but apparently it's written in stone.

Laura explains that when she first moved here seven years ago, Hyacinth was her first home, and she had exactly the same deal. Now she lives in Black Rose, another of the cottages, with Matt and the girls, plus her older children when they're back. Nate is away in Liverpool, studying to be a vet, and Lizzie is working in London as a social media manager for a record label.

'I miss them both like crazy,' she tells me. 'Even though I have Ruby and Rose with me, and they're quite a handful—mum code for absolute nightmare, that, isn't it?—I still find myself sometimes sitting in Nate and Lizzie's rooms, remembering when they were little.'

I completely understand. I was the same when Ben left for college in Manchester. I knew it was good, knew it was part of the natural flow of things. But that didn't stop me bawling like a baby when he left, and still doesn't stop me from turning into a full-on overbearing mum when he comes home for the holidays. When we were getting the house ready for the tenants, we packed up our personal stuff and stored it in the attic. Even then, I had a little cry as I took his dartboard down, and put his football trophies into a box.

He'll be finishing up his semester in December, and I don't know if he'll join us here, go to his dad, or stay up north. My heart breaks a little at the thought of the last two options, so I decide not to think about it. It's hard work, this mothering lark. For so long all you think about is your kids, and then suddenly, as if by magic, they're gone, on to the next stage of their life without a second glance.

Once we're wrapped up, we leave together, lights switched off and doors locked, Laura using a torch to guide us back down the path. The wind is behind us now, so we all comedically look as though we are skipping down the hill, the gusts pushing us forward a lot faster than we want to go. The rain is still bucketing down, and I'm looking forward to being warm and cosy in my new bed.

Laura sits in the front to give me directions, and tells us she'll get Matt to help us unpack the roof box when we're there. Sophie is in the back seat with Gary, her eyes half-closed.

'On my first day here,' Laura says, sounding faraway, caught up in the memory, 'I couldn't reach my roof box. I'd packed everything really badly, and when Matt—I didn't know his name then—came to help us, he opened it and all my underwear fell out. One of my bras—not even one of my nice ones—landed on his head. And then, dear reader, I married him!'

I know from my chats with her that it wasn't quite that simple, that she was still grieving for the husband she'd lost, that the kids were a mess, that she'd been determined to leave at the end of summer. But here she is, loved up and mummy to twins. Maybe I should start throwing my bras at random men and see what happens. Probably just some funny looks and possibly a restraining order at a guess.

She directs us up through the village, past the still lively pub, and inland towards the Rockery. It takes less than ten minutes, but it's hairy. A bit like a scene from *Twister*, with debris flying out in front of us and the rain slashing against the windows. I can only hope a herd of cows doesn't come crashing from the sky.

As we pull through the gateposts of the complex, Sophie mutters: 'Hyacinth House. That's the name of a Doors song, isn't it?'

Personally I have no clue—I wasn't into cool music even when I was young. Sophie's tastes are more eclectic, and she likes anything from Nicki Minaj to Nirvana.

'It is! Ten points to you, Sophie!' says Laura, turning around to grin at her. 'All the cottages at the Rockery are named after bands or songs from the sixties and seventies. As you might have guessed from meeting Cherie, she was quite the girl in her day. Still is. Tomorrow, when Linda has buggered off, you can walk around and see if you spot any more you recognise. It's like one of those trails they do in art galleries to keep kids interested, but for grown-ups!'

'Do I get a prize if I get them all right?' she asks, as I park in the spot Laura indicates.

'Only if you don't use your phone, and even then you only get … umm, I don't know, actually. A free can of Guinness? Matt always has those knocking around, and I hate the stuff.'

Sophie makes an appreciative noise, as she is not fussy when it comes to booze. Even though she's old enough to drink now, I think she's still mentally at that stage where she'll mine-sweep anything at all.

We clamber out of the car, battling doors that want to squash us, and I let Gary have a wee before following Laura through a little archway in the stone wall. It's dark and wet and cold, but I can still see that this is a very pretty place. There's an oval-shaped green, and around it are rows of little cottages. Most have their lights on, and I catch glimpses of people inside, living their lives. I always love that—seeing people through their windows, and imagining who they are and what they're up to. I suppose, like Sophie always says, I'm just a very nosy person.

Our feet crunch on gravel as we walk, and Laura points out the big detached house on the corner, telling us that's Black Rose—a Thin Lizzy song, apparently. Hyacinth is further back, down a little winding pathway, next to the swimming pool. I didn't know about the swimming pool, and find myself quite excited about it until I remember I don't have a costume with me. Still, I suppose there are probably shops somewhere nearby, even in deepest Dorset.

'So,' Laura says, chattering on, raising her voice over the

gusts of wind, 'it's a nice little cottage, and more private because it's tucked away back here. Three bedrooms, so big enough in case your son comes to stay, and you have your own garden at the back where you can see the best sunsets. Obviously this isn't ideal weather, but it's only September, and there'll be plenty of nice days left once the storm passes. You can sit out and have a glass of wine and watch the birds; it's really lovely. Plus it's the perfect size, you know—you won't feel crowded, but it's also really cosy, and—'

She halts abruptly as we turn the corner, and stops dead in her tracks. I walk right into the back of her, and Sophie walks into the back of me. Gary looks up at us with his wise golden eyes like we're all idiots.

I follow her gaze, my hair whipping in the wind, and see that Hyacinth House does not look cosy at all. In fact it barely looks like a house. Something has gone badly wrong, and the ground in front of it is strewn with smashed tiles and broken masonry and chunks of plaster.

More tiles are still falling, some catching on the wind and flying, and it looks like the tall brick chimney stack has collapsed, smashing open the roof on its way down. The little planter trough outside the door has been broken in two, pottery and squashed flowers mashed up by the falling roof tiles, and one of the windows has been broken, the lights shining from inside illuminating the wreckage.

'Oh no! Oh no!' mutters Laura, her hand going to her face, tears in her eyes. 'What's happened?'

She looks utterly devastated, and I suppose she is seeing

a little piece of her personal history falling to pieces before her eyes. I move us all back a bit, not wanting to get caught by a flying brick, and stare at the scene in front of us. I can see, through that broken window, how lovely it is inside— or at least how lovely it was.

Fresh flowers had been placed on the table, but the wind has blown the vase over, and water is dripping onto the floor. A bottle of wine has fallen onto its side, and the chintzy sofa nearest the window is covered in rain and bits of rubble that have been blown inside.

If I ignore all of that, and focus on the wood-burning fire and the basket full of logs, I can see that it would have been the perfect cosy refuge for us. That effect is ruined by the disintegrating roof, and the fact that the floral curtains are twisting around in the wind, as though they're trying to warn us off.

'I think, um, maybe there's been an accident?' I say, lamely. Sophie gives me a 'you think?' look, and I shake my head at her. This is bad—no getting away from it—but for us it's just an inconvenience. We can find a hotel, or at worst sleep in the car. For Laura, this is something more.

An especially powerful gust of wind howls around us, and more tiles slip from the top of the building, shattering into pieces when they crash to the ground. I put my arm around Laura, and steer her away from the cottage, back towards the path. She barely resists, and I can feel her body trembling beneath my hands.

'I'm so sorry,' she says, voice weak with emotion. 'I

wanted it to be perfect for you, just like it was for me. I wanted everything to be right.'

'It doesn't matter,' I say, leading her back around to the lawn, heading towards Black Rose. 'It can all be fixed, I'm sure. Everything looks worse at night. Come on, let's get you home now.'

She seems to pull herself together a bit, either because of my words or because she doesn't want to risk her girls seeing her so upset. She nods, and manages to reply: 'You're right. I'm sure it'll be okay with a glue gun and a bit of TLC.'

Sophie and I share a look at this, because there's no way that roof is going back on with a glue gun. This isn't the time to mention that, though, as Laura is just about holding all her pieces in.

When we walk through the door to Black Rose, Midegbo greets us with a woof and an excited gambol towards Gary. Our poor little fella is a soggy doggy again, and I know exactly how he feels. As the warmth of Laura's home hits me, I realise exactly how cold I am. I glance at Sophie, and see that her teeth are chattering. I usher her towards the fire that is roaring away in the living room just as Matt walks in, barefoot in pyjamas. He does a bit of a double-take when he sees us all standing in front of the fire warming our extremities, which is understandable.

I only met him very briefly earlier, and he spoke maybe four words to me. It's not that he was rude, just quiet. Probably that works well for him in Budbury, because everyone else seems to talk all the time. He nods at me, quickly covering up his confusion, his eyes going straight to his wife.

She runs towards him and into his arms, and despite the fact that she is soaked wet through, he simply wraps her up in an embrace. He drops a kiss on her curls, and murmurs comforting words, even though he presumably has no idea what's wrong. As I watch her cling to him, see him offer such sweet consolation, I feel a flutter of envy. It's not my proudest moment, and obviously it's not that I don't want Laura and Matt to be happy... I suppose it's just that I miss having that myself. It's only when you're single that you realise the world is full of couples.

Sophie and I stand by the fire, looking away from them, because it somehow seems like an intrusion to watch. After a few more moments, I hear him ask: 'Okay, so is somebody going to tell me what's wrong?'

'It's Hyacinth!' Laura says. 'She's fallen down!'

Hyacinth is a girl, apparently.

'It's not that bad, I don't think,' I chip in. 'Looks like the chimney stack has been blown down, and it's taken most of the roof with it. Lots of loose tiles, some damage downstairs. Might be a bit of a mess upstairs, I'd imagine, but it's still standing! It'll be all right, Laura.'

Somehow, I realise that I feel guilty. Like it's my fault that her favourite building in the whole world collapsed on the night we were supposed to move in.

She swipes tears away from her eyes, and comes over to give me a hug.

'I know, I know,' she says. 'I'm just being a drama queen

because I love it so much. And thank you for reacting like you have. This was supposed to be your fresh start, your first night in your new home, and I can't imagine how it must have felt seeing that instead. Don't worry. We'll sort you out.'

Even as she says this, I see a flicker of doubt cross her face. She'd be terrible at poker, I think, because she's clearly not good at hiding what's worrying her.

Matt has listened to all of this while getting a big waxed jacket from the hallway and putting it on, along with a pair of wellies.

'The girls are asleep,' he says, gesturing upstairs. 'I'm going to go and check out the damage, and I'll call Gabriel and see if he can come round. We might need to try and get a tarp up, or at least fence it all off so nobody tries to use the pool in the morning.'

'But it's so late!' Laura replies, looking aghast.

'It's only just gone ten, and you know what he's like. He won't be asleep anyway. Neither will Cherie if you want to call her. You stay here, and get some hot drinks and snacks going, okay?'

That is exactly the right thing to say to Laura, and evidence of how well Matt knows his wife. As soon as he mentions catering, she seems to transform into a different person: suddenly steady and calm, because now she knows what she has to do, and she is perfectly capable of doing it.

She gives Matt a kiss and tells him to be careful, blocking Midgebo from the door as he tries to follow him, and tells us she'll be back in a jiffy.

As she bustles around in the kitchen, and we sit close to the fire, I look around properly for the first time. It's a big room, but also a full room—five-year-old twins will do that to a place. But behind the clutter, I see good proportions, a nice high ceiling, a big bay window that looks out to the green. Nothing matches—the curtains, the wallpaper, the furniture—but somehow that adds to its charm. It'd be called 'eclectic' on one of the shows I watch.

If I was doing it up, I'd get some shelving built in to the alcoves—something nice, high quality crafts, dark wood—and then the random books and games and photo albums would have somewhere to call home. I'd probably paint it all, maybe a rich deep burgundy, and an old leather Chesterfield would look fabulous in here. At the moment there's a carpet, and a couple of rugs that I suspect have been strategically positioned to hide the signs of wear that young kids and lively Labradors tend to leave. I'd get rid of that, sand down the floorboards, and varnish them.

Laura and Matt's house is, of course, gorgeous the way it is; it is a lived-in family home drenched in comfort and familiarity, a place full of laughter and love and belonging. My little mental survey of 'what I'd do' isn't to criticise them; it's to calm my own mind. It's a thing I enjoy doing wherever I go, to distract myself. During my lowest moments, I've actually been known to browse the Rightmove website, looking for dilapidated houses and imagining how I'd redesign them. Sad but true.

Right now, I need that distraction, because I am starting

to feel the aftereffects of seeing our alleged new home collapsing before my eyes.

I'd focused on Laura right then, because she was a mess, but now I feel a low-level tremble spreading through my body. It's mainly internal, a kind of hum of anxiety, but as Laura passes me a huge mug of tea, I see that my hands are shaking slightly. Sophie has crashed out in a big armchair and has her eyes closed, her skin pale and wisps of dark hair glued to the side of her face. She's almost asleep; I can tell from her breathing.

Laura seems fully recovered from her shock, just in time for me to start experiencing my own. We're like a tag team. I sip my tea, and after a few moments I ask: 'Who's Gabriel?'

'Oh! Well, he's relatively new here—by which I mean he's been around for a year or so. He inherited a little smallholding a few miles outside the village, from Mr Pumpwell.'

I bite my lip and try not to laugh at the name. Pumpwell? That's so funny, and now I know Sophie is definitely asleep, or she'd be on that straight away. I remind myself that if Gabriel inherited a property, then Mr Pumpwell is sadly no longer with us, and I need to show some respect. Still, though.

'We were all a bit surprised, because none of us even knew he had relatives—he was a bit of a loner, Mr Pumpwell. Pumpwell, Pumpwell, Pumpwell. Yes, I see you there, Maxine Connolly, trying not to giggle! Anyway, Auburn, Willow's sister—redhead, sang "A Whole New World"—was pretty close to him. She used to take him his prescriptions and have a chat, and … well, I don't suppose that matters. He was in his late eighties, so it wasn't exactly a shock when he died, but it's never nice, is it? Everyone stepped in to re-home most of his animals, and take care of the one that was left, and the farmhouse was mothballed.

'Then one day—this was high drama in Budbury, as you can imagine—a mysterious *stranger* drove into town…'

'Are you sure he drove? Didn't he actually ride in on a piebald pony, then walk into the local saloon and ask for a sarsaparilla?'

'Hush now! And kind of. He was driving an old-fashioned Land Rover and came into the café and asked for a coffee. Turns out he was Mr Pumpwell's great-nephew, and he'd been living abroad. Nobody really knows, there are all kinds of rumours about him. Like he was in the SAS, or M15, or the French Foreign Legion.'

'Why? Is he soldier-y?'

'Well, not really, not to look at. But there's something about him that's a bit different, I suppose. He's very *private*!'

She says this as though it is the worst thing that has happened, ever, in the entire universe. I get the feeling that although the Budbury ladies are absolutely adorable, they make my levels of nosiness look like disinterest. I can only imagine how much of a torment it's been to have this man so close, and for him to remain a mystery—and that's resulted in them creating a mythical history that casts him as Jack Reacher. It's funny, and I can't keep the smile off my face.

'Right. I feel your pain. So why is Matt calling him now?'

'Because he's also single-handedly renovated Mr Pumpwell's place, and also done some other building jobs around the village, and he's just one of those blokes, you know? The ones who always know which wall is a structural wall, and who has ladders that go to the moon, and can just *fix* anything?'

'You sound like you're in love with him, Laura. Or at least like he could be the star of one of those rude movies where a hot man comes around to fix the washing machine, and ends up taking a spin cycle in the bedroom…'

She laughs, blushes slightly, and replies: 'I know what you mean. Though to be honest, I'd prefer a man who just fixed the washing machine and left. But what can I say? I'm only flesh and blood … and he *is* easy on the eye. Like a combination of Poldark and the guy out of *The Last Kingdom*. Did you ever watch that?'

She sounds a little dreamy as she asks, and I second that emotion. There's not a boxed set out there I haven't watched, and I spent a delightful few months lost in the world of the Vikings and Anglo-Saxon England not so long ago.

'Oh yes. Uhtred of Bebbanburg. I wouldn't mind him fixing my washer.'

We both giggle like schoolgirls, and I'm glad Sophie is asleep. She is but young, and she doesn't quite understand that just because women hit their later years, they don't magically grow up. Inside, our teenaged selves are always lurking, waiting for the chance to escape.

It's a pleasant distraction, and one that I needed. I'm exhausted now, and the creeping doubts that I'd only just started to shed are sneaking back into my mind. Has this all been a terrible mistake? Is it too late to cancel the tenants? Am I the world's unluckiest woman?

Some of this must show on my face, because Laura reaches out to pat my hand, and says, 'It'll all be okay. What's life without a few challenges?'

'I don't know. Easy?'

'Easy is overrated. Look, you guys can stay here tonight, Lizzie and Nate's rooms are free. And longer term, we'll sort something, all right? This is Budbury. There's always a solution. Don't sit there fretting, wondering if you've cocked up, because you haven't. It's just a storm, not a cosmic message. I know I overreacted when I saw what had happened, but I'm made entirely of mush. Everything will be good in the end. I need to make a few calls, and maybe have a hot shower. Are you okay down here for a bit? The kitchen's just through there if you want anything, and there's a fresh Victoria sponge on the counter. Help yourself, but just make sure you don't leave anything within Midgebo reach, okay?'

The dog, who is lying with Gary in front of the fire, looks up at the mention of his name. One ear twitches, and his eyes seem to say 'who me?'

I nod, and assure her that we will be fine. I finish my tea, and feel comfy enough here to put my feet up on the sofa.

That is my last memory for an unspecified amount of time, as I seem to defy all the odds and drift off to sleep. It could have been for a minute, or it could have been for hours, but when I wake up my eyes are crusted together and I have drool on my chin. Nice.

I glance over to Sophie, see that she is still in the land of nod, and begin the process of stretching out my limbs and reacquainting myself with reality. I can hear quiet voices coming from the nearby kitchen, and listen in.

'All the cottages at the Rockery are booked,' Laura says. 'I checked with Cherie, and we'd only blocked out Hyacinth. She called Cal, but the farmhouse is full—Frank's grandson is over from Australia, Martha's back, and they've hired some new hands for the season.'

'What about Tom's place? Briarwood?' Matt asks.

'Also full. Apparently they just got a fresh batch of residents in. Edie has a spare bedroom, but only the one, and nowhere else in the village is empty. There's Tom's motorhome, but that's only got one bed too. What are we going to do? I feel so bad for them!'

I hate being the source of this whispered debate, and get to my feet to join them. Gary comes over and gives my hand a lick, fulfilling his role as my moral support dog.

A new voice chips in, deep and male and unrecognised as I make my way to the kitchen.

'She can stay at mine if she wants to. It's not luxurious, but there are bedrooms that are just about usable. I don't have beds, or blankets, or any of that stuff, though.'

I presume this is the mysterious Gabriel, and I pause a

few feet away to listen in. He sounds grumpy, and the offer he's just made doesn't sound enticing.

'Beds or blankets or that stuff'—he says this as though it's a spa bath and underfloor heating, not a basic necessity. More than that, though, I am taken aback by the reluctance I hear in his tone. Everyone I've met here so far has been so welcoming, so friendly, and this man speaks as though he's just offered himself up to be injected with a live dose of ebola. But what do I know? Maybe he sounds like that even when he's opening his Christmas presents.

'Well, we could get the furniture, that wouldn't be an issue,' Laura replies, and I can almost hear her brain working. 'That's a manageable hurdle. But are you sure? I know you, erm, like your own space … and she does have a dog, too?'

There's a pause before he replies, and when it comes it's a humdinger: 'The dog isn't a problem. And yes, I do like my own space … but the house is big enough that I can avoid them. They just need to try and stay out of my way. I'm not a nanny.'

Wow. I feel a flush of anger, and am considering marching in there and telling him he's more than welcome to his solitude. I think I'd rather go back to Birmingham than be such an inconvenience.

'Okay, well, maybe that could work,' says Laura, sounding relieved. 'I really want it to work. She's so nice, and so is Sophie, and I'm … well, let's just say that I'm emotionally invested! I want this to work out, for them and for us—we do need the help at the café now Willow's leaving, and Cherie likes her too. She's not been herself since Frank died last year, and I think having someone new around will be good for her. She really perked up once she started chatting to Max on video call. Like it gave her something different to think about. She's not been firing on all cylinders for a while now.'

This new information stops me in my tracks. Who was Frank? Cherie's husband, son, brother? And if the Cherie I've met is missing some cylinders, what on earth is she like with them all in working order? She already seems like a force of nature.

Whoever Frank was, I am sad for Cherie—I know how much the life sapped out of me after I lost my mum. Grief is sneaky, and ambushes you at the most inconvenient of times. But Laura, I suspect, is overestimating my importance. I'm just a temp, and I'm sure she can find another one from an agency.

Gabriel makes a kind of growly 'humph' noise, and answers: 'I don't know Cherie well enough to comment on that, but she's been good to me—you all have—and if I can help, I will.'

His words are nice, but he is still using that same gruff tone. I wonder if he's even aware of the disconnect?

'Oh Gabe, that's wonderful. And she's only small, you'll barely notice her!'

'Huh,' he retorts. 'She didn't look that small to me, and there's two of them … but I'll do it if it'll help you and Cherie.'

Laura gushes her thanks, and I quiver a few feet away, feeling a mortified blush blossom on my cheeks.

'It might not be for too long anyway,' he adds. 'If the weather cooperates and you can get the labour in, you could have Hyacinth back in working order in a couple of weeks. It's a mess and you should try and get experts in, but if you can't find anyone, I'll do what I can.

'The roof will need completely replacing, and the upstairs is a disaster zone. The whole chimney crashed right through into the bedroom, and part of the roof came in on the bathroom. I've tarped it up the best I could, but in this weather, I wouldn't be surprised if the rest comes off overnight. I turned off the utilities just in case. I'll come back tomorrow in daylight and have another look, but for now I've done as much as I could. Let me know.'

I realise they are maybe about to start making goodbye noises, and suddenly I feel embarrassed to be lurking by the door and earwigging. I don't know why—I'm not twelve, and it's me they're discussing after all. If I had any backbone, I'd walk my un-small self right in there and own the situation.

Except I'm not doing especially well for backbone these days. In fact I'm practically an invertebrate. I dash quickly back over to the sofa, and drape myself back down on it. As the three of them walk through into the living room, I make a show of waking up and stretching my arms, yawning as though I've just come back to consciousness. And the Oscar goes to...

'Max!' says Laura, grinning at me. 'Everything's going to

be fine. You can stay at Gabriel's for a bit, until we sort Hyacinth! It's a few miles out of the village, but you have a car, and you'll be working anyway, and … um, is that okay?'

Maybe I'm not getting that Oscar after all, because I find that I can't quite forget the words I overheard. I can't quite get over the fact that the man hovering behind her made his kind offer in such a blatantly reluctant way.

It doesn't help that he is, to put it frankly, drop-dead gorgeous. He's over six foot, broad-shouldered but lean, with the kind of dark good looks that immediately make me think of Heathcliff. His hair is dark, thick, wavy, touching his shoulders, wild and damp from the weather. His eyes are a deep shade of shining brown, and his features are strong and imposing: high cheekbones, a slightly Roman nose, a wide mouth. He'd be an absolutely breathtaking specimen of manhood if it wasn't for the glower, and the way his expression seems carved from stone. If he smiled, I suspect his face might crack in two.

He's made it perfectly clear that he doesn't really want us around, and the feeling is entirely mutual—the thought of spending time with this buttoned-up, arrogant arsehole doesn't exactly fill me with joy either.

'I don't know,' I reply slowly, feeling my way through the next few thoughts. 'I mean, I don't know Gabriel at all, do I? It's not just me I have to think about either; it's Sophie as well. She might not be happy with staying with a strange man.'

At this exact point, Sophie rouses and stares at us all in

confusion, obviously having that weird sensation when you wake up somewhere new and wonder where the hell you are.

Gabriel's nostrils have flared at my comment, and I wonder if I've offended him. If I have, I decide, then that's fine, because it's also a valid point. Laura herself has said she barely knows anything about him. I see Laura's gaze flicker between me and Gabriel, and Matt looking uncomfortable behind them.

'Well,' announces Gabriel, shoving his hands into the pockets of his coat and staring at me. 'Please yourself. Laura knows where I am if you change your mind.'

He strides out of the room without a backward glance, and I hear the door slam. Sophie rubs her eyes, and says blearily: 'Who was that?'

Chapter Six

We end up spending the night in Nate's room because he has bunk beds, and both of us feel the need not to be separated after a long, strange day. Plus I have an instinct to stay close to my daughter, in case any other disasters strike. I'd hate to be in a different room if there was a pterodactyl attack, or the mattresses came to life.

We're both wiped out and despite the sound of the wind howling outside, we sleep solidly until just before ten the next morning. As soon as I wake up, I lie in bed, disorientated by the bunk above me, and check my phone. Before I crashed out last night, I'd emailed the letting agency, asking if there was any wriggle room with the tenants.

I let out an audible sigh when I see the reply. They'd strongly advise against withdrawing at this stage, as everything is signed, deposits have been paid, and I could be sued for breach of contract. The agent also added a more personal note, explaining that the couple moving in are young, just starting new jobs, and really lovely. I'm frustrated but also a little relieved; I don't want to be the kind of person who messes anyone around.

'You okay?' Sophie says, dangling her head over the side of her bunk, her hair flowing down like a curtain.

'Yep. I just checked if we could go back to the house, and, well, we can't. So that's a bit tricky.'

She clambers down the ladder and sits next to me. She's still wearing last night's clothes, as am I. We probably both smell gorgeous. Matt had unpacked some of our stuff for us and even though we were too tired to root around for PJs, at least we have clean things to wear today.

'I don't want to go back anyway,' she says quietly. 'I know this hasn't started off the way we'd hoped, but there's still a lot to like. I mean, it's beautiful here, and the people are lovely, and I … well, I think we should stay.'

I knew she would. This whole crazy plan was her idea, and she's not ready to let go of it. She's probably feeling bad about everything, and I sit up and give her a quick hug.

'I know you do,' I reply. 'But the reality is more complicated than that.'

'No it's not. We go and stay with Gabriel. For a bit, anyway. He can't be as bad as you think, and we'll probably barely even see him. It's not like it's for the whole time, is it? Plus, he was kind of hot, in a wild-man way. Looked a bit like Poldark, didn't he?'

'A bit, yeah, but he was also rude, and didn't really want us to come, and he called me fat, and basically he can stick his tricorn hat where the sun doesn't shine as far as I'm concerned.'

'He called you fat?' she repeats, looking shocked. 'That's out of order. It's okay for me to call you fat, but not for someone we only just met!'

'Well, technically he called me "not small", but that's what my brain translated it to. And that doesn't matter anyway. I just don't know, love. Maybe we could find an Airbnb or something.'

I sound unconvinced as I say this, because a very quick look last night revealed that our choices in this area are limited. We could have a shepherd's hut with a double bed and an outside loo, or a luxury villa with swimming pool and tennis court that costs six gazillion quid a night.

'Anyway,' I announce, pushing her off the bed so she falls onto the floor—something about the bunks has brought out my inner child—'I'm going to get a shower. I smell like a dead gerbil.'

She rolls around on the ground for a bit, pretending to be injured, and as I leave the room she shouts: 'Mum, don't forget to take your anti-asshole pills. I think you're off your meds!'

I grin as I make my way out onto the landing, and karma immediately strikes as I trip over a random child-sized wellington boot that has been left outside the door. The whole landing is strewn with detritus: shoes, books, Lego, colouring pads, and chunky felt-tip pens. I pause and listen up—it's quiet, which means the girls have gone to school. I'm guessing they set up base camp outside our door in hopes of waking us up and seeing us before we left. Laura probably banned them from knocking but they did their best anyway. It is a tribute to our exhaustion that we didn't hear a thing.

I walk towards the bathroom, and both Gary and Midge come belting up the stairs to sniff me and tell me how excited they are. I'd expected Gary to want to sleep with us, but there was no budging him from Midge's basket downstairs, where he'd curled up in a little ball with his new friend.

I give them both a fuss, do my thing in the shower, and feel like a different human being by the time I make my way down the stairs. Amazing how restorative a clean pair of knickers can be.

I find Matt sitting at the kitchen table, sipping coffee and eating his way through a ginormous pile of fresh toast. The bread is obviously home-made, and it makes my tummy rumble. He gestures for me to join him, and I soon feel the not-so-gentle nudge of Midgebo beneath the table, waiting for scraps. Gary is by his side, looking mischievous.

'Laura's doing the school run then heading into the cafe,' he says. 'I'm opening the surgery later so I can get started on Hyacinth. Or arrange for someone else to get started on it, at least. You okay?'

Matt is the village vet, I already know, amused at how he ended up with such a boisterous dog.

'Yeah, I'm fine. Slept surprisingly well.'

'Despite Ruby and Rose doing everything they possibly could to wake you up? Ruby was actually playing her recorder at one point…'

'Gosh. I'd forgotten that recorders even existed. I suppose we were tired enough to block it all out. Was Laura all right this morning? She seemed so upset.'

'She was, but now she's okay. Now she's on a mission. She's worried you're going to leave, and she'll probably be heading straight to the café to have a pow-wow with Cherie about how they can persuade you to stay. I hope you do. Stay, that is.'

I nod, and butter some toast. I'm not quite sure how I feel right now, and silence seems the best option. As Matt isn't exactly the chattiest of people, I fear we could be here all day without uttering a word.

'I know it's a lot,' he continues, proving me wrong. 'Moving here at all. You took a chance, and it probably feels like it's backfiring right now. But I promise I'll do everything I can to get Hyacinth ready for you as quickly as possible, and in the meantime, you could at least consider Gabriel's offer.'

'I don't know him, Matt, and he seemed … well, he seemed a bit rude.'

'I get what you mean; he can be abrupt. But people think that about me sometimes. Not everyone is a little ray of sunshine. It doesn't make him an axe murderer either. I probably know him better than most around here—I've been out to see his donkey, Belle, and we've been to the pub a few times. He's a decent bloke, and pretty funny when you get to know him. We wouldn't suggest it if we didn't think it would work.'

'He has a donkey?' I ask, for some reason fixating on that. I bloody love donkeys. Richie once adopted one from a sanctuary for me for my birthday. There's something about their grumpiness and their less-than-supermodel looks that just endears them to me. They're like the poor relations of their leggy, glossy horse cousins.

'Part donkey, part demon. She's old and vicious and she's lived on her own too long. Donkeys are social animals; they should be at least in pairs. They don't do well alone.'

I wonder if he's making some sort of subtle analogy to me, and decide I'm being paranoid. I carry on eating my toast, and weigh everything up in my mind. I can't go back home. There doesn't seem to be much accommodation within striking distance that I can afford. Sophie is desperate to stay, and I also now seem to be an integral part of some kind of Cherie rescue mission.

'Who's Frank?' I ask, realising as I do that I've potentially given the game away—I was allegedly asleep when they were discussing him. 'I heard someone talking about him last night.'

Matt raises his eyebrows, and I suspect he has some suspicions, but he replies: 'Frank was Cherie's husband. He died last year of a heart attack. It came as real shock, because he looked as fit as a fiddle even though he was in his late eighties. He was out in the fields at his farm when it happened, though, which is maybe the way he'd have wanted it. Him and Cherie ... they found each other later in life, were friends for years before they got married. It hit her hard, and we're all a bit worried about her. She misses him. We all do. He was part of this place, you know? Sometimes I still walk into the café and expect him to be sitting there, eating a burnt bacon butty and reading the papers.'

He is suddenly silent again, as though he has revealed too much. He's a big, brawny man, but obviously a sensitive one. These people all seem so connected, so laced in and out of each other's lives in a way I've never really seen before. I don't know if I love it or hate it, but decide that I should at least probably give it a go.

'All right,' I say finally. 'We'll stay. With Gabriel. Unless it becomes unbearable, and then…'

'Then,' he says, grinning at me, his usually serious face lighting up, 'you won't be able to bear it, and we'll all understand. But at least you'll have tried. Thank you, Max.'

It takes a half-hour or so for us to mobilise, and then I drive first to the café to see Laura. The day has dawned with pure blue skies, sunshine, and not a whisper of wind. The legendary calm after the storm, I suppose. Sophie and I get to properly admire the view from the walk up the path, and it is breathtaking. The sea is almost turquoise, racing in to the golden sand, and if it wasn't for the slight chill in the air I could almost believe we were in the Med.

Up in the garden there are signs of the storm—the upturned table, the loose fairy lights, a fence panel that's blown off—but other than that, you'd never guess the destruction that Linda caused the night before.

Sophie stays outside. There's a little paddock for dogs,

and Gary wants nothing more than to chase Midgebo around it. Poor Midge doesn't stand a chance—our Gary definitely has some whippet in him. We should have changed his name to Usain Bolt.

Inside, I find Laura with a group of people, some of whom I remember meeting the night before, some I don't, and they're giving the place a deep clean after the party. Everyone seems a bit subdued, which I guess is a combination of hangovers and a touch of sadness because Willow and Tom have left.

I get given a cleaning spray and some cloths to do the tables with, and while I work I chat to a heavily pregnant blonde woman called Katie. She has a toddler with her, and a nine-year-old in school. She's married to Van, Willow's brother, I soon learn. I start to understand why they need files to keep all of this straight in their heads. I might suggest name tags.

'We're all really excited for her,' she says, looking on as her three-year-old son, Zack, helps Laura, and by 'help', I mean kicks the bin bag she's trying to hold open and empty her brush pan into.

'She's had a hard time—they all have. Their mum, Lynnie, developed early onset Alzheimer's years ago, and Willow looked after her. The other two—Van and Auburn— did as well, but not for as long. It's complicated. But basically her older sibs were off travelling the world while she stayed back. Lynnie died six months ago and obviously they were all devastated. But it was one of those situations, you know, where if she wasn't actually your own mum, you'd be thinking maybe it was also a bit of a relief? For Lynnie at least, because it was really bad by the end. For ages you'd still see flashes of the old her, knew she was in there somewhere, but then … well, lockdown, and cancer. It was awful.'

'I can imagine. And I know what you mean. Even though they never wanted to lose her, there's part of them that knows it was time, and then they beat themselves up about thinking that, and feel like the worst humans in the world.'

'Exactly! Is it something you've been through?'

'I'm still going through it,' I reply, marvelling at Laura's patience as she persuades Zack to hold the bag instead of jumping on it. 'My mum passed away a year and a half ago. She had COPD, and selfishly I never wanted to let her go, even though she'd made her peace with it. Then I had all this free time, but whenever I tried to enjoy it, the guilt would come along and I'd feel like I'd been hit by the proverbial bus. Which I suppose is better than being hit by a real bus, even though it doesn't always feel that way.'

'I'm sorry,' Katie replies, her hands on her belly as she rocks from side to side. 'That's terrible. I think they felt the same, especially Willow. All she'd ever known was looking after her mum, her whole life was regimented and built around it. Even after she married Tom, he moved in with her and her mum. It took us ages to convince her she could let go. That it was her turn to live a little, you know? So we're all glad she's gone, but we'll also miss her. I'm glad you're here, though. She made a little leaving speech this morning and said she knew we were all in safe hands!'

'Oh lord, I don't know about that,' I reply, surprised. 'But thank you. So, I need to go with Laura, and move us— temporarily—into our new accommodation.'

'Oooh, where's that then?' says Edie, the elderly lady we met last night, who has approached us by stealth from behind. She's carrying a tray of fresh pastries, which she places down on the nearest table before picking up a pain au chocolat as big as her face. I notice she already has one packed up in Tupperware to take home as well.

'With someone called Gabriel, on Mr Pumpwell's farm?'

Edie's wrinkled little face breaks into such a big smile that her eyes disappear completely.

'Oh, he's so nice, that Gabriel! Such a lovely young man. He came round and fixed my sink for me, you know? I'd mentioned one day that the tap wouldn't stop leaking, and that afternoon he just turned up. Lickety-split, he had it sorted. Wouldn't let me pay him or anything. And while he was there, he noticed a few other things that needed doing, and he's been coming back whenever he has the spare time. Always stays for a cuppa too. Doesn't say much, mind, but he seems happy enough to let me witter on! Not bad-looking either, is he, if you're into that kind of thing?'

'What kind of thing?' I ask.

'Sexpots.'

'Oh. Right. Well. I didn't really see him for long; it was all a bit chaotic last night, as I'm sure you've heard.'

I go back to scrubbing my table, because it's less

confusing than talking to Edie. I had Gabriel firmly placed in the 'bit of a dick' category in my mind, and her version doesn't quite sit with that. I suppose it's possible that I overreacted, and I remind myself not to do a *Pride and Prejudice* and make assumptions. Like Matt said, not everybody can be a little ray of sunshine, and at the end of the day he did offer to let two complete strangers stay in his home just to be a good neighbour. He sounded rude, but maybe actions speak louder than words on some occasions.

I meet a few more people as the morning wears on, including Laura's sister Becca, and Zoe who runs the bookshop, and a man whose name I can't remember who turned up with a crate of home-made cider at lunchtime.

Sophie's been in and out, and spent a bit of time with Martha, who is Zoe's god-daughter. She's older than Sophie, early twenties somewhere, but they bonded over a mutual love of David Bowie, Nandos, and the fact that they are wearing the same Doc Marten boots. Martha graduated from Oxford then started a post-grad degree before realising it wasn't for her. She's come back to Budbury for 'the free rent and cake' apparently, both of which seem like very valid reasons.

The clear-up soon starts to show every sign of turning into another party, with lots of food being wheeled out of the kitchens and the cider being cracked open, and I wonder if it just goes on like this: an endless cycle of party-clean-party. I suppose it could be worse.

Eventually, though, several hours later, Laura declares herself happy with the state of everything, and we set off to

Gabriel's place. She's over the moon that we've taken up the offer, and as soon as Matt told her this morning, she got to work sorting out beds for us. Van, Katie's husband, who presumably has a van as well as it being his name, was dispatched to 'the retail park'. No idea where that is, but I'm assured it's a veritable fleshpot of earthly delights, complete with a McDonald's, a Pets at Home and several outlet furniture stores. Wowzers.

We follow Laura's car out of the village, through winding country lanes that come with the most jaw-dropping views out over the coast and across the hills. It is gorgeous here, the kind of pretty that you see in films and on postcards. Every twist and turn we take plunges us even deeper into a wilderness of ancient woodlands and Iron Age hill forts and frothing rivers that are tumbling their way to the sea.

It's probably only five miles away as the crow flies, but the roads here are like crows if they'd drunk a bottle of Baileys and then dropped some acid. They wriggle and curve through the landscape, past signs for places with names that sound as old as time: Nettlecombe, Powerstock, Dottery, Whitchurch Canonicorum. We drive up; we drive down; we drive in what feels like an impossibly random way along roads that sometimes turn into narrow one-way tracks. I'm sure I'll get used to it, but for now I'm glad the traffic is light and we see little else but the occasional tractor, or a car at a passing place.

Finally, Laura indicates and turns in through an open iron gate, tooting her horn as she drives onto a gravelled courtyard. Off to one side is a small paddock, presumably home to the infamous Belle, complete with a little stable. There's a run-down garage, and signs of recent building work: bags of cement, a mixer, a stack of dismantled scaffolding. A pile of tree branches, maybe torn off by the storm, is weighted down beneath netting.

As I get out of the car, I see that the cottage itself is a strange mix. The central part looks old, made of mellow gold stone with mullioned windows and a big wooden door freshly painted a deep blue. Around it are various extensions, which I'd guess have been added over generations of working and living, giving the whole building a ramshackle look with its different heights and different materials. A barn further back looks more run down, its roof sagging and one of the big wooden doors off its hinges. I can't tell if it's always like that, or a victim of the storm.

Despite the work-in-progress vibe, the location is idyllic, in the middle of lush fields bordered by hedgerows and drooping oak trees. We're in the base of a valley, the road dipping suddenly down, surrounded by velvety green hills and grazing sheep. I see a flurry of swallows swooping in and out of the barn, and it makes me smile. They'll be heading off to warmer climes soon, I'm sure.

Gary is running around having a good sniff at everything, Midge by his side, and both of them seem to be having a contest to see who can manage the final pee against the gate post. They came; they peed; they conquered.

As soon as the big wooden door opens, they both look up, ears cocked, alert for threats or treats or both. Midge immediately dashes over, obviously familiar with the human who emerges, and Gary cautiously follows. A small, petty part of me secretly hopes that he doesn't approach him, doesn't respond to him, but the traitorous beastie does his I'm-nervous-but-brave slink towards Gabriel, who is squatting down to put himself at dog height.

Within seconds, Gary is getting his ears scratched, and licking his fingers like they're old friends. The swine.

I feel an instant bite of tension when he stands up and walks towards us, taking in the chunky fisherman-style sweater, the battered Levi's spattered with paint, the scuffed steel toe cap boots. Despite the working gear, there's an aura of something exotic about him, like he could have just left his artist's studio. Maybe it's the tanned skin, or the longer-than-usual hair, I don't know. Somehow, he seems slightly too striking a creature to find in an old farmhouse in the English countryside—as though he should be migrating, like the swallows.

The smile he had for Gary and Midge fades as he approaches, and he meets my eyes and gives me a single nod.

'Nice dog,' he says gruffly, and although it's not much, it does melt me a little. Your dogs are like your babies, aren't they?

'He is,' I agree, deciding that I will always match him word for word. He speaks two, I speak two. If we keep it like that, there's no chance of things going wrong.

'Van's already been round. We moved the stuff up to the rooms.'

Ah, shit. I realise that this will be harder than I thought. If I have to count his words every time he speaks, I'll miss what he's saying. How many was that?

'That's great!' says Laura, saving me the effort. 'Did he bring everything? I asked him to call into Dunelm and get duvets and things.'

'I don't know what Dunelm is, but he brought a lot of stuff with him. Are you any good with building flat-packs?'

Laura laughs out loud, scaring up a few nearby magpies, and replies: 'Of course I'm not! That's one of those times when I think sexism is a really good idea, and declare it's a "man's job". Sorry!'

'Mum is,' Sophie pipes up helpfully. 'She's an absolute whizz with them. Give her a screwdriver and a set of instructions in Swedish, and she's in her happy place.'

Laura looks surprised, and Gabriel simply nods.

'Good,' he says.

'Great,' I mumble.

'So,' Laura continues, obviously realising she needs to fill a conversational void, 'I need to be getting off to collect the girls from school. Matt had a roofer out, Gabe, and he agrees with you on the estimates, so hopefully we'll have Hyacinth restored to her former glory before long. I've brought some food obviously, because I'm me. I'll leave that with you and be on my way. Is eight okay for you tomorrow morning, Max?'

'That's fine. I'll see you there. And thank you, for everything.'

She makes hush-now noises as she retrieves several containers full of food from the car, stacking them up on the floor before she departs in a flurry of curls, Labrador woofs and honks on her car horn. In response, I hear the sonorous boom of a donkey hee-hawing, and see the famous Belle amble towards the edge of her paddock.

'Oh my God,' Sophie mutters. 'A donkey! Also her happy place.'

I can't argue with that, and I walk over to meet her. Gary runs by my side, and takes a tentative sniff at the fence before deciding it's a no for him and retreating a few feet away.

Belle is not, to put it bluntly, the prettiest of animals. She's old—her teeth are terrifying—and one of her ears points out at a wonky angle. I don't care; she looks gorgeous to me.

'Be careful,' says Gabriel, at my side. 'She doesn't like people. I've tried winning her over, but—'

'Your natural charm has failed?'

There's a hint of a smile at that, and I realise it's the first I've seen from him—aimed at a human, at least. There's a bag hanging on our side of the fence, containing carrots and apples, and I decide on a carrot. Less chance of losing my fingers.

Belle lets out a ferocious roar, the kind of sound you could use in a TV show set in the bowels of hell, and batters Gabriel's shoulder out of the way with her bulky head. I ignore that, and offer up the carrot, making soothing noises as I do. She turns her attention to me, and her teeth seem to get even bigger. There's a stand-off for a few seconds, then she grabs the other end of the carrot and starts gnashing it in her mouth. While she's distracted, I manage a quick stroke of her head, running my fingers gently over the thick, bristly hair.

I don't push my luck, and back off straight away afterwards. She glares at me with shining brown eyes, and shows us her substantial rear.

'That's closer than I've got in over a year,' Gabriel says, shaking his head.

'Mum has a lot in common with donkeys,' Sophie replies. 'They're like her spirit animal. They're both grouchy, stubborn, sometimes affectionate. Short, stumpy legs, awful hair…'

I throw a handful of hay in her face and she splutters as she swipes it off. Maybe I do have more in common with Belle than I thought.

I run my hands over my hair, suddenly self-conscious. There's nothing wrong with my hair, I tell myself. It's normal hair—dark with a few hints of grey, long, thick. Okay, it has no style whatsoever, but I've started to think that's much easier; no need for trims or colours or trips to the salon for me. Here in Budbury, I fit right in. It's when I'm comparing myself to women like Valerie that I come off badly.

Gabriel has watched our interaction without comment, his hands shoved into his jeans pockets as though protecting them from the donkey. He waits until we're finished, then strides off back to the house. I assume we're supposed to follow him, even though he doesn't say a word. Sophie and I exchange a brief 'WTF' look, and go after him.

The door opens straight into the kitchen, and I stand still for a moment admiring the room. There's an old Aga that looks like an original, with pretty cream enamel doors. The floors are made of stone, and that's even older than the Aga; you can see all the little indentations and smoother shining paths where countless feet have walked it down over the decades.

The walls have been stripped back to bare brick and whitewashed, and I can tell the cupboards and counters are new, even though they're made of antique-looking pine to fit in. The ceiling is freshly plastered, little spotlights shining down on us. A big pine table sits in the middle of it all, and I run my fingers over it. I'm guessing this came with the house, and bears the scars and bruises of many mealtimes.

'This is beautiful,' I say, spinning around to soak it all in. 'Did you do the work? I love the Aga!'

Gabriel looks borderline embarrassed, and replies: 'I did. And as for the Aga, have at it – I've no clue how to use the thing. I stick to the microwave, the toaster, and that.'

He points at a little two-ring electric hob that he has set up on the counter.

'Can we see the rest of the house?' Sophie asks. I see her

phone in her hand and suspect there will be pictures before long.

He shrugs, and takes us through into the living room. It's big and roughly square, with a low beamed ceiling that he has to duck under. The floorboards have been sanded down and painted a very pale shade of green, almost white but with a hint of apple, and the windows look out over the darker green of the fields beyond—it's almost like they match. I'm sure an interior designer would say something clever, like 'bringing the outside inside'.

Only one wall has been painted, the rest is exposed whitewashed stone, rough and characterful beneath my fingers. Looking around, I see what amazing potential this space has, but right now it feels empty and unloved.

There's one small two-seater sofa, the type that has a button you press for the feet to pop up, and stacks of books. And ... that's it. There's a huge coal fire grate with a beautiful old surround that's made of cast iron—the kind you'd pay a fortune for at an antiques place—but literally nothing else. No art, no photos, no TV. Just one small coffee table next to the sofa. It feels spartan, unused, like nobody even lives here.

I glance at Gabriel, and see him in a slightly different light. Maybe he's the one who has things in common with Belle, not me—living this solitary life, miles away from anyone. I picture him sitting on his recliner after a long day of work, rewarded with a microwave meal and a mug of tea. That's probably exactly the way he likes it, but somehow it makes me sad.

I tell myself off—I'm projecting—and remind myself that this is the life he chose. I'd be lonely, but then again, I'm really quite pathetic.

'Where's all your … stuff? Where's your *telly*?' Sophie says, looking incredulous.

'I don't have one. And this is all my stuff. There's another room on the other side of the building. Loads stored in there, plenty of old furniture and things from when my relative owned the place. There might be a TV, I don't know. I was just leaving it there while I worked on this. You can look if you like, makes no difference to me.'

He's clearly uncomfortable at the scrutiny, and turns back towards the kitchen. A narrow, steep set of stone stairs leads up to a spacious landing, still carpeted in some awful seventies pattern that is a relic from the last owner. He shows us into the rooms we will be using, and both are similar—medium sized, bare floorboards, paper stripped from the walls but not replaced. Both have big windows that offer the kinds of views that make the presenters on *Escape to the Country* sigh in delight.

I see the flat-packs and bundles of bedding, and say: 'Shall we get started? I can probably manage to do it on my own—Sophie wasn't lying—but it'll be easier with two if you can spare the time.'

At that point, after consulting her phone, Sophie pipes up: 'I think you've got this situation handled, grown-ups. Is it okay if I go back to the village for a bit? Martha's invited a few of her friends to the pub and I'd like to meet them.'

I feel immediately unsettled at the thought of her

leaving. Partly because I'm protective, partly because I'm not sure how I feel about being left here alone with Mr Chatty. One look at her pleading face overrides the second concern, but the first still remains solid.

'I'm not sure it's a good idea to go to the pub and drive back,' I say. 'These roads are going to take some getting used to.'

'Well, I won't get used to them if you never let me drive them! And I promise I won't drink, not even the two I'm allowed. I'll stay totally sober.'

'And if it's dark when you come back, will you remember to put your headlights on?'

'Of course! I *never* forget that.'

She always forgets that. But I can see how keen she is, and understand that much as she loves her dear old mum, meeting people of a similar age is important to her.

'I don't know why you even bother meeting in a pub,' I say. 'All you'll do is look at your phones.'

'Ah, that may be true, but when we see an especially good TikTok, we can lean across the table and show it to each other. There's not much of a Wi-Fi signal here, and you can't expect me to quit cold turkey, that's child abuse! Please please please!'

'Okay, jog on then, but be back before midnight, or I'll beat you to death with a pumpkin, all right? And reply to my messages!'

I've noticed with both of my offspring that while they are permanently glued to their phones, they seem to have a magical ability to 'not see' my WhatsApp messages.

'Will do!' she yells, already running back down the stairs. Gary goes with her, then runs straight back up when she leaves. He looks giddy with all the new stimuli.

Gabriel ignores all of this, staring at the boxes, and says: 'I can spare the time. Back in a minute.'

He comes back up bearing a Stanley knife and some tools, and gets to work cutting open the boxes. Unusually for a man, he takes the time to look at the instructions before we begin, passing the sheet to me once he's done.

Without even a word being shared between us, he slices the boxes open, and we pull out the various mysterious sticks of wood and bags of screws. I love doing this stuff; it's just like a big puzzle that needs to be solved, and at the end you win the prize of fully-assembled furniture.

We work silently, and with surprising ease. Both of us clearly know what we're doing, and we quietly get on with it, passing parts and holding legs and tightening screws. It's almost choreographed, as though we've done it a million times before, and it's a deeply pleasant way to pass some time. The silence isn't awkward because we're busy, and while we might not be compatible on a social level, we're a great match when it comes to DIY.

We get the first one done in just over an hour, complete with mattress, then move to the other room to repeat it all over. I lose the tip of one fingernail and he trips over some discarded plastic packaging at one point, but other than that we escape pretty much unscathed. It's definitely easier with two, and by the time we finish, although my back is sore and I'm sweating, I feel the familiar sense of satisfaction I always get when I'm working on a project.

'I love doing stuff like this,' I announce, as much to Gary as to Gabriel. 'I don't know why, but it always makes me feel really peaceful.'

'It's because the results are there, right before your eyes,' Gabriel replies, crunching down the cardboard for recycling. 'It's tangible. You work hard; you achieve something real. The rest of life isn't like that.'

He's right, I think. That's exactly it. When we moved into the new house it was an absolute shit-show, and so was I. I was still reeling from Richie, and losing my job, and beneath all of that, there was the slow, poisonous current of grief over my mum. I had zero self-confidence, and no hope for my future, but working on the house gave me the perfect distraction.

I bought it partly because it was cheap, and fitted my new financial circumstances, but also partly because it hadn't been decorated since the eighties, and still had an avocado bath suite. It still does, I just tarted up the whole bathroom and made a feature of it, going for a kitschy vibe with framed pink flamingo prints and old-fashioned cocktail shakers as toothbrush holders. Still an avocado bath suite, but now it looks like it belongs in a quirky themed hotel in Vegas. It's the kind of bathroom Frank Sinatra would have had.

Doing that work didn't just distract me, it gave me something positive to focus on, something I could control, that I was good at, that was building a brighter future for me and the kids. And now here I am, doing it all over again.

'I'll leave you with the duvets and covers,' he says, hefting up the cardboard. 'That's girl stuff.'

I raise my eyebrow at him, wondering if it's at all possible he just made a small joke.

'What?' he responds. 'Laura can be sexist but I can't? Anyway. I've got my own work to do. Barn door needs fixing.'

I shout a quick 'thank you!' to him as he clumps off down the stairs, because I have manners. I spend the next few hours in blissful productivity, unpacking the bedding and making everything up. Van has obviously hedged his bets and opted for plain white duvet covers and sheets, and only made one mistake: buying king size when the beds are double. No big deal, and I'm grateful for the effort that everyone has gone to to make this happen for us.

Laura has given me the impression that Cherie is quite the sneaky entrepreneur, owning several properties and businesses, and that the expense isn't something I should worry about, but all the same, I appreciate it. If I was at home I'd have washed and dried everything first, drenched it in fabric softener to make it feel and smell nice, but I'm very much not at home, and I don't even know if Gabriel has a washer.

I make a couple of trips outside, and finally get to unpack, at least for a while. There aren't any drawers or wardrobes in our rooms, so for the time being I simply fold everything in piles, and vow to take him up on his offer of going through the old furniture he has in storage. At the very least I need a bedside table; where else am I going to put my glass of water and my Rennies?

I venture into the bathroom in a state of high trepidation, but am delighted to see that he's already worked on it. In fact it's gorgeous—a big old claw-footed tub in one corner, and a nice shower with a fancy rainforest setting on the sprinklers.

As I expected, there's not much in the way of personal belongings—a toothbrush, and an old-fashioned bar of soap. On the corner of the bath, though, I spot a bottle of luxurious-looking liquid—green glass, and a label that tells me it contains organic oil of basil and lemon. Looks like Gabriel has at least one human weakness: he likes a nice soak in the bath. The well-thumbed paperback copy of a Michael Connelly crime thriller next to it gives me a hint as to what he likes to do while he's soaking.

I add mine and Sophie's bits and bobs, and it completely changes the feel of the room. The simple presence of Lush shower gels, brightly-coloured bottles of shampoo and conditioner, our small box of fizzy bath bombs and the pink towels I brought from home transform it. Whether that's something Gabriel will appreciate or not remains to be seen.

As I walk back out onto the landing, Gary at my side, I can't help taking a quick sneaky peek inside the last room, the one that must be his. Part of me knows this is wrong, an invasion of his privacy, but the rest of me is so nosy I can't resist. I can hear the whizz of a power drill outside, so I know he's busy, and I guiltily push the door open a few inches and stick my head around.

My quick glance takes in a bookshelf, full to busting, with more books piled up beside it. One of those portable hanging frames, with a few shirts dangling from it. An ugly chest of draws, and a bedside cabinet—graced by a book, but no Rennies, the lucky devil.

The whole room is dominated by a huge bed, bigger than king size I'd say, with a very old and intricate brass bed-frame. It's a beautiful thing and wouldn't look out of place in a stately home, but what really catches my eye is the fact that there is no duvet, no blankets, no sheets. Just a thick khaki- green sleeping bag. It looks so incongruous, so out of place; a tiny scrap of comfort swimming in all that space.

I close the door quietly behind me, and steady my breathing. I feel unsettled by what I've seen for some reason. What does it matter to me how Gabriel sleeps? Why should I care if he prefers a sleeping bag to a duvet? It's none of my business, and I am reminded, not for the first time, that being nosy is sometimes a dangerous thing. Because now I feel sorry for him, and I'm sure that's something he would hate, and also gets in the way of my decision to simply tolerate him for the next few weeks.

Gary follows me down the stairs, and I let him outside to do his business. It's nice to not have to use a lead, and it makes me smile as he scampers around investigating everything, making sure he gives Belle's paddock a wide berth.

I get out my phone, and call Ben, who shockingly actually answers. He's walking from one place to another, surrounded by traffic on a busy road, the sound of car horns and sirens in the background. It couldn't be more different from my current location.

'Ben! Look, there's a donkey!' I say, holding up the phone towards the field. Right on cue, Belle spots me, and rumbles over, screeching at the top of her voice. I pull back the phone, laughing. It's entirely possible she'd have crunched it with her mammoth teeth.

'Jesus, Mum,' Ben says, grimacing. 'That's not a donkey. That's some kind of lab experiment gone wrong. How's things? Sophie said your house fell down and now you're living with some bloke who doesn't talk.'

'Um, yeah. Well, he doesn't talk much. So far anyway.'

'It's good that you can talk enough for two then, I suppose. Can I call you back later? I'm late for a lecture. I was up late at bible study class.'

'By bible study class, do you mean you were getting hammered in the college bar?'

'I can neither confirm nor deny. But I have got to go. Love you! Don't get eaten by a mutant donkey!'

I grin at Belle, and she glares at me in return. I think she likes me. By this time Gary is disappearing off around the side of the building, and I follow him.

He has run straight over to Gabriel, who has apparently managed to reattach the barn door and is swinging it backwards and forwards to check it's working okay. He's taken off his chunky sweater, and is wearing a plain black T-shirt beneath. I don't want to notice the muscles flexing in his arms as he moves, or notice how snugly it fits across his shoulders, but I do anyway. He's good-looking, and has one of those fit bodies that comes from being active, not going to the gym, and I am only human. I must forgive myself the occasional lapse from sainthood.

His dark hair is loose on his shoulders as he leans down to pet Gary, and again I see the full wattage smile that only seems to come out for canines.

'What's in there?' I say, making my presence known. I walk up to him, peering inside the open door and seeing only murky darkness and the outlines of unidentified objects.

'Old machinery at the moment,' he answers, standing up and arching his back in a way that says it aches. 'A rusty tractor, a very old combine, pitchforks.'

'It sounds like something from a horror film. Like when the teenagers go somewhere scary on Halloween, and the ones who snog first get hacked to death?'

He looks at me as though I'm mad, and I remind myself that this is a man who lives in the middle of nowhere without a bloody telly. He's not likely to get my pop culture references.

'If you say so. Better warn your daughter. Eventually, I'm going to get it cleared. It'll fetch something for scrap, and some of it might even be of interest to the agricultural museum.'

'What will you do with it then? It'd make a lovely conversion.'

He frowns, as though this is a conversation he's had with himself before, and replies: 'It would. But if I'm planning on staying here, I'm not sure I'd want anyone living that close.'

'And are you? Planning on staying? Is this, like, your ancestral home?'

He actually laughs at that, and his whole demeanour changes. It's like he's a different human being, a softer one. A happier one. As quickly as it happens, though, it stops, and he slips back into his resting grump face.

'No. I grew up all over the place—military family—and I never even met him.'

'Mr Pumpwell?' I ask, trying not to giggle at the name, because it might well be Gabriel's too, and that would be rude.

'Yeah. He's technically my great-uncle, but it was a complicated family situation. My mum died when I was sixteen, and she never even mentioned him. Neither did my grandma, who outlived her, and he was her brother. Nobody ever talked about that side of the family. My dad's still around, but we don't speak much. I do remember him saying my gran was the "black sheep" of her family, and he knew no more than that.'

'Oh gosh,' I say, intrigued. 'How weird ... and fascinating. I wonder how you could find out more? Maybe Edie knows?'

'Maybe she does, but I have zero interest in the subject. The past is the past, no use poking at it. It was a surprise, when the solicitors finally tracked me down. I was living in

France at the time so it took a while. When I first saw the place and the state it was in, I was just going to sell it. But ... well, you know what this place is like.'

I nod, because I do, even though I've only just got here.

'Let me guess. You called into the café for a cappuccino, and before you knew it, you were persuaded to stay?'

'Espresso, but yes, that's about the size of it. I suppose it came at a good time for me. I'd just ... well, again, that doesn't matter, it's in the past. But I spent one night here, nursing my first donkey bite, and realised it had potential. That the location is perfect for me. That I had nothing to lose. I can still sell it. I'll just be selling it for more once the work is done.'

This is, by far, the longest conversation we have shared, and I can tell it is making him uncomfortable. He swipes his hair back from his face, takes a swig from his water bottle, and announces that he's going to clean up. Without a backward glance, he marches off, back to being borderline rude again.

I tell myself that I don't care, and have a little walk around the land that surrounds the farmhouse. From what Laura told me, it was once part of a much bigger family farm, but the late Mr Pumpwell never married or had kids, and sold most of it off.

By urban standards, though, it's huge. I have a tiny courtyard barely big enough for a small table and chairs. This is a whole different way to live, and the autumn sunshine makes it look enchanted. The light is filtering through the red and gold leaves on the trees and dappling onto the grass, and there's a whole section of garden that's been taken over entirely by late-blooming wildflowers. I can hear skylarks singing, and the mild breeze is rustling through the branches like a whispered lullaby. Somewhere nearby, there's a brook or a river, the water gurgling away in the background.

It's like a patch of land that time forgot, and if you squint, it looks completely untouched by modern life. If you don't squint, though—and you can't do that for long or your eyes hurt—then it's not quite as perfect.

There's a lot of debris, piles of bricks, and mysterious metal objects heaped under tarps. The side of the barn looks like a scrap yard, and there's a metal skip filled with the old kitchen cupboards, the shell of a bath, the wreckage of a lawn mower. It's a combination of English countryside idyll and building site, and I actually find that even more exciting. It's a place in flux, in a state of change. Waiting to be moulded into something new and lovely.

Gary disappears off into the patch of woods at the back of the barn, and comes back bearing a stick so big he can barely carry it. He drops it at my feet and woofs, reminding me that he needs feeding. As do I, now I come to think of it. Before I go back inside I take a few pics to send to Ben, and then see a message from Sophie, an old-fashioned text one to make up for the fact that we don't have much Wi-Fi out here. 'I am alive', it says, followed by a string of random emojis. That'll do. I tap back telling her to make sure she eats something other than crisps, and head back inside the house.

I can hear the sound of Gabriel moving around upstairs, and wonder if he's going to have a soak in the bath. Then I wonder what he'd look like naked and wet, and then I wonder if he has chest hair, because I really like chest hair. Then I wonder if I should shoot myself in the head. I'm sure there's a shotgun in the barn.

I give Gary his dinner, and busy myself in the kitchen. I don't know how to use an Aga, but I'm sure Laura does. I'll ask her to give me some tuition so I can cook properly. For the time being, I root in the fridge, which is clearly a new addition, one of those gorgeous curvy Smegs in pastel green that looks like it belongs in the Fonzy's kitchen.

Inside I find all of the tubs that Laura left for us, along with what I presume are Gabriel's rations. And 'rations' is the right word, as the entire contents add up to nothing more than butter, cheese, some bacon, and a six-pack of lager. The fruit bowl is full, though, with wonky-looking apples and pears that suggest they've come straight from the tree.

I investigate Laura's donations, and am thrilled to find a home-made lasagne, bowls of salad with a lemony dressing, and some slabs of ginger loaf. She's also left some granary bread and a bottle of wine. What more could a girl want?

I put the lasagne in the microwave, and rummage around the kitchen cupboards, familiarising myself with the locations of the mugs and plates and cutlery. There's more than I expected—Gabriel seems like the sort of man who would function perfectly well with one of each—and some of it is really nice. There's part of a Wedgwood dinner set, and some cups and saucers that I swear could be Clarice Cliff. I'm basing this on my extensive watching of *Antiques Roadshow*, so I can't sure, but the vibrant colours and geometric patterns have me convinced.

It's odd, delving into all of these small mysteries, the combined wordly goods of a man I barely know, and one I will never meet. But as I bustle around, I realise that I am also quite content. I haven't thought about Richie since we got here, which is a minor miracle as he's usually always hovering in the back of my mind. As soon as I think his name I chase it away like the woman with a broomstick in *Tom and Jerry* cartoons. Begone, foul beast, this is my new start, and you have no place here.

I realise as Gabriel walks into the room that I have said the last few words aloud, and he looks understandably confused.

'Not you!' I say quickly. 'You're not a foul beast, and this is your house. I was just, umm, thinking aloud. Do you want lasagne? It smells amazing.'

His hair is damp on his shoulders, and he smells even better than the lasagne—basil and lemon, I suspect, which perfectly complements tonight's menu.

I wonder if he'll say yes, and how we will go about this business of living together as strangers. Will he set the table and pour us a glass of wine? Will we sit in silence, or snark at each other, or chat? I know he said he wanted us to stay out of his way, but it's not always going to be that easy.

'Yes, please,' he says, his nostrils twitching. 'But I'll eat in the other room.'

His tone isn't rude exactly, but it is dismissive. As though he wants to nip this communal nonsense in the bud before it gets the chance to take root. Maybe he's worried I'll want company, or that he'll have to act as my nanny.

I nod, and silently go about the business of dishing up. He duly takes his plate away, and I sit down at the dining table, like a civilised person. I add in a glass of wine, like a civilised person. Then I wolf down my food like a very uncivilised person: I was starving, and this is delicious. I'm glad Laura will be doing most of the cooking at the café, because there's no way I'll match this level of culinary skill.

When I'm done, and my dishes washed, I get out the files that Laura gave me, the ones that will allegedly tell me everything I need to know about both my new job and the people I will be serving. Some of it is mundane—hours, responsibilities, menus, instructions—but some of it is captivating.

I learn all about the various regulars and their comfort foods, and a lot about their lives. The files come with photos, so I can put faces to names as well as see the ghosts of parties past. Once I've absorbed as much as I can, I read through the *Game of Thrones* style document that Willow compiled, laughing at all the various comments. It was obviously created a few years ago, typed and printed out, but someone—Cherie, Laura?—has kept it updated with little scribbled additions.

Some of the additions are lovely: Tom and Willow getting married on the same day as her sister Auburn (the singer with the long red hair) and her boyfriend, Finn; Katie and Van moving in together, and Katie giving birth to Zack; Laura's daughter Lizzie getting a first in her Marketing degree; her son Nate getting accepted to veterinary school; Martha graduating from Oxford; Becca's daughter, Little Edie, starting school. It's all there, the love, the laughter, the sense of community as these people's lives grow and evolve.

But the flip side of that evolution is darker, and sadder, and altogether too poignant. There are losses as well as gains, including a photo of pink-haired Willow and the lady I presume was her mum, Lynnie, and a grey-muzzled Border terrier on her lap. 'Always missed, Lynnie and Bella Swan', says the caption.

That makes my eyes swim, and the next thing I see pushes me over the edge. It's a little broken love heart that someone has doodled next to Frank's name, along with his dates of birth and death and an RIP followed by kisses. I sit at the kitchen table with my glass of wine, and feel overwhelmed with emotion.

As ever with these things, they creep up on you. One minute I'm laughing at a photo of Sam—the surfer-looking man who is the partner of Laura's sister, Becca—holding his comfort food, a chicken and mushroom Pot Noodle, aloft. The next I'm weeping at the death of Willow's mum. Then, of course, I'm crying about everything else as well, because tears have no mercy, and they do not discriminate.

By the time Gabriel walks into the kitchen, I am lost, a soggy mess of a woman. He takes one look at me and seems to consider turning around and heading in the other direction. I really wouldn't blame him. Nobody wants to deal with this level of dysfunction.

'I'm okay!' I say weakly, gathering up the scattered papers. 'You don't need to worry!'

He freezes in the doorway like a hunted animal, then seems to come to a decision. He walks in, and gets a glass of water from the tap. Then he leans against the big Belfast sink, and looks at me.

'I'm not an expert on these things,' he says, after sipping his water, 'but you don't look very okay. Has something bad happened?'

'Probably, to someone, somewhere. I'm just … upset. Laura gave me all this stuff to read. About people who go to the café, and people who live in the village, and it was all lovely but also a bit upsetting, and … well, I'm actually crying because I'll never get the chance to make Frank his burnt bacon butties, and that was his comfort food, and now he's gone, and Cherie's heart is broken, and Van and Katie's kids will never get to know their grandmother, Lynnie, and … well, it's all so sad!'

It all rushes out in a jumble of words, and even I can see how mad I sound. Gabriel shakes his head, and says: 'You've probably become more involved in this community in one day than I have in over a year. I can't say you're a good advert for it right now, though.'

'I know! I'm sorry. I was laughing earlier, I promise. What can I say? I'm better at building beds than I am at managing my emotions.'

'You and me both, Max, you and me both. Look, I'm not

the right person to comfort you. I'm rubbish at all this stuff. But I'm also not quite as much of a prick as I might first appear. I'm not made of stone.'

I choke out an unexpected laugh at this comment, and at the blunt language he uses in his self-assessment.

'I never said you were a prick.'

'No, but you thought it, and that's okay. I think it too, sometimes. Have you got wellies with you?'

This is an unexpected turn for the conversation to take, but I nod dumbly.

'Right. Well, get your boots on, and come with me.'

Chapter Seven

I have no idea where we are going, or why Gabriel has insisted I wear one of his fleece jackets instead of my own. Even more curious is the fact that he sniffs me before we set off.

'You're not wearing perfume are you?' he asks.

'No. Do I smell bad?'

'You don't. But they don't like perfume or other strong human scents. My fleece smells of the woods, not wherever it is you've come from…'

'Birmingham.'

'Whatever. Are you ready?'

I have no idea what I'm supposed to be ready for, but the small flurry of activity has at least distracted me from the emotion-bomb that was the Comfort Food Café file. I suspect that was the whole point.

Gary is left behind, and he gives me a baleful look as I betray him and walk out the door. He's like kids who cry when their mums take them to school: he'll be fine once my back is turned. He has his basket and a chew toy and is a championship-level sleeper anyway.

I follow Gabriel down to the back of the barn, and we take a narrow path into the trees. The sun has faded but is still just about shining, and the autumn leaves are dappled with gold as we make our way into the dense woodland.

I recognise oak and yew and beech, and the floor is scattered with ferns and mushrooms, some of them plain little white caps, others spectacular displays of twisted form and colour. I wonder which would make a nice omelette and which could be used to murder someone, and decide to see if Zoe has a book about them.

The ground underfoot is soft and squishy with fallen leaves and mud, and the storm has thrown up a few obstacles—branches in our way, and on one occasion a complete tree trunk barring our path. We clamber over it, and continue on into ever-thickening woods, the light now almost completely blocked by the canopy of green and gold. Gabriel has a torch with a weird red beam, and he goes ahead, waiting for me to catch up when I fall behind.

Eventually he stops, and whispers to me: 'We have to be quiet now. I've got a notepad and a pencil, and I'll write down anything you need to know. It might take a while, but don't talk. I know that might be hard for you.'

I'm not sure if this is a sly dig or a simple statement of fact, but I do a mime of zipping my lips up and follow him. We emerge into a little clearing, the ground seeming to dip in a bowl shape in front of us, the surface rough and lumpy with clumps of leaves and gnarled tree roots. He leads me to a small wooden hut with one of its sides missing, and inside there is a bench. The front of the hut has a hole cut into it that runs horizontally, creating a kind of viewing zone of the clearing.

I'm still not sure what we're doing here, and am desperate to ask, but I can't because my lips are zipped up. We settle down on the bench, and I'm uncomfortably aware of how much space my arse is taking up, and how closely we are squashed against each other. I look up at Gabriel, and see his profile in the dusky light. He seems totally relaxed, and has clearly gone into some kind of meditative state.

I'm not so good at meditative states, and struggle with sitting still and not speaking. I let my mind wander, flittering from subjects as disconnected as 'I wonder how Sophie's getting on?' to 'When is the next series of *The Traitors* starting?', and 'Wouldn't it be funny if Daniel Craig came into the café for a cheese and ham toastie tomorrow?'

Eventually, he nudges me in the side, putting his fingers to his mouth to remind me to be quiet. He points outside the viewing window, and places his torch on it so it casts a diffuse red glow.

I don't know quite what's happening at first. The ground seems to start moving, and my mind immediately goes to that Kevin Bacon film, *Tremors*, where the monsters tunnelled through the earth.

What actually happens is that a little creature emerges, popping its head out from a hidden hole burrowed between two twisted tree roots. It has to knock some debris out of the way, possibly scattered there by the storm last night, and then sticks its face out into the world beyond. I suck in a breath as quietly as I can, and lean forward, taking in the long muzzle and the black and white stripes across its head. It's a badger. I'm watching an actual badger, climbing out of its hobbit hole, whiskers twitching as it sniffs the evening air.

I feel completely enraptured as I watch him, as bit by bit he slithers his whole body out, deciding it's safe and emerging fully into the clearing. He's much bigger than I'd have expected, with a chunky grey body and a fluffy, stubby tail. His little black eyes seem to swivel around, and he's clearly scouting about to check for danger.

Gabriel passes me the little notepad, and there's just enough light for me to read: 'That's Carling. The dad.'

I nod, and carry on watching as Carling starts to scamper around the earth, digging into it with claws, investigating with his nose. Next out is a slightly smaller animal, and Gabriel tells me this is the mum, Estrella. She follows the sit-and-sniff routine, then starts to amble around, rooting in the grass and ferns, every now and then running back to the burrow with a clump of something.

I'm completely entranced by their behaviour, and even more so when the next two come out. They're smaller, more streamlined, and they tumble out into the clearing in a flurry of fur. They roll around in a ball together, playing and fighting, before going their separate ways to forage.

These, I get told, are 'the cubs—Stella and Artois'.

I realise, somewhat belatedly, that Gabriel has named all of the badgers after brands of lager, and I have to bite in a laugh. The animals are frolicking in front of us, and even the slightest sound will spook them.

We sit there for maybe an hour, watching the badgers go about their badgery business, as the final stripes of sunlight disappear and the chorus of blackbirds starts to silence. The dad takes off at some point, but mum stays with the cubs. The babies themselves seem to be mainly eating, and mum is making return trips to and from the entrance to the burrow with twigs and grass and leaves. I'm guessing she's thinking about keeping them warm for the winter, and the cubs are thinking about their stomachs—it was ever thus.

They have a strange gait, walking and running in a way that is both graceful and comedic, and I suspect I could watch them all night long. They play, and eat, and groom each other, and the whole experience is so uplifting that by the time Gabriel nudges me and makes a 'time to go' gesture, I feel like I could actually float all the way home.

I nod, and we quietly tiptoe out of the hut. I see Estrella go on alert, sitting up tall, head swivelling and whiskers wobbling, before she settles again. I cast one final glance at them before we leave, seeing one of the cubs swipe his sibling across the face before running away. They're so much like human children.

Once we've been walking back down the path for about five minutes, Gabriel whispers: 'You can talk now. But quietly. If they don't feel safe in this sett, they'll move on.'

The route home seems tougher in this direction,

probably because it's fully dark now, so I am concentrating on where I put my feet as I reply: 'That was amazing! Thank you so much for sharing that with me. How old are the babies?'

'Apparently badger cubs are born in February, and I first saw them around April. They were much smaller, and almost unbearably cute. Hard to believe then that they'll grow up to be the biggest land predator in the UK.'

'What do they eat?'

'Pretty much anything they can get their claws on. Earthworms, rodents, berries, nuts, seeds. Even hedgehogs. You sometimes see them foraging near people as well, rooting in the bins. If that happens while you're here, don't approach them. I know they look like pets but they're not.'

'Do you feed them?'

'Sometimes I scatter some peanuts on the clearing—they like those—but mainly no, they'd become dependent on me.'

'And that's a bad thing?' I say, as we clamber over the fallen tree trunk.

'Yes. They're wild animals; they should be self-sufficient. And I don't like having anything dependent on me.'

'You're like the badgers,' I say. 'Self-sufficent. But not as cute.'

He laughs, short and sharp, and it feels like a victory. Every human response I get from this man feels like a victory, because while he is self-sufficient like the badgers, he doesn't have their sense of community. They are part of their own little family, and he is alone.

This, I tell myself, is not a bad thing. It might not be everybody's ideal, but who am I to judge what is right for him? Nobody forces him to live alone in splendid isolation, with only his sleeping bag for company. He's a very attractive man—he'd be a huge hit on Tinder-for-grown-ups—but that doesn't seem to be what he wants. He lives like this because he chooses to, and I don't really know the first thing about him, plus I'm definitely not in a position to feel sorry for him, given the disaster zone that is my own life.

We emerge back in the grounds of his property, and I ask: 'Why did you name the badgers after lager? Because I assume they didn't pick those names themselves.'

'No, and even if they did, I don't speak badger so I wouldn't have understood. If they have their own names, they're something like cheek-a-cheek-a-waaaaah-grrrr-yeeek.'

He says this completely deadpan, but delivers it as a series of grunts and squeals that is a pretty good imitation of the various sounds the badgers had been making.

'Dunno,' he continues, shrugging. 'I suppose I just like lager?'

I nod in acceptance—it's as good a reason as any—and we make our way back around to the front. It feels completely different here now it's nighttime, and other than a few birds still calling and the distant hoot of an owl, it is totally silent. I'm not used to this, and find it slightly unnerving.

Luckily, my nerves are settled by something more familiar: the sound of a car horn honking as Sophie swerves the Toyota into the courtyard. The wheels squeal and gravel flies up from the impact, and I see Gabriel's eyes widen.

'I know,' I murmur. 'I'm sorry. My spirit animal might be a donkey, but hers is Lewis Hamilton.'

I'm relieved to see her home at a relatively early hour, and even more so to see that she is stone-cold sober. Mums can always tell.

'What have you two been up to?' she asks, after getting out of the car and slamming the door. I hear Belle bellow her objections from the paddock.

'We've been badger-watching!' I announce, with some glee. I can't wait to tell her all about it.

'Oh, is that what the kids are calling it these days?' she responds, giving me a saucy wink. 'Why are you wearing Gabriel's clothes?'

'Because mine smelled too weird for the badgers, and his smell of woods and trees and dirt, and they like that.'

I realise that this doesn't sound very complimentary, but I needn't have worried—he's already walking away and leaving us to it. He opens the door, turns to give us a nod goodnight, and disappears into the house without a word.

'So, how was it?' I ask, putting Gabriel and his quirks out of my mind.

'Good, yeah! I mean, it was hardly a wild night out as you can tell, but I get the feeling everybody has a different body clock here. Circadian rhythms adapted to countryside hours or whatever. But I met some cool people. Martha's ex, Bill, was there, and his brother, James. He's my age, and he's doing an apprenticeship on "Frank's farm", which seems to be still called that even though Frank is sadly RIP. And I met a girl called Jess, who's second year in her A-levels and lives in the next village. And I met Martha's dad, Cal, who is Australian and a complete DILF. Looks like a cowboy version of Chris Hemsworth. He wears a hat and everything!'

The words spill out of her in a rapid-fire ramble, and I can see that she's happy. She has a thick veneer of confidence, my daughter, but I know that beneath the surface she can be shy and sensitive. Finding a little tribe she feels comfortable with will make our time here much more enjoyable for her.

'Plus, I think I've decided I will do resits. Term's already started, but I'm sure I can catch up— Miss Edmonds said she'd arrange access to online lessons for me. Martha went to Oxford, you know, and it sounded really fun. I might try that.'

I blink, and try to nod encouragingly. Sophie got two Cs and a D in her A-levels, so I suspect she might be overreaching. But who am I to put her off? She'd initially wanted to study psychology, but who knows now? She seems to be in a constant state of change.

'So did you really see badgers?' she asks. 'And not, like, the dead ones on the side of the road that always make you cry?'

She's right. My empathy sponge goes into overdrive when I see roadkill. Most people see a dead hedgehog and go 'aah, that's a shame', and forget about it. I will spend the next half-hour pondering the poor hedgehog's life, and the babies it might have left undefended, and wondering if Mr or Mrs Hedgehog is sitting at home worrying about them.

'I did! They were gorgeous, Soph. You'll have to go and watch them. It was like nothing I've ever done before. They're so cute.'

We walk back into the house as we chat, and I automatically start to speak more quietly once we're in the kitchen. Gary has other ideas and runs towards us woofing and wagging, unbearably excited at our return.

Sophie looks at me, and I look at her, and we both make 'who knows?' faces, because we have no idea if Gabriel is still downstairs, or what he's up to, and basically it's a bit weird. We have to navigate a whole new set of rules here, and that's hard because I have no idea what the rules are. Are we allowed in the living room, where he sits on his solitary recliner and reads? Do we need a bathroom rota? What time does he go to bed, and should we tiptoe around in case we wake him?

I put the kettle on for a cuppa, and realise as I make it that there's nowhere to sit and drink it other than the kitchen table. That'll do for now, I suppose.

As I'm pouring in the milk, Gabriel himself appears, as though I've summoned him. He stares at me, and I feel nervous. It's like he's never seen me before, and is wondering what this strange woman is doing in his kitchen. Gary rushes over to sniff his crotch, which at least breaks the moment.

'Tea?' I ask, holding up a mug, as though demonstrating what 'tea' looks like.

'No. Thank you. Look, I just wanted to tell you that you might hear me moving around in the night. I don't sleep much. So, that's it. Goodnight.'

He nods, as though satisfied that he's delivered his message, and disappears off up the stairs.

'He's so weird,' whispers Sophie as we sit down. 'But I think I like him.'

Chapter Eight

My first day working at the Comfort Food Café is a mixed bag, but on the whole has to go in the 'win' column on the spreadsheet of life.

My usual working hours are set as eight until three, with every Monday off and one other day as well, sorted between us. When I arrive, Laura is already there, creating something that smells of apples and cinnamon in a mixing bowl. As soon as she sees me, she wipes her floury hands down on her apron, and comes over to chat.

'How was your first night at Gabriel's?' she asks, a slight hint of concern in her voice.

'It was fine,' I say. 'Ate your excellent lasagne. Watched badgers. Slept like a baby.'

The last part isn't entirely true, but she doesn't need to know that. It always takes me some time to settle into a new place. I'm the same even when we go on holiday. Every building has its own character, its own creaks and groans, and until I'm accustomed to them I seem to have some kind of adrenaline reaction. I did hear Gabriel as well, doors opening and closing, him coming up and down the stairs a few times. Gary is in with me, and every time it happened, he tried to get out and find him, which didn't help. I suppose it will just take time, and we're not going to be there for long.

He was already up and out by the time I staggered into the kitchen on my traditional coffee hunt, leaving behind a few signs of his presence: a single washed mug by the sink and the smell of toast in the air. I was relieved he wasn't there, to be honest, because he's unpredictable, and I'm not good in the mornings. Plus, I was wearing a ratty old dressing gown and looked like poo.

Sophie comes into work with me, and has a busy day planned. She's taking Gary up into the village to explore 'the shops'—which I can't imagine will take her long—and then is coming back to set herself and her laptop up to do some school work. Her teacher has set her up for her online courses—psychology, English lit and history—and she seems very determined about it. I'm pleased. She's been a little directionless of late, and it's good to see her so motivated.

She could have found a uni course that would have accepted her with her lower grades, but came up with some very logical reasons why it wasn't a good idea: the cost, mainly, and the fear of ending up massively in debt with a degree that wasn't much use to her.

I'd assured her there was money in the savings pot if she wanted to go, but she still stayed at home. She said she just wasn't ready but I've always had a sneaking suspicion that she actually meant *I* wasn't ready. I think she was worried about leaving me when I was vulnerable, and that is a topsy-turvy relationship dynamic that has always upset me. If nothing else comes of our adventure in Dorset, at least she'll know that I'm now capable of change, of embracing life, of building something new.

She called in briefly to say hello to Laura, then disappeared off up towards the village, basking in a burst of autumn sunshine. It's a glorious day, a vague chill in the air, but the pastel-blue skies make up for it. Down on the beach, I can see plenty of people walking and playing, dogs and toddlers and couples, already out and making the most of the weather. At this time of year, with October staring us in the face, every warm day feels like a gift.

Once she's gone, Laura gives me a brief tour of the café kitchens, which I note with surprise are decked out with all mod cons. The main café itself might be quirky and cluttered, but the business end of things is a different matter.

'We won't get many customers in for another half-hour or so,' she explains. 'So for now, it's all about the prep!'

I follow her instructions and start chopping salad and plating up sandwiches for the cooler, and putting jacket spuds into the potato oven for later. She's making muffins, and has already got a raspberry cheesecake chilling in the fridge. As we work, she tells me about her plans to test out a Halloween menu, and completely loses herself in her enthusiasm for it.

I smile as she goes into ecstasies about pumpkin spiced soup and cookies in the shape of ghosts and Red Velvet cake designed so it looks like it's dripping in blood. Laura is a woman who was born to do this job; I'm just a woman who can do this job, but will never feel it in my bones like she does.

We pass the time in pleasant companionship, and once I'm done in the kitchen, I go out into the café and check everything is shipshape. I notice more random items that hadn't registered before: an antique sewing machine, a giant conch shell, a collection of tiny silver spoons, and a few framed photos from what looks like the Second World War.

When I ask about them, Laura tells me that one of the girls in the pictures is our very own Edie May, back when she was in the Timber Corps, which was like the Land Army but with more trees. Edie is apparently ninety-eight, which is astonishing—she seems fitter than I am.

Our first customer of the day is Becca, Laura's sister, who calls in after dropping her daughter and Ruby and Rose off at school. She looks nothing like Laura, really, and it's only the easy banter they share that tips you off about their relationship.

'Mum and Dad want to know if they can have the girls for a couple of nights in half term,' she says, sipping her coffee and perching on one of the tall stools by the counter. 'I've told them they can have Little Edie permanently if they like.'

'You don't mean that!' says Laura, flicking her with a tea towel. 'What would you do without her?'

'I'd watch TV that doesn't feature cartoons or annoyingly perky presenters, read books, go for long walks, eat cake, have enormous soaks in the bath, go to art galleries, visit the cinema, take a trip to London and see a show, have lie-ins, go clubbing, learn how to ride a Segway, and have spectacular sex with my boyfriend without having to be quiet. Especially that last one. I'd do that a lot.'

I can't argue with that list, and Laura gives up and laughs.

'Okay, fair enough. Tell Mum and Dad it's a yes from me. I also have a husband I'd like to enjoy some personal time with. Do you think they'd take Midgebo as well?'

'No, because they're not stupid. I think you're stuck with your hooligan animal. You'll just have to shut the door while you and Matt have a bonkathon. How's it going, Max? Settling in? Overwhelmed by the Budbury madness? Feeling like the world and his wife wants to know every last thing about you?'

'Well,' I say, wiping down the counter in the absence of anything else to do, 'I'm staying with Gabriel, so no to the last question.'

'Ah yes. Gabriel Moran, Mystery Man. He's quite the enigma, hidden inside a puzzle, and wrapped in a stud-muffin exterior. He's nice enough, just takes a bit of getting used to.'

I nod, and leave it at that. I can already see Laura's gossip antenna whirring inside her brain and don't want to fuel it. I'm also strangely relieved that he's not actually called Pumpwell.

After Becca, a few other people start arriving, fresh from early-morning walks and looking to warm up with a cosy hot chocolate and a treat. I make toast, and grill bacon, and serve up muffins, and generally make myself as useful as I can be. Sophie comes back just before lunch, and bags herself and Gary a little table in the corner, where she works at her laptop. It's nice having them there.

The work is pretty plain sailing, and as it gets busier, I enjoy it more. Sophie was right about me, of course: I am nosy, and I do like chatting to people. I suppose I'd just forgotten that about myself, wallowing in self-pity as I was. I'm a far happier person when I have something useful to do, and ideally people to talk to while I do it. This isn't unlike my old job on the tills, but with more cake and walking around.

By half past two, the lunch rush has passed, and we mainly just have a few stragglers coming in looking for sustenance. Pretty much all of the fresh food for the day has sold, and Laura is clearing up outside.

While she's doing that, I'm attempting to make a takeaway latte for one of the last customers, which is probably foolish as I've had minimal training, and the coffee machine looks like something from a steampunk convention. It's huge, intimidatingly loud, and has more metal tubes and buttons than I know what to do with.

Everything seems to be going well until there's a big

gust of steam, and the machine starts making a low-pitched hissing sound. I suddenly remember this bit from my instructions, but can't remember what I'm supposed to do when it happens.

I faff around randomly pressing things, dodging the steam and apologising to the customer, all while the hissing noise is getting higher and higher. Much like my stress levels.

I'm about to run out into the garden and scream Laura's name when Cherie appears at my side. She's popped down from her flat a few times, but retired for a 'siesta' a while ago. She looks bleary-eyed now as she strides towards me, grabbing hold of a small hammer that's hanging from a chain next to the coffee machine. She gives the machine a giant whack on the top, and the hissing sound immediately stops. Unfortunately, other sounds begin … like the sound of Cherie crying.

It starts slowly, a few tears trickling out of the sides of her eyes, followed by a sad sigh. Then she cries a bit more, and pretty soon she is standing there in front of the coffee machine, holding the hammer in shaking hands, full-on sobbing. I quickly finish up the latte for the customer, giving it to them on the house, and turn my attention back to Cherie.

I take the hammer from her hands, and put it back on its hook. She's holding her face in her fingers, and the tears are streaming, and her whole body is trembling. She's a large woman, but I try and put my arms around her and console her, patting her back and telling her everything is okay. I've no idea what's going on, but her pain is contagious, and I'm desperate to comfort her. She lets out a soul-splitting cry and throws her head down on my shoulder, her arms around my waist.

I simply let her sob, stroking her hair and waiting until the moment passes. Eventually it does, and she pulls away from me, taking a deep breath and making a very obvious effort to calm herself down. Sophie is looking on in concern, and I give her a nod to tell her everything is all right.

Cherie smoothes stray strands of silver-grey hair from the sides of her face, and swipes at her eyes. She gazes down at me, and suddenly lets out a very unexpected laugh.

'I'm so sorry, my love!' she says, pointing at my T-shirt. 'I've gone and got you all soggy, haven't I?'

'That doesn't matter,' I reply, shaking my head dismissively. 'It'll save me having a shower later. Are you okay?'

'Course I am … now. Snuck up on me, that one did. That was Frank's job, see? Looking after the coffee machine. He could dismantle it and put it back together again quick as you like, that man. Always said it was temperamental, like a woman, the cheeky bugger. I need to replace it really, it's old as the hills, but … well…'

'It'd be like replacing a bit of him?'

'Exactly, my sweet. You understand. And although I'm sorry you were on the receiving end of that little display, thank you for your kindness. I've spent years comforting other people in this place, and now suddenly it feels like I'm always the one in need of a soft word and a shoulder to cry on. I'm not sure I like it, to be honest. Makes me feel less super-human than usual!'

'Well, your secret's safe with me, Wonder Woman,' I reply. 'Don't worry. I have two shoulders, and they're both always available to cry on, all right? We all need a little weep now and then.'

She nods, and reaches out to stroke my cheek. It's a gentle gesture, warm and motherly.

'See?' she says wisely. 'I knew Laura hadn't got it wrong about you. Now, tell me, what else have you got planned for the day?'

At that moment Laura walks back in, and does a quick scan of the two of us.

'You both okay?' she asks. 'Do I need to crack out the emergency Baby Guinness supplies and get the shot glasses?'

'It's all good, love,' Cherie says, winking at me. 'There was just a bit of a malfunction. Mechanical and human. Max here was just about to tell me what she has in store for the rest of the day.'

'Well,' I tell them, 'I was going to pick up a bit of food from the farm shop, and I was wondering if one of you could show me how to use an Aga at some point? I've watched a few YouTube videos but it'd be much easier with some pro tips, and I'm sure you're both pros. Gabriel only uses the microwave.'

'Oh I know!' exclaims Cherie, horrified. 'We send him

out care packages, but he's a prickly one, just like Mr Pumpwell was. Took us ages to wear him down as well. Nice bit of home-cooked food will be just what the doctor ordered. I'll come, love. Laura's got the girls, and I'm at a loose end. Shall I meet you there in an hour or so?'

Sophie and I make our farewells and drive home, calling off at the shop for some supplies on the way. I don't mind the occasional TV dinner, but it seems a shame to have that beautiful Aga, and not use it. The kitchen is beautiful, and it should feel like the heart of the home. I can only hope that making some tasty meals will result in that, and not in me burning the place down.

I've bought some fresh carrots for Belle, and when she sees me at the side of the paddock she runs at me at top speed. It's terrifying to be honest, especially when she bares her massive teeth, and for a moment I think she's going to crash through the fence and eat me alive. Instead, she slows down right in front of me, and lets out a sound that's half-bray, half-scream. I hold the carrot towards her and she snatches it from me, missing my fingertips by an inch. As before, while she's distracted I stroke her head, and this time she stays for a few more seconds before she snubs me. Slowly, slowly, catchee donkey.

There's no sight of Gabriel when we get back inside the cottage, so I make the most of the chance to jump in the shower and change clothes. It's been a while since I did a day's work, or did anything new, and I'm not going to lie, I'm pretty knackered. But in a good way. A satisfying kind of knackered.

I've just put the kettle on when Cherie arrives, tooting her car horn in a way I am starting to realise is traditional out in the wilderness, a way of saying, 'Hi, I'm here!'

She seems a lot more together now, and is wearing a spectacular maxidress covered in sunflowers. She also comes bearing cake, of course, and lays it down on the table before she inspects the Aga.

'Oh, this is nice,' she comments, after poking and prodding it a bit. 'The range itself is old, and I'd guess originally it used coal. But somewhere along the line it's been converted to gas, which is a lot easier. It's in good nick. Mr P must have looked after it. Just needs a bit of a clean ... and to be honest, love, probably a service as well. You don't want to mess around with this stuff, and I wouldn't recommend using it straight away. Once it's up and running, though, it'll work a treat!'

She gives me a little guide on how to use it, and although there's a lot to remember, it's not that complicated really. She talks me through how the stove-top hot plates can be used, and the different functions of the various oven compartments. It's a lot more versatile than the little four-ringed cooker we have at home, and I can see why it was beloved of olden-days families cooking all their meals from scratch. This is a mighty beast, made for multi-tasking and heating a home.

For the time being, we're stuck with what we've got.

'I'll make a stew,' says Sophie, peering into our bag of food. 'There's chicken and veg, and even Gabriel has salt and pepper. I can do it on the little hob thing. We can dip that crusty bread we got into it. It'll be delish! Plenty for all of us.'

I leave her to it—she enjoys cooking—and accompany Cherie as she walks around the downstairs of the house. It feels weird having her here, and I wonder if I'm breaking some kind of rule by inviting a guest. Then I remember the things Gabriel said when he was talking in Laura's kitchen that night; he is clearly fond of Cherie.

She pulls a face at the living room, and says: 'Bit basic, isn't it? I know he's a man and all, but still. It needs more ... everything!'

'I know. It's a gorgeous room, and so full of light. I'd get some new curtains for a start, maybe deep green velvet to go with the floor. I'd leave the stone walls—I think they look lovely—but the beams need a bit of attention. They've obviously been painted at some point in the past, and it needs stripping off. And look at that, just a bare light bulb hanging from the ceiling! That's barbaric! It needs a shade, and the whole room would be much nicer at night with some lamps, making it all cosy. Then I'd add a nice rug in the middle of the room, maybe even something a bit exotic, with an Aladdin vibe? The room's big enough to carry that.'

I walk around, visualising it all, and add: 'It needs some proper furniture, obviously. Doesn't need to match, but you could easily have two sofas in here. Big ones, pale colours, don't you think? And some bookcases. Pine would look best. You have some gorgeous framed photos of the coast and countryside in the café. Imagine bigger versions of those on the walls, maybe even canvas rather than frames?

It'd be such a lovely combination: the traditional beams and walls, but with that modern touch? And flowers. Every room looks better with flowers, doesn't it? You could have a little table here by the window, and vases full of them...'

Cherie looks bemused as I wander around the room, gesturing and imagining. I suddenly feel embarrassed, and shut up.

'Sorry,' I say. 'I do go on a bit.'

'No need to apologise, love. Nothing wrong with a bit of passion! That all sounds gorgeous, and I'm a bit jealous. Everywhere I live ends up looking like a squat in Marrakesh. You clearly have a gift. Is there anything we can do now?'

'Well, Gabriel did say there's another room full of stored furniture and Mr P's stuff, and he also said it was fine for us to see what we wanted ... but I'm a bit concerned because this is his turf, isn't it? His territory. He might not like me messing with it.'

'You make him sound like a dog who's cocked his leg everywhere! Why don't we go and have a look? See what there is? If he's not happy, you can put it back.'

I consider it for a few moments, then agree. Truth be told, I'm bursting with curiosity, and the state of this place is hurting me.

We head to the room he's shown me, on the other side of the house in one of the extensions. Inside, we find pretty much the entire contents of a junk shop. I switch the light on, and sneeze as dust assaults me. Clearly nobody has been in here for a while.

It's all arranged pretty sensibly, with larger items of furniture at the back and smaller at the front. It's a big room, long and thin, lacking the charm of the older part of the cottage, but still useful. I spy a small battered bedside cabinet as soon as I venture in, and immediately hoist it up. It's ugly but solid, and once it's been painted it'll look lovely. I put it outside in the hallway, and go back in to forage for more.

As I carry out a visual survey of the furniture, Cherie is having a fine old time rooting around in boxes and drawers, occasionally holding up random items and making comments. Some of them are funny—a spectacular pirate's hat, a half-deflated blow-up flamingo, a massive jug with a donkey's face on the front—and some of them are a bit sad. Like a pill box that still rattles, and stack of unused blood sugar testing strips. A half-filled in crossword book. The signs of age and solitude.

I concentrate on the more practical stuff, because if I go down that rabbit hole, I'll never escape it. I find a small round coffee table with turned legs that I salvage for Sophie's room, and a couple of dusty but usable velvet footstools in a surprising shade of deep pink. Nearer the back, I see a nice old wardrobe that would definitely be useful, and a long dark pine sideboard that would look fantastic in the living room.

I make a mental inventory, and then shout to Sophie to come and help. Between us we manage to clear a path and carry the sideboard through, and I place it under the window. Leaving Cherie to her explorations, I go outside to the wildflower meadow. It's autumn, so most of them are fading now, but there are still some plentiful patches. I don't know their names, but they're vibrant in yellow, purple, and white. I gather some up, and spend a few minutes trimming and arranging them in water in the donkey jug.

I smile as I place it on the sideboard, delighted with the way the sunlight streams through the window and casts floral shadows on the wood.

Back in the storage room, Sophie is just as thrilled when she comes across a huge old dirt-streaked television, one of the chunky ones with a massive plastic back.

'It's a CRT!' she says, clapping her hands together.

'Does that stand for crappy random tat?' says Cherie.

'No, it stands for… Actually, I don't know what it stands for. But these are brilliant for gaming. And before you say, Mum, yes, I'll keep it in my room so I don't disturb you old people while you discuss the weather and play lutes or whatever!'

I was about to suggest that, damn her. Apart from the lutes. I tell her I'll help her carry it upstairs later, and continue rummaging. I find a lovely antique-looking lamp with a brass stand and lavender-coloured glass panels, and take that through to the living room. Amazingly it still works, and I set it up in the corner nearest to where Gabriel reads. If I could only get rid of that ugly recliner, we'd be set.

Right at the far end of the long storage room, I come across a tall wing-backed chair. It's a Chesterfield style with brass studs, made from deep burgundy leather. It's gorgeous, and I get Sophie to mule-train it out for me. Once it's in the living room, I wipe over the leather, and place one of the velvet footstools in front of it. Now two people can sit in here in comfort. Though I wonder if that's one person too many for Gabriel.

All of this takes some time, and before we know it, Sophie dashes to the kitchen and announces that 'the best stew in the world' is ready. We all wash our hands and settle down at the table, and I wonder out loud if Gabriel might want to join us.

Cherie nods and gets out her phone, presses call, and says: 'Gabe, darling, where are you?'

I can't hear his reply, but she says: 'Right. Well. I'm sure the fence will still need repairing tomorrow. I'm currently sitting in your kitchen and dinner's ready. Come and join us, you grumpy sod!'

We leave the stew on the hob while we wait for him, and I realise I feel nervous about the small changes I've made to his living space. He did give me permission to look for things, but this is different.

When he walks through the door to an enthusiastic welcome from Gary, he stares at the three of us, standing frozen.

'Yes, there are people in your kitchen,' says Cherie breezily. 'Just go with it. Wash up and join us.'

There's a moment where I see him considering a refusal, but Cherie is hard to say 'no' to. Once he's sitting, Sophie dishes up, placing a big platter of crusty bread in the middle. There's enough wine left for a small glass for us three, and he cracks open a can of Fosters. Sophie puts some music on her phone—presumably a playlist for awkward dinner parties—and we tuck in.

Cherie declares that *is* the best stew ever, and even Gabriel nods appreciatively. The next hour passes by far more easily than I'd expected, the conversation flowing in the way it does when three chatty women are in a room together. Even Gabriel chips in, telling us about the place he lived in the south of France, where he renovated an old property and worked as a handyman. Sophie asks him if he speaks French, and he tells us he can have a fluent conversation about plumbing and replacing windows, but not much else.

By the time we wave Cherie off just after eight, it's dark outside. She seems to have enjoyed herself, and there was no sign of her earlier grief, so that's a job well done if nothing else.

Sophie enlists Gabriel to help her hoist the CRT television upstairs, and I know she'll be happily lost in a world of treasure-hunting and puzzle-solving and coin-gathering for the rest of the night.

When he comes back down, I say: 'Um, I made a few changes in the living room. If you don't like it, I'll rewind.'

He nods, and walks through into the lounge. I've left the lamp on instead of the overhead light bulb, and personally I think it looks lovely. I see him take in the new additions, and stare at the donkey jug full of flowers, and wait tensely at his side.

'It's … nice,' he says finally. 'I love the donkey. And it feels better with the dimmer lighting.'

'Yes!' I reply, relieved. 'Less like a prison cell! I'm so glad you don't mind.'

'Were you worried I'd be furious and demand you turn it back into a prison cell?'

I nod, and bite my lip.

'I'm not an idiot. I can see how much better this is,' he says, wandering over to the new chair and stroking the leather. 'It's not even changed that much, but somehow it has… Did you find all of this in storage? I mean, I remember lumbering stuff in there, but I wasn't paying much attention. None of it looked like it had much potential.'

'Well, that's all in the eye of the beholder. I like doing this kind of thing. I've got a few more items I'd like to use, if it's okay. Bit of sanding, lick of paint, that kind of thing. And a wardrobe for upstairs if you can help with that. Plus, if you're okay with it, I could maybe get some new curtains, do a bit of decorating when I have time…'

He nods firmly, and answers: 'Yep. Fine by me. Keep track of costs and I'll reimburse you. You've obviously got a flair for it.'

I feel a little warm glow at the praise, and then tell myself off for being so needy. I *am* good at this; there's no need to be over-modest.

'Sounds like a plan. It'll be my way of thanking you for letting me stay. Do you want to see any more of the stuff? Or will it be weird, because he was your family?'

'I don't really believe that blood is thicker than water, and I never even met him. I'll come and look, see what else there is.'

As we walk back through, past the stone stairs, I hear Sophie in her room shouting: 'Mario, you crack whore!'

He raises his eyebrows at me, and I shrug. Let him think what he will.

Back inside the storage room I point out a few more items I think can be saved, and he makes a note of them on the little pad he always seems to have. There's a sofa at the far end that is currently adorned in hideous tasselled green velvet, but the bones of it are good enough to reupholster. There are some wooden chairs which I can paint and re-cover for the bedrooms, and quite a few items of pottery that I think might be worth getting valued.

I find a writing bureau hidden beneath a pile of old bedding, a beautiful thing made of golden oak. Even Gabriel can see that one is special, and I can only imagine he was in some kind of fugue state when he started storing things in here.

I pull open the front panel, and it lies flat to make a desk, little compartments behind it. I see a few old bills, and a file that turns out to contain copies of insurance documents going back decades. Even Belle was insured, presumably against third-party damage. There's a pile of receipts, including one that tells me when the Aga was last serviced, and paid invoices for deliveries of hay. Right at the back, I come across a big envelope tucked away on its own. As I pull it out, a small pile of photos flutter to the ground.

Gabriel picks them up and flicks through them, and I see his face register surprise.

'These are pictures of me,' he mutters, staring at them. 'One when I was a baby. A school photo. When I joined the Army, my wedding… This is weird.'

I blink away my surprise at the mention of a wedding, and lean over to take a peek. He looks serious in his school picture, a strained grimace revealing a gap where his front teeth should be. The Army one is different; he's in full uniform, his dark hair cropped, and he looks young and happy and confident. The wedding photo … well, that's pretty special too. I'd guess he was somewhere in his mid-twenties, still in his Army uniform but with a few more pips on his shoulder and a medal pinned to his jacket. The bride is stunning, blonde, elegant, gazing up at him with adoration.

'You never met him, but he still has these?' I say, deliberately not asking about his wife. Of course I'm almost incandescent with nosiness, but I understand that we have come across these clues to his past by accident, and it might not be something he wants to discuss.

'Yeah. Like I said, weird. There are letters here too. I don't know whether to read them or bin them.'

'What! How could you consider binning them? They're part of your history. Don't you want to know who wrote them, and what the family rift was all about?'

'I'm not sure I do, no. What good would it do? Nobody's left alive.'

'Other than you, Gabriel. You're very much alive, and…

Look, it's up to you, obviously. But to me that's like buried treasure.'

'That's where we're different, Max,' he replies, passing me the bundle. 'I just see the emotional version of an IED. It might mess with my head, and my head doesn't need any more messing with. You read them if you like. Then if you think I should know, tell me.'

'No. That's too much responsibility. I either read them and tell you what's in them, or I don't. You can't expect me to decide what is or isn't important. That can't be my choice.'

He considers it and nods, obviously unsettled by the whole thing. He announces that he's going upstairs for a bath, and I head to the kitchen. There's cake, and I might need it.

I make a mug of tea, and sit down to go through the contents of the envelope. I set the pictures to one side, and find that the letters are all dated. Apart from one, all of them are addressed to 'Dear Norman', who I assume is Mr P. All of them are signed 'your loving sister, Marjorie'.

I take a deep breath, put them in order, and plough straight in. It's a strange thing to be doing, immersing myself in the lives of these dead strangers, and it takes me over an hour to read and digest all the nuances, piecing the tale together. When I'm finished, I get two cans of lager out of the fridge, and walk into the living room. I heard him come down earlier, and find him on his recliner, hair damp, reading a Stephen King novel.

I hand one of the lagers to him, and take a moment to

appreciate how warm and cosy it feels in here now, the remains of a fire smouldering in the grate. He looks up at me and raises one eyebrow. I sit down on the leather chair, and plonk my feet up on the velvet footstool.

'So,' I say, sipping my beer. 'Do you want the long version of the short version?'

'Short, for now.'

'Well, some of this I've put together from the dates and contents of the letters, and some of it is conjecture, just to be clear. Without bringing in a psychic, I can't be certain about any of it.'

'Understood.'

'Okay. Your great-uncle—Norman—was two years younger than your grandmother, Marjorie. Sounds like neither of them wanted to stay and run the family farm. He wanted to go to university, had his heart set on being a doctor. Marjorie was engaged to a local man called Philip, and he came from a family who owned another local farm. It seems like some kind of deal had been reached: she'd marry Philip and the two farms would merge; that way it would stay in both families. Except she didn't go through with it.'

'She called the marriage off? My grandmother?'

'Not exactly. Sounds like she met another boy she liked better, a visiting archaeologist who'd come to do a dig at one of the hill forts.'

'That fits,' he replies, nodding. 'My grandfather passed away before I was born, but he was an archaeologist. Gran's house was like a cave of wonders, filled with artefacts and aerial photos of sites. I used to love going there as a kid. So, how does this relate to Norman?'

'Well, she—Marjorie—eloped with her beau. Ran away to London and got married before anybody could stop her, and that left Norman stuck at home, with the burden of the farm now resting on his shoulders. It's hard to imagine now, isn't it? A young person accepting that kind of fate? But from the tone of your grandmother's letters to him, she knew that once she left, he wouldn't be able to. He was fifth generation on this land, and the pressure piled on for him to continue. Seems like he didn't have a choice: one of them had to stay, and she'd taken that decision out of his hands.

'She didn't start writing to him until the eighties, so it's not like this was a rash decision on her part. It seemed to just take her that long to ask for him to forgive her. As far as I can tell, they had had no contact at all before that, and there's reference to the fact that their parents essentially disowned her once she eloped, and never spoke to her again.'

'Right. Well, I was born in 1981, and her husband had died in 1980. Maybe that's what started it?'

'I think so, yes. Her first letter mentions both of those things. Apparently you looked like Winston Churchill marinated in a vat of port when you were born, by the way. I think it was a crossroads in her life, and she decided to reach out. She basically apologised, and said she knew what she was leaving Norman behind with, but she hadn't been able to sacrifice herself to a loveless marriage just for the sake of a farm and some history.'

He cracks open his beer, and stares into the red embers of the fire, taking it all in.

'Like you say, it's hard to imagine,' he repeats. 'But it was what happened. Norman Pumpwell didn't become a doctor. He didn't follow his dreams; he stayed here. He ran the farm, and presumably looked after his parents as they aged, and then he aged himself. I know he sold off most of the land, just kept a few animals for company. So the irony is that the farm ended with him anyway.'

He looks around the room, soaking up its age and its history, and adds: 'It's so strange to think of my grandmother living in this house as a child. She was a lovely lady, a lot of fun. She basically raised me, and I still miss her now.'

The barely concealed sadness in his voice is hitting a little too close to home for me, and I don't want to start blubbing so I push on.

'So, by the eighties, she's had your mum, who in turn has produced you. Your grandfather had gone, and maybe Marjorie just felt lonely? Started thinking more about the past? This is all pre-internet, so it meant letters, sent to the place where she last knew her brother lived. She talks about all kinds of things in them—her life in London, your mum, you. Mainly you. I bet she spoiled you rotten!'

He grins a little, and nods.

'Didn't he ever reply to her? Did you get the feeling that she was answering back, or was it all one-sided?'

'The latter I'm afraid. She just carries on with her news, and there's never any hint that he's responded. She's just writing into a void. Until the last letter in the envelope, which isn't by her. It's by him, Norman, your great-uncle. That one's a bit of a heartbreaker to be honest. It's dated early in 2022, which is maybe the year he died?'

'It is. And the year after she died. He never knew it, but he was writing to a ghost. And he obviously didn't send it, either.'

'No, he didn't, and it's a shame he didn't do it earlier. Maybe you'd have had a chance to meet him. So, his letter basically says he's forgiven her, was sorry he'd ignored her for so long, and that he would love for her to bring you for a visit. He said he'd been living alone too long and got "set in his ways", that he was basically a recluse until "those terrors from the village" dragged him back into the world.'

'The visits from Auburn?' he says, obviously knowing a bit about it.

'Yes. Then Cherie started sending out care packages and organising events at the café. She told me he was dead set against it at first, but eventually they won him over.'

'That sounds about right,' he grunts, a smile offsetting his words. 'Hard to refuse, aren't they? You fit right in.'

'Thank you.'

'I didn't necessarily mean it as a compliment.'

'Well, I choose to take it as one. Anyway, I don't know why he didn't post the letter. Maybe he had second thoughts, or maybe he got sick? And from what you've said it was too late anyway. It's all a bit sad, isn't it? All those lost years. But I suppose there's proof he still always loved her, the fact that you're here now. Doing this place up. It's nice in a way. Do you believe in God?'

'That's an unexpected question. And the answer is I don't know. Why?'

'I don't know. I'm the same as you I suppose. But it would be nice to think that maybe they're up there somewhere together, and looking down on you bringing their childhood home back to life? Even if you just decide to sell it in the end, you'll have brought it back to life.'

He gets up and pokes the fire, sending up a shimmer of hisses and sparks.

'Are you okay?' I ask, worried about his earlier IED comment.

'Yeah. Just a bit shaken. So much history I never knew about. I wish I'd met him. Auburn says he was a curmudgeonly old git, but she always smiles when she says it.'

'Wow. The genetics must run strong in your family.'

'Ha! Fair point. And thank you, for doing that. I'd have probably chucked them in the fire if you hadn't been here, but I'm glad I didn't. I like the idea of doing what you said.'

'What did I say?'

'That I could bring this place back to life. I'm not a sociable man, in case you hadn't noticed, and there's a real risk I'll also end up as a hermit with no company but a murderous donkey. Maybe it is genetics, maybe it's coincidence, but I wouldn't be shocked if that was my fate. Before I reach that stage, though, I think I would like to bring this place to life again. For the memory of my gran if nothing else. I think it's pretty obvious that I need some help on that front. So, I suppose what I want to ask is, will you help me?'

I look around at the bare room. At the man standing before me. I feel a little sliver of excitement curling in my tummy, and I'm not sure which causes it.

'I'd love to,' I say firmly.

Chapter Nine

After those first few days, life settles into a busy but fulfilling routine. I head to the café with Sophie in the mornings, and it's hugely enjoyable. It barely feels like a job at all apart from the aching back at the end of a shift.

I get to know the locals a lot better, learn how to make chocolate-bar milkshakes in the blender, and master the art of whacking the coffee machine with the hammer. I meet a lot of tourists from all over the world, and enjoy talking to them about their lives. I'm especially entranced by a fossil-hunter from Austin, Texas, who has come all the way here just to hammer at stones on the beach.

I manage to get down to the beach myself, and on clear days spend my half-hour break perched on one of the big boulders, zoning out while I listen to the waves. It's incredibly peaceful, even when there are children playing and dogs barking in the background—somehow the sound of the water seems to override them. The hiss-suck-hiss melody of the sea racing into shore and then running away again is almost hypnotic.

Sophie carries on working hard, and also enjoying herself with her new friends. I suspect there may be a budding romance with the farming apprentice called James, but I don't push on that. She'll tell me when she's ready. She helps out in the café when it's especially busy, and to be honest she's better at it than I am—Laura's already recruited her to help with her Halloween menu.

Later in the afternoons and on my days off, I carry on at the farmhouse, and I am loving every moment of it. The work on Hyacinth has, predictably, taken longer than expected, but I don't mind. In fact I'm secretly delighted.

In the last few weeks, we have achieved so much. Gabriel gave me the greatest gift a man can give a woman— a Farrow & Ball colour card—and mine and Sophie's bedrooms are now complete with lining paper on the walls, painted in beautiful matching tones of pale green. The upstairs landing is in a colour called Brassica, a rich shade of lavender, and the floorboards up there have been sanded down and painted white.

We've stripped back the beams in the living room and painted them matte black, which gives it a bit of a Jacobean feel that works really well. All of the doors have been sanded, re-hung and had nice vintage handles added to them, and I've upcycled several pieces of furniture from the storage room. The big old sofa at the back is getting reupholstered in deep red velvet, and should be back with us soon, which means the recliner's days are numbered.

Like the day we built the flat-packs, Gabriel and I work well together. We're a good team. He is still quiet, still doesn't like to talk about himself, or in fact about anything much other than the job at hand. But the silence is companionable rather than awkward, and I talk enough for two of us anyway.

I've found a few nice antique shops in the area and picked up some lovely items: pictures, vases, a set of vintage tea and coffee canisters in the same pastel green as the Smeg fridge. The little touches make me just as happy as the big jobs, and I'm planning on attending a few fairs and car boots as well.

In short, I am extremely busy, and extremely happy. I am so tired by the time I fall into bed that I sleep almost immediately, listening to the sound of the owls and wondering what the badgers are up to for a few brief moments before I drift off. I still get woken up by Gabriel moving around the house sometimes, but I've gotten used to it I suppose. I have no idea how he functions on so little sleep.

I still miss my mum, and find myself wishing I could bring her here and show her this place. She'd love it—the locals and their quirky sense of humour, the scenery, the cake. Mainly I think she'd love seeing me so content, doing things that I love in a place where I feel safe.

The dark cloud that Richie's betrayal cast over my life has been chased away by the autumn sunshine, replaced with more of a sense of who I am without him. I think that was part of the problem: with no job, no mum to care for, no small children, no husband, I had no clue who I was. My whole life had been defined by those relationships, and once they disappeared, my foundations crumbled.

Now, slowly but surely, I'm building new foundations, ones that are based on *my* life, not other people's. It's pretty awesome, to be honest, but I don't want to get too carried away in case some disaster occurs, or I wake up in Solihull and realise it's all been a dream.

Today, after we turn the café sign to 'closed', I am having an especially nice time. Katie is here, enjoying a rare break as both her sons have been taken to work with their dad, and Cherie is on fine form. She got enlarged copies of the photos in the café, sunsets on the beach and snow on the fields, printed onto vast canvases for us to hang at the farmhouse. They are absolutely gorgeous, and I know they'll look perfect.

'They were taken by my late husband,' she explains, 'and he'd be thrilled to see them used.'

'Frank?' I ask.

'No, the one before that, Wally. I'm like the black widow of Budbury!'

She lets out a guffaw at this, so I'm not concerned about her. Katie laughs along, picking at a slice of chocolate fudge cake and looking enormous.

'When are you due?' I ask, glancing at her bump.

'December 20th. The other two were both late, though,

so knowing my luck I'll be spending Christmas Day with contractions. I can't wait to meet him, though.'

'Is it a boy?'

'It's always a boy. I'm doomed to putting the toilet seat down for the rest of my life. It'll be hard work, I know, having three … but I love it. I just need to get through the sleepless nights part.'

'Is Van not much help on that front?' I ask, surprised, because now I've met him a few times, he seems like the perfect dad.

'No, he's not. He's brilliant in every other respect, but somehow, he just never wakes up, no matter how much crying is going on!'

'Ah. Yes. Well, I suspect that's biological. Men seem to be programmed to be able to sleep through a crying baby.'

'But,' says Laura, joining us, 'somehow they can hear a bra strap being unhooked from three miles away!'

At that point, Sophie walks into the café, looking flustered. She stares around the room, looking for something, and we all watch as she walks around searching. It's entertaining, and none of us offer to help.

'I've lost my purse,' she announces. 'I went up to Auburn's chemist shop—eye-liner emergency—and only realised when I got there. She let me have it anyway.'

'You've lost your purse again?' I ask, shaking my head. This is a common occurrence with Sophie, and can be frustrating.

'Yes, but don't use that disappointed tone, Mum! I've

only lost a purse, not a stock of decommissioned Russian uranium!'

Cherie snorts at this, and I try not to laugh myself. Sophie eventually emerges triumphant, having found her purse tucked down the side of one of the sofas. She waves it in the air, and comes to sit with us.

'What are you lot up to?' she asks suspiciously. 'Plotting world domination?'

'Just chatting,' I say. 'And eating cake. Obviously.'

'Lame. Can I have some money to pay for my eye-liner?'

'I thought you'd just found your purse?'

'Yeah, but it turns out to be empty. I need to get a job…'

I see Laura and Cherie exchange looks, and Laura pipes up: 'You can work here if you like.'

'Why? Is Mum screwing up?'

I give her a gentle slap on the back of the head, and she threatens to call Child Line. I am a bit concerned, though. Are things not going as well as I'd thought?

'No, not at all,' says Laura. 'She's doing brilliantly. All the customers love her. We got a review on Tripadvisor the other day that specifically thanked her for the welcome. But you've been helping me with the Halloween menu, and then there'll be a Christmas menu, and you're really good at it. I know you're busy with your studies as well, but if you wanted to pick up some shifts here, they're available. Maybe that could free your mum up a bit to do more of her … *renovations*.'

Somehow she manages to imbue this perfectly innocent

word with a world of innuendos. *Carry on at the Comfort Food Café*. I know it's driving her mad, having a spy in the Gabriel camp and me not reporting back to her with every detail. She'll ask me questions about the work on the house, which I'm happy to discuss, and then randomly throw in something like: 'Oh, you painted the window ledge? Very nice. But do you ever bump into him wearing nothing but his boxer shorts?'

Laura is a very happily married woman, but she definitely has an appreciation for the male form. Cal, the Chris Hemsworth cowboy, is one of her idols, and I suspect she feels the same about Gabriel. I always deflect, even though the answer to that question is 'almost, yes'. A few days ago, I came out of my room just as he was emerging from a shower, and there was an awkward moment where we danced around each other in the confined space. All with him wearing nothing but a white towel tied around his waist.

I now know that he is an extremely lithe and well-muscled man, and that yes, he does have chest hair. I stare at my fudge cake and try not to blush at the memory. Some things you cannot unsee. My relationship with Gabriel works fine just as it is. Anything more would unbalance it.

'How's it going, the work?' Cherie asks, as she makes us all a fresh coffee.

'Good!' I reply. 'Really good. He's put adjustable lighting in the living room, and is considering underfloor heating in the bathroom. We've done a lot of the decorating, and … well, it's coming along.'

'Do you fancy doing Hyacinth after?' Cherie asks,

passing the drinks over. Katie's off caffeine and has an enormous hot chocolate instead. 'I know it's dragged on, but the roof is almost done, and the damage to the upper floor is on its way to being repaired. But to be honest, it needed a refurb anyway, and you've obviously got a knack for it. I'd be paying someone else to do it, and I'd rather pay you.'

'She has got a knack,' mutters Sophie, nose deep in her own fudge cake. 'It's like her superpower. The Amazing Doer-Upper.'

I'm surprised by what Cherie has suggested, but also intrigued. It's never even occurred to me that I could earn money doing what comes naturally to me, even though I'd never actually accept cash from Cherie. She's done enough already.

'But there are lots of cottages at the Rockery,' I say eventually. 'Wouldn't you want to do it wholesale, so they had a theme?'

'Good lord no!' she says, shivering in horror. 'Why would I want that? I hate things that all look the same. I'm more of a mismatched kind of gal! Have a think about it anyway. As for Gabriel's, tell him we'll be expecting a grand house-warming party once everything's done, won't you?'

'I think you can tell him that yourself, Cherie. I can't imagine it'll be top of his wish list.'

'I know, but it'll come better from you, my love. You're like … the Gabriel Whisperer! You've clearly won him around with your home cooking and your domestic skills.'

'And her huge boobs,' adds Sophie, cheekily.

'Gabriel is not interested in my boobs!' I snap. 'Gabriel's type isn't scruffy chubby women from the Midlands.'

'Oooh,' says Laura, leaning closer and smiling. 'What is his type then? Please say it's scruffy chubby women from Manchester!'

I suddenly feel pinned down, trapped, and way too much in the spotlight. This is probably how he feels all the time. Of course, the only thing I based that comment on was seeing the wedding photo by accident, and catching a glimpse of his beautiful, tall, very slender, very blonde wife. But that is not something I would ever share with these ladies, no matter how lovely they are, because that is not their business, and I would never betray Gabriel's trust.

I know the letters between his grandmother and Mr P have had a profound effect on him, and he's said that he might go and visit Edie to find out more, as she was around at the time. It was probably a huge scandal when Marjorie ran away with a visiting archaeologist, and even thinking those words makes me realise how fantastical it sounds, like something from a film. I know he's interested, almost against his will, because he loved her so much. It was easy for him to disconnect from his great-uncle because he never knew him. But his gran is different.

If and when he decides to talk to Edie is up to him, although he has now read the letters for himself. The one that described his mother's death obviously affected him, and he disappeared off to his room for the whole night. I think Mr Pumpwell's story has also really moved him, as it did me. Knowing that the man had lived a tough and solitary life, but that his last few years were enriched by the café, by the community, by the women currently sitting around me speculating on whether Gabriel is a breast man or a leg man.

'We should do a test,' Laura announces firmly. 'We can arrange a lineup. Auburn is all legs, and Max is all boobs, and Becca's a bit of both. Get them all dressed in bikinis and see which one he stares at the longest.'

'It's too cold for bikinis!' Katie points out, as though that's the only possible problem with this scenario.

'You're right,' Laura says, frowning. We're well into October, and the temperatures are plummeting along with the leaves. 'Maybe they can all wear slutty nurse outfits for the Halloween party?'

I shake my head, and ignore them. It's Halloween next week, and shockingly, they've decided to have a party. I have quickly realised that anything from a birthday to somebody recovering from a nasty cold is cause for a celebration here.

They chat among themselves, moving happily away from Gabriel's sexual preferences to safer subjects like cocktails—apparently Cherie will be whipping up a batch of her 'famous' Pumpkin Spice Punch, along with some jugs of Murderous Martini. Sophie is planning on making chopped-off fingers from marzipan, and Laura is speculating about the best way to make eyeballs float in the trifle.

As the talk moves on to costumes, I find that my mind has drifted to Hyacinth House. To a seaside theme, with nautical touches in the bathroom, and driftwood from the beach on the living room shelves. To cupboards that look like onboard cabinets, and pale blue curtains, and sea shells that let you hear the sea when you hold them to your ears. I can see it all clearly, and know how great it could be.

'I'll do it,' I say, interrupting a debate about whether *Twilight* is a horror film or a comedy. 'Hyacinth, I mean. I'd love to do the refurb for you, Cherie.'

Chapter Ten

Getting the sofa back makes a huge difference to Gabriel's living room. It's gorgeous, and now it's been revived, it has deep squishy seat cushions covered in super-soft velvet that I want to keep stroking. I know velvet takes some maintenance, but it looks amazing.

Gabriel and the delivery man carried it through, and we spent an entertaining few minutes where I asked them to move it to various different places before finding its perfect spot.

I'd initially imagined paler colours for the furniture, but finding the leather Chesterfield armchair changed all of that. It works surprisingly well with the touch-of-green floorboards, giving off a bit of a National Trust vibe that suits the age of the building.

I've hung new curtains, and they swoop to the floor behind the sideboard, which I've sanded and polished and now glows with new life. It still bears the donkey jug, which

I regularly refresh with cut flowers, and who knows? Maybe one day Gabriel will finally give in and get a television.

The new lighting is in, and between that and the lamp and the open coal fire, this big room is now capable of feeling small and cosy. When I'm gone and he returns to his old patterns, at least he won't be sitting reading a book in a prison cell.

I found him a gorgeous oak bookcase in an auction one town over, and his vast collection of paperbacks now has somewhere to call home. Cherie's canvases are up, looking smashing, and it's almost done. I just need to find the right rug, and maybe add some more personal touches, which is tricky, as this isn't my home. If it was, I'd have pictures of the kids up on the walls, including some extra embarrassing ones just for fun.

It's my day off as I ponder the nearly there room, and I have a casserole slow-cooking in the Aga. It throws off a huge amount of heat, and as it's only going to get colder from now on, that's a good thing.

Gabriel walks into the lounge to find me standing there with a mug of tea, surveying his kingdom. He's been mucking out Belle's field, which is a task that requires nerves of steel and nimble feet. The cantankerous old beast and I continue to have a truce, and she now even lets me scratch her ears. I know he's talked to Matt about finding another rescue donkey to keep her company, and apparently it could go two ways – either she'll take to it, or she'll try and kill it.

'Something smells good,' he says, gesturing back to the kitchen with his head. It's been drizzling outside, and his thick hair carries a sheen of mist.

'Hopefully it'll taste good as well. Have you thought about maybe putting some family pictures up? Making it feel like, I don't know … *your* home, not just *a* home?'

'No, I haven't thought about that. I have some. Of my mum. And the ones that we found in the writing bureau.'

The bureau itself is still in storage, because once that room is empty of clutter, it'll make a wonderful centrepiece for it. It could be an office-cum-library.

'That one of you with no front teeth is super-cute,' I reply, grinning at the memory. 'And maybe you have some of your gran too? It'd be nice to find one of them together, wouldn't it? Her and her brother?'

'It would. But I've not come across anything like that. In fact I'm wondering if Norman got rid of any photos he did have. I mean, it wasn't common back then, taking pictures, was it? But there should have been some.'

'I know. I thought the same. Maybe he fed them to Belle. I think it's worth asking Edie, though. She was the librarian before she retired; she probably has all kinds of local history knowledge. I hope so anyway, as it would be fascinating. This was their childhood home and we have no idea what they looked like back then. These days everyone takes photos all the time, like, of their dinner and their new shoes, thinking nothing of it. Even when I was growing up it was usually just holidays and Christmas and weddings.'

'Well, there won't be any wedding pictures going up on the walls, that's for sure.'

I nod, and sip some tea, and realise that I literally can't hold my curiosity in for a moment longer. I've told him about my life—probably way more than he was interested in—but he has remained predictably tight-lipped about his.

'What happened?' I ask quietly. 'I assume you're not married anymore?'

This is, of course, potentially rocky terrain, and I see him tense slightly. I'm familiar with his body language now, which is often the only way he really communicates. I know when he quirks his head to one side that he's amused and trying to hide it, and when he clenches and unclenches his fists he's trying to behave well in a situation that doesn't feel comfortable for him, like being in a room full of people. I know if he folds his arms across his chest and looks into the distance he's ready to bail, and when he stands with his hands on his hips he's considering saying something, but thinking it over first.

This move—the barely noticeable upwards squeeze of the shoulders—can go one of two ways. Either the tension carries on through the rest of his body and he'll shut down and walk out of the room, or he'll do this thing he probably doesn't even notice: take a deep breath, and nod as he lets it out. That's his 'this is freaking me out but I know it shouldn't' ritual.

I hold my own breath while I wait to see which one wins out, and eventually he nods, and meets my eyes.

'No, not married anymore. The woman you saw on the

photo was Helen. I was twenty-five on that, and like most people, thought it was forever.'

'Forever is a long time.'

'It is. We were fine when I was enlisted. When I was away, and only home on leave, it was all good. I suppose it made it exciting, and I was in the Army when we met, so we'd never known anything different. We'd never actually properly lived together. I left seven years ago, and I'd been deployed all over the world. Iraq, Afghanistan, Nigeria. I don't talk about that part of my life, so don't ask. I suppose, to be fair to Helen, the man she ended up with wasn't the man she signed up for. It changed me, and by the time we tried to make a go of it in civilian life, I was … different. Maybe a bit damaged.'

I stay silent, not wanting to break the spell or even remind him that I'm here, and he continues, 'It didn't work. We fought. I didn't talk, and she hated that. She had her own life and friends, and I didn't fit in. It was a mess, and we hurt each other. Then she had an affair, and that was the end of it. I don't blame her, not really, but it was bad. She'd been seeing him for a while before I found out, and it messed me up even more. Combination of wounded macho pride and genuine pain.'

My heart breaks for him, and I struggle not to reach out and touch him. Console him. I know exactly how that feels, and it was bad enough without throwing in the aftereffects of active military service and having to adapt to life in the outside world.

'I'm so sorry, Gabriel,' I say. 'That must have been awful.

That kind of thing makes it almost impossible to trust anyone.'

'It does,' he says, nodding sharply. 'But God loves a trier, eh? We're both trying, in our own way, Max.'

'We are. She was … very beautiful.'

I don't know where that comes from, and it's totally irrelevant. I suppose I just have that wedding day photo frozen in my mind, remembering how gorgeous and happy they looked. Like they had the world at their feet.

'On the outside, maybe. Plus she really worked at it— she was always on a diet, and never ate carbs.'

'What?' I say, shocked. 'Never? Not even a roastie at Christmas? That must have put her in a very bad mood! But I suppose that's why she looked like a model, and I … umm, don't.'

Right now, I'm looking especially un-model like. I've not gained weight since I've been here, despite all the cake. I suppose the walking and the active work have offset it. But I'm also aware that I'm wearing a pair of paint-spattered jeans and a shaggy old jumper with a hole in the armpit. I'd been planning on cleaning all the windows today, and nobody dresses up for that.

'There's nothing wrong with the way you look, Max,' he says, his dark eyes sweeping over me. 'You have a beautiful smile, and really pretty hair, and lovely eyes. I like the fact that you eat carbs. They look good on you.'

I'm so shocked at the compliment that I can't even speak. I stare at him, my mouth open, my fingers going to my messy ponytail in surprise. The shock is followed by pleasure, and the pleasure is followed by something altogether warmer. I blink rapidly, my heart suddenly racing, a blush blooming across my cheeks.

'Thank you,' I say eventually. 'I … um… You called me fat when you first saw me.'

He looks horrified, and quickly replies: 'What? I didn't! I wouldn't … even if you were. Which you're not.'

'Technically, you said I was "not small". You were talking to Laura and Matt the first night I was here. I was eavesdropping.'

His eyes narrow as he tries to recall the conversation, and then he says: 'Right. I was a bit freaked out about having people in the house. I didn't mean you were fat, Max, just that you were a human, and I … I'm not so good with those. Even if you'd been the size of a gnat, I'd still have been a bit concerned. I'm sorry if I hurt your feelings, though. and I meant everything I just said.'

'That's okay. I was probably oversensitive. And, well. You're not so bad yourself.'

We stare at each other for a few moments longer, and then he abruptly turns around and walks out of the room. Strange, and unsettling, and not altogether unpleasant.

I've always been aware of how attractive Gabriel is, but in a kind of detached way. He's so far out of my league that he might as well be George Clooney, and I've never entertained ideas about any kind of romance between us. Well, strictly speaking, I suppose I may have had a few saucy thoughts, but that's between me and my conscience. I definitely never imagined that he'd feel anything more for me other than tolerance, and even that was pushing it.

I tell myself that I'm being stupid, that nothing has changed. A man can compliment a woman without fancying her. Sam, Becca's husband, is the world's biggest flirt; he compliments every single woman he meets, and even flirts with Edie. None of it means anything. It's just the way he's made.

This, though, is Gabriel, and getting words out of his mouth at all is a small miracle. He doesn't say much, which makes everything he does say feel even more significant.

It's all too confusing, so I shove it in a mental bin bag and forget about it. I carry on with my work list for the day, and clean the windows, inside and out. After that I check on the casserole, feed Belle a carrot, and chat to Ben on the phone for a bit. Anything to distract me, I suppose.

When Sophie gets home from seeing her friends and suggests we start planning our Halloween outfits, I leap on the idea with so much enthusiasm that she narrows her eyes at me suspiciously.

'What's up?' she asks. 'Are you on drugs?'

'No! Well, I did have an ibuprofen about an hour ago, but I don't think that counts. What are you going as?'

'Well, we've all decided to be vampires. It's not original, I know, but it's easy, and that makes it good. Martha's going to a fabric shop in town to buy a load of black velvet for our capes, and Auburn says she'll order in some face paints and white powders and stuff. But obviously, I'll be going as a *sexy* vampire, because that's what Halloween is all about. What about you?'

'Oh. Well. I thought I'd just get an old white sheet, cut some eyeholes in it, and be Maxine the Friendly Ghost.'

'Mum, that's the lamest idea I've ever heard. Did you not hear what I just said about Halloween being *sexy*?'

'Halloween might be, but I'm not. I'll be more comfortable as a ghost in a sheet.'

'Right. Well, that's pathetic. Comfortable is a word for armchairs and jeggings. It's not a word for women in their forties who still have a lot of living left to do. You could be Elvira, or a slightly squashed Catwoman, or a really wicked witch!'

'I don't have the stuff to make those outfits.'

'That's what shops are for. Come on, we'll go looking together. It'll be fun, mother-daughter bonding time! Let me give you a makeover!'

I'm about to say no when Gabriel joins us, nose twitching at the smell of the almost-ready casserole.

'Gabriel!' Sophie exclaims, jumping to her feet. 'What are you wearing to the Halloween party?'

'I don't think I'm going,' he replies, running the tap for a glass of water. He avoids my eyes, and I suspect he's feeling awkward around me after what he said earlier. It'll pass, I know.

'Of course you are!' she says. 'What is it with you old people? Have you completely forgotten how to have fun?'

'Nope,' he says, shrugging. 'We just have different ideas about what "fun" is.'

She ignores this, and carries on, 'You'd be a good vampire, too. You've got that dark and mysterious vibe, and the hair. Or Lucifer. Or a Roman soldier—'

'How is that scary?'

'It doesn't need to be scary! Just fun, and different, and hot. You can do it. I believe in you!'

'I'm not Tinkerbell,' he says firmly. 'Is dinner ready?'

'Ten minutes,' I say, amused at their exchange.

He nods, and leaves again. Sophie is chuffing away in disgust, and it makes me laugh out loud.

'Okay,' I say after a few moments' thought. 'Wicked witch doesn't sound too bad.'

Maybe, I think as she celebrates, she's right: maybe I need to aim for something more than 'comfortable'. Maybe it's time I started thinking of myself as someone who is capable of being sexy again. Not for Gabriel, or Richie, or any other man, but just to remind myself that I can.

Chapter Eleven

The party takes place a few days after Halloween, on a Sunday because the café is closed the day after.

Sophie and I get ready in her room, while Gabriel makes himself scarce. I think he'd rather snog Belle than be dragged out to the bash, and I have to admit I'm a little disappointed. I don't know quite what's going on in my brain, but I realise with some horror that maybe I was harbouring a little fantasy about me looking like such a sexy witch that something would happen between us.

I know it's stupid, and I know I'm not even ready for a relationship, but for some reason there's a big fat gap between what I know and what I feel. I've gone from thinking he was hot but rude to thinking he was hot but misunderstood, and now I don't seem able to get past the 'hot'. It's his own fault, of course, swanning around looking fit and macho, fixing things, using power drills while he swings his hair around. It's like living in a razor advert.

I've always been aware of him, but since his comments a few nights ago, it's like everything has stepped up gear. I find myself thinking about him in ways that are not entirely appropriate, and undoubtedly wouldn't be welcome. Richie made it perfectly clear what he thought about my sex appeal, and there's no reason to think Gabriel would feel any different.

Despite understanding all of this, part of me has definitely turned into a teenage girl. I'll be scribbling his name on my pencil case next.

The actual teenage girl in the room is looking at me appraisingly as I squeeze myself into my outfit. It's a dress with a swishy skirt covered in netting, and a bodice-style top that forces my boobs up like watermelons.

'I look ridiculous,' I announce, running my hands over my waist. 'I'm too old for this.'

'You're forty-three, not dead! Anyway. Look at that chest, Mum—you could rest your pint on those! Why didn't I get your genetics?'

'Dunno, but be grateful, they're a pain. Plus you have lovely long legs and can wear skinny jeans and look good in them.'

'This is true. Okay, well, your hair looks great—bit of volume, bit of va-va-voom, very witch-like, good with or without hat—and the dress really is nice. I know you feel self-conscious, but that's because you've been hiding your body for the last gazillion years. We're not in LA. Nobody here is a body fascist. This is Budbury, a village that is fuelled entirely by cake! Anyway, make-up, I was thinking we could try a nice smoky eye?'

'Just the one? Won't that look weird?'

'Shut up and sit on the bed.'

I do as I'm told, because I'm not great with make-up and she is, in that way her generation can be. They learnt at the feet of YouTube masters. She takes ages, and I do worry she's actually painting a clown face on me for kicks and giggles.

'I watched a tutorial,' she says, as she dabs me fiercely with a sponge. 'On contouring for old people.'

'Is that what it was called?'

'No, it was something more polite, like contouring for mature faces, but it means the same. Anyway. You look great, as if by magic!'

I actually do look great, I think, as I do a little spin in front of the mirror. More glamorous than I have for decades, possibly ever. I do a little shimmy to make sure the girls won't pop out while I'm dancing, and we set off for the café. I'm driving us there, and Becca, who doesn't drink, will be ferrying people who live any distance away back at the end of the night.

Inside, we find one wall lined with trestle tables full of food, and Sophie shows me the bloody marzipan fingers with pride. She also points out her cupcakes decorated with spider webs and the little sandwiches she made earlier, all cut into the shape of ghosts. She grabs herself a glass of punch, and joins the gang of other young vampires on the sofas. They all cheer when she turns up, and it makes me smile. She's doing so well at the moment.

I gaze around the room and take in the various outfits. Katie, obviously stuck for costume ideas in her pregnant state, has simply wrapped a load of bandages around herself and come as a mummy. Auburn, Willow's sister who runs the pharmacy, and her husband, Finn, have painted their faces green and added head-dresses made of wire coat hangers. I'm not entirely sure but maybe they're aliens?

A few young people are here from Briarwood, the research centre that Finn manages. I'm told it's some kind of hothouse residential for talented kids from the world of STEM, and they've already patented several lucrative inventions. One of them is dressed as a Rubik's Cube, another as old-school Luke Skywalker.

Edie and Becca, Laura's sister, have come as Laurel and Hardy, but with blood spattered over their suits, and Cherie is a magnificent Bride of Frankenstein, her massive wig adding to her height. I notice she keeps getting it tangled up in the mobiles that dangle from the ceiling, and suspect its days are numbered.

There are several children running around, including Katie's boys, Little Edie, Ruby, and Rose. They are in a variety of outfits, including Doctor Who, a zombie cheerleader, and glow-in-the-dark skeleton onesies. It's all very cute, and reminds me of trick or treating nights of yore. I used to love taking my kids out when they were young, and even now I always make sure I have a big stock of Love Hearts and lollipops to give out. I wonder if the tenants in my house will do that, or if they'll be the types who switch the lights off and pretend they're not in.

As I help myself to a Murderous Martini, Laura floats towards me and puts a platter of pizza bats on the table. I know it's her because she's carrying the food, and saying: 'You look gorgeous, Max!' as she approaches. I can't see her face, though, because she has a sheet over her head and has come as a ghost. She stole my idea, the sneak.

'Thank you,' I reply. 'I feel a bit exposed.'

'Have some alcohol. That'll cure it. Where's Gabriel?'

'He's not coming, I don't think. He's been in hiding all day. Probably scared I'll cast a spell on him and force him to enjoy himself. Do you need any help with anything?'

'No, don't worry, Sophie was great today, and it's all out now. I'm about to get spectacularly drunk, though I'm not quite sure how I'm going to drink through this sheet…'

I go and chat to Sam, Becca's husband, who is dressed in the wetsuit he uses for surfing, but with a plastic knife glued to his back as though someone has stabbed him. I take Laura's advice and drink my way through my nerves, and soon calm down enough to enjoy myself.

There's boogying to a classic Halloween playlist, and apple bobbing, and someone has set up a limbo dancing bar in a corner. At some point a confetti canon is blasted over the crowd, and we all end up covered in tiny glittery black cats.

It's all a lot of fun, and I make sure to snap plenty of pictures to show Ben. I'm hoping he'll come when term ends, and get to see it for himself.

I enjoy the night, and love the sense of belonging I have here now, but I'd be lying if I said I wasn't also aware that someone was missing. I keep gazing at the door, wondering if he will make an arrival. I even left out Mr Pumpwell's pirate hat on the kitchen table just in case he had a change of heart.

By the time Becca is rounding up me and Laura's family for our lifts home, I'm ready to go. I've had a couple of Murderous Martinis, and although I'm not drunk, I'm tipsy enough. As we're about to leave, Sophie runs across and asks if she can stay over at Frank's farm, where there is apparently an after-show.

I have a word with Zoe about it, and she assures me it's fine. At least I think it's Zoe; she has all of her bright curly hair over her face like Cousin It, complete with sunglasses and a bowler hat. She adds the proviso that there won't be any adult supervision, because 'me and Cal will be there'.

I agree, which earns me a big hug from my daughter, and I give her the car keys so she can drive home the next day.

Becca shepherds us all down the hill through the rain, and I keep a tight hold of my witch's hat as we make our way to Matt's big seven-seater car. Laura sits in the back with him and Ruby and Rose, Laura belching and then giggling about it.

When I get back to the farmhouse, Gary is waiting by the door, and yips and jumps around my ankles in excitement. I let him out to do his business, and as soon as he's back in, I close the door against the weather. He immediately curls up on his bed and goes back to sleep. Lazy bones.

I stand in the kitchen drinking a glass of water, the warmth from the Aga wrapping itself around me in a welcome blanket. It's quiet in here, and when I tiptoe through to the living room I see the lights are off, and the fire guard is up. I feel a flash of disappointment, like the idiot I am. What was I expecting? That he'd have waited up for me? And why am I thinking like this at all?

I put the dimmer lights on as low as they can go, and decide to slip my shoes off and have a little lie down on the squishy sofa. It's still relatively early by normal-world standards, and I'm not quite ready to admit defeat yet.

It's warm and pleasant and relaxing, the only sounds the odd hiss and crackle from the dying fire, and perhaps inevitably I drift off for a little snooze. Even witches need the odd power nap.

When I wake up, I'm startled to find Gabriel kneeling on the floor next to me, about to cover me up with a blanket. My eyes widen in shock, and he looks as surprised as I am. He's wet, and he's wearing the pirate hat, and I'm very confused.

'Sorry,' he says quietly. 'Didn't mean to disturb you. Just wanted to tuck you in, it's getting cold.'

'That's nice of you,' I say, looking up at him. 'Why are you wearing the pirate hat?'

It looks fantastic on him, of course, with his dark hair and brooding features.

'I went out to watch the badgers, and it was raining.

Seemed to make sense at the time. You have little black cats stuck to your … self.'

I follow his gaze, and realise exactly where the little black cats are lurking. He quickly looks away, obviously embarrassed at being caught looking at my cleavage.

I don't know quite what happens then, because I seem to suddenly become possessed by the spirit of someone far more adventurous than me. Someone far more confident. It could be the martinis, or it could be magic. Whatever it is, I see my own hand reach upwards, almost as though it had a mind of its own. I touch the side of his face with my fingers, running them over his cheekbone and his jawline.

He freezes, and says: 'What are you doing?'

'Touching you.'

'Why?'

'Because I want to.'

His face is silhouetted by the glow of the fire, and his eyes flash dark and dangerous. He takes my hand in his, and for a moment I think he's going to simply shove me away in disgust. But he holds it to his mouth, and kisses the soft skin of my palm. It's such a gentle thing, barely even there, but the sensitive skim of his lips on my flesh sends shivers right through me.

He releases my hand, and it floats to his shoulder. His top is damp, and I can feel the outline of his muscled frame. It is every bit as divine as I had imagined it would be. He reaches out and winds his fingers into my hair, stroking it back from my face, and every flimsy moment of contact feels like paradise. Maybe I'm dreaming. Or maybe I've simply started something that I've wanted for a long time now. Maybe I've started something that I need. His face is so close to mine I can feel his breath wisping against my skin, and I murmur: 'Take me to bed.'

'Are you tired?'

'No.'

He nods once, and stands up tall, holding out his hands to pull me up. I land against his chest, and gaze up at him, thinking again how beautiful he is. Neither of us speaks, but my body is trembling with anticipation, and when his hand goes to the small of my back and pulls me closer, I can tell that he feels the same.

He leads me out of the room and up the steep stone stairs, and I absolutely refuse to let my mind start whirring away. If I start thinking, start questioning this, then it will stop—and I don't want it to stop. I know this is probably a mistake, that it will be messy, but I don't care. I want to feel his body against mine. I want to feel his lips on me, his hands on me. I want to know what he tastes like.

We reach the landing, and he pauses. He pushes me back against the wall, one palm against it on either side of my face, trapping me. I feel a rush of blood to parts of my body that have lain dormant for years now, and suck in a breath.

'How drunk are you?' he asks, as I twine my fingers into his thick hair.

'Why?'

'Because I don't want to take advantage of you.'

'That's very gentlemanly, Gabriel, but you can stop it.

I'm fine. I want this, and I don't need you to be polite about it.'

I am shocked at my own words, at my own behaviour, as I grab hold of his jean-clad behind and tug him closer to me. He might be saying gentlemanly things, but his body is betraying him, and it's not feeling polite at all. I sigh a little, and lean into him, revelling in how solid he is. He wants me as much as I want him.

That seems to push him over the edge, and his hands are suddenly in my hair, turning my face upwards. His lips are on mine, and there is nothing gentle about it anymore. It is hot and demanding and passionate, his whole body crushed against me, my hands sliding under his T-shirt and glorying in what I find there. His skin is soft as velvet, but what lies beneath is hard as iron, and it is a combination that leaves me wanting more.

When we both run out of breath, he grabs hold of me and hoists me so my legs are wrapped around his hips, and I squeal in surprise. It almost breaks the moment—I don't see myself as the kind of woman who a man can lift—but he shuts me up with another kiss, this one slower but just as demanding. My hands are around his shoulders, and my tongue is dancing with his, and every part of me is alive.

His lips drift down the side of my neck, finding sensitive places I didn't even know I had, trailing kisses and nipping at my flesh and making every single cell in my body light up.

He lets out what sounds like a growl, and carries me through into my bedroom. We fall onto the bed together, and he is there, hard and gorgeous and annoyingly fully clothed between my legs. He carries on his explorations, his mouth roaming my neck, my throat, down to my breasts.

I hear my dress rip, and he unhooks my bra, and good lord, he does things to my nipples that they've never experienced before. Every suck, every lick, every touch, drives me more wild, and I'm bucking up against him, moaning his name as he expertly plays with my senses. Hands, fingers, tongue, all of it combining to make me groan in need.

He suddenly pulls away, and I am momentarily devastated until I see that it is only to pull his T-shirt over his head and his jeans off. The pirate hat got lost somewhere on the way. He stands before me, naked and magnificent, his body lean and ripped and ready, and he is so perfect that I could almost cry.

He lays a hand on my leg, running it slowly and torturously up my inner thigh. His fingers feel insanely good against me, and I wonder how I've lived without this for so long.

'You're so fucking beautiful,' he mutters, staring at me hungrily. 'But are you sure this is what you want? I'm not a simple man...'

'I never thought I'd say this, Gabriel,' I reply desperately, 'but stop talking. Less thinking, more doing. Please.'

Chapter Twelve

There is quite a lot of doing after that, and it is so insanely good that it should be illegal. It is the Class A drug of the sex world, and my mind is truly blown.

I have only ever been with two men, my first boyfriend when I was seventeen, and then Richie. Like a lot of couples, I suppose over the years, our sex life took a back seat to the rest of life. I was always tired and busy and preoccupied. I put weight on, ran low on energy, and felt self-conscious about my flabby bits. None of that is a recipe for spectacular sex, and eventually I started seeing it as a chore rather than fun.

Part of me even has some sympathy for Richie on that front; he was a typical bloke, always up for it, but I was inhibited and reluctant, and often rejected him. If he came to bed later than me, I'd pretend to be asleep, and even when we did it, afterwards I'd think 'Well, that's another job ticked off the list; he should be okay for another month.' I totally lost my mojo, and never thought I'd find it again.

Now, though, my mojo isn't just back; it's throwing a party. I don't know whether I'm just at a different place in my life, or it's down to the mystery of chemistry, or whether Gabriel is simply better at sex, but I have more orgasms in one night with him than I did with Richie in the last decade of our marriage.

We wake up several times during the night and repeat the whole thing in slightly different and crazily exciting ways, and when we drift off for the final time, I fall asleep with a satisfied smile on my face.

I know that things might look different in the morning, that the glorious simplicity of the night will fade as reality assaults it, but I just don't care. Tomorrow is, after all, another day.

When it does arrive, though, it's not quite how I'd imagined. I know Gabriel isn't a good sleeper, and I haven't shared a bed with a man for a long time. I expected that neither of us would be able to get any proper rest, that I'd wake at seven with the sky still dark outside, and Gabriel already gone.

Instead, I am shocked awake by the familiar sound of a car outside, doing the toot-toot-I'm-here horn honk. I shoot upright, completely naked, and stare around in surprise. It's light out, and Gary is barking, and a quick glance at the bedside clock tells me it's almost eleven.

Gabriel is next to me, his hair splayed across his face,

one leg and an entire butt on display. I take a moment to appreciate the view, then shake him roughly.

'Get up, get up!' I say, jumping to my feet and grabbing my pyjamas. I hop around the room trying to get my legs in them, and peek through the curtains. My car is parked up outside, which means only one thing.

'Gabriel, come on, shift yourself. Sophie's back!'

I look outside again, and as she opens the door, Gary comes streaking out, obviously needing a wee. Poor baby. I have been a bad dog mama.

Gabriel looks as stunned as I do as he staggers out of bed, rubbing at his eyes and tracking down his jeans. He pulls them on, then adds his T-shirt, both inside out and back to front, so the label is on display. He dashes out, and I laugh as I hear him stumble and swear in the landing. I do a quick survey of the room and notice his boxers on the floor. I kick them under the bed together with my witch dress, which is now ruined because Gabriel literally ripped my bodice. Swoon.

I dash to the bathroom, and when I see myself in the mirror I almost scream. My hair is wild and tangled; last night's make-up is smeared and crusted; my lips are swollen and I have dull red marks on my collarbone. I look like a woman who has been well and truly shagged, and quickly start splashing cold water on my face and trying to smooth down my hair.

By the time I make it into the kitchen, Sophie already has the kettle on and is giving Gary his food. He looks up at me with accusatory amber eyes, and I give him a stroke to assure him he's still my number one guy.

Sophie leans against the counter and looks me up and down, narrowing her eyes.

'You look like shit,' she announces. 'Hangover from hell?'

'Yes. Too much punch.'

'These things happen. I'll make you a coffee, because I'm officially the best daughter in the world. Possibly the best human being. I called in at the café and did some clearing up, and I'm working the rest of the day. I've got mocks coming up in December and I'm chasing those As, baby. Then tonight I might go and hang out at Jess's house and play video games.'

Oh God, I think, the clear-up. I need to go back to the café and help out, even though it's the last thing I feel like doing. My body is aching in places I didn't even know I possessed.

I chat to Sophie, and I don't think she suspects a thing until Gabriel walks into the room. He's looking better than I am, but not by much.

'What's your excuse?' she asks, making him a coffee too. 'I know you weren't at the party.'

'Had a wild night in with a six-pack of Stella.'

'Right. And were you wearing a pirate hat while you did that, because I found one on the living room floor? Plus, FYI, you seem to have a glittery little black cat stuck to your neck. Just saying.'

She cackles as she exits the room, leaving Gabriel peeling the feline evidence from his skin. Oops.

I sit down with my mug, because I'm not sure I can rely on my legs this morning. He leans against the sink and gazes at me over the steam cloud.

'Last night was…' he says, then trails off. I'm convinced he's about to say 'a mistake', but he surprises me by grinning and adding, 'Amazing.'

He looks completely different when he smiles. His brown eyes sparkle, and little laughter lines appear on his face, and he seems to shed that black cloud he often has hovering around him.

'It was, wasn't it?' I reply, sipping my drink. 'I thought you were going to get up and be all mean and moody about it.'

'Yeah. I thought I would too, to be honest. Maybe I'm still under your spell. That's the only logical explanation. You actually are a witch, and you've enchanted me. I can't be held responsible for my actions.'

I nod, and accept this. It's been a long time since I felt like I could enchant a man, and it doesn't feel unpleasant.

'What do you have planned today?' I ask.

'I'm going to start clearing the barn, maybe give Belle's stable a check over before winter kicks in. And then, if you had any interest in this whatsoever, I thought we might find some time alone so I can do that thing that makes you go cross-eyed.'

'Which one?'

'All of them.'

I feel my pulse hammer away at the thought, and blush bright red. This really isn't going the way I'd expected. Gabriel is not a man who flirts, or engages in casual conversation, or makes plans that involve other people. It's not unwelcome, but it is confusing.

'I'm starting to wonder,' I say, 'if while I was at the party you were maybe abducted by aliens, and this is a fake Gabriel, sent to gather intelligence about our species.'

He smirks a little, and raises his eyebrow as he answers: 'Well, if I was, I'd say I did a pretty good job of it last night. And … yeah, I know. You're right. I'm behaving out of character, even I can see that. But I actually slept, for hours on end, for the first time in years. It made me feel almost human. And if it reassures you, I did just spend ten minutes in my room telling myself I should end this before it even begins.'

'Okay. That sounds more like Gabriel. And?' I reply, clamping down on the little churn in my stomach. I'm not sixteen, and this isn't a fairytale. One night of sex, no matter how good, doesn't change reality. We're both battered, both cynical, both too cautious to rush into anything too serious this soon.

I shouldn't be sitting here expecting Gabriel to be the reluctant one; I should be gathering up my own reluctance, and using it as a shield around me. I need to be careful, I know that, but something about this man simply undoes me, in all kinds of ways.

'And I realised that I don't want to do that. Look, Max, I have no idea what's happening between us. But I do know that I enjoy your company. That I feel relaxed around you. You've kind of snuck under my skin, and after last night, I don't want to lose all that just because it disrupts my life. Maybe my life needs a bit of disrupting.'

'You make me sound like bad weather!'

'Well, you did bring a storm. I'm probably not explaining myself well, because I'm not used to this.'

'Communicating?'

'Exactly. I know I'm bad at it, and I promise I'll stop soon. I don't know what you think or feel about this, but do we have to make it a big deal? Is there a way we could just … God, I can't believe I'm about to say this—I think you might be right about the aliens—but is there a way we could just have fun? If that's not something you're interested in, if last night was just a one-off, then that's totally fine. I accept it completely. Anyway. Piece said.'

I can see the tension creeping back into his body as he speaks, the way his shoulders are bunching beneath his inside out T-shirt. His face, reassembling itself into its normal distant demeanour.

'I don't know what I'm thinking or feeling,' I say honestly. 'I'm still a bit giddy, truthfully. Give me some time to think about it.'

He nods once, with his usual abrupt style, and disappears back off upstairs. I feel a bit bad about leaving him hanging, but I really can't be expected to make decisions like this before I've even finished my first coffee. It's too important.

I sit in silent contemplation for a few minutes, Gary

curled up at my feet like a comforter, and let the caffeine seep into my veins. I try and weigh up what I might lose, and what I might gain. I tell myself to take my time, because this needs time. I tell myself that I must not rush this.

I wash the mug, and put it on the drainer.

I walk up the steps, and ease my way past Sophie's room. I hear the sounds of one of her online lessons, a man discussing symbolism in *A Streetcar Named Desire*, as I tiptoe by. I knock once, very quietly, on Gabriel's door, and slide inside.

I find him with his top off, and stare for a moment at his smooth, tanned skin, and the sinuous movement of muscle beneath the flesh.

'My T-shirt was back to front,' he murmurs, looking befuddled. 'And inside out!'

'I know. Look, I've now thought about it … and the answer's yes. Let's have some fun. I think we both deserve it.'

Chapter Thirteen

'I feel a bit seedy,' I say, gazing out of the hotel room window and out across the moonlit sea. 'But in a good way, you know?'

'I do. I kind of wished we'd checked in as Mr and Mrs Smith, just for laughs.'

'Exactly! It's so boring that we're actually allowed to do this kind of thing now!'

'What kind of thing did you have in mind?' he says, walking towards me. He has that look in his dark eyes, the one that makes me want to squeak. The one that says he has plans for me, and that I will enjoy every single second of those plans. The one I still find a tiny bit frightening, because I know that it means I will be completely out of control within minutes.

Since Gabriel and I decided to have fun together, I've had to adjust to a few things. Firstly, the sneaking around. Sophie has her suspicions, but I'm not ready to talk to her about it. Mainly because I don't really know what 'it' is. It's not been easy carving out alone time while also sharing our lives with a teenager, a belligerent donkey, and a whole village full of nosy neighbours who would be delighted by our news.

I've also had to get used to that feeling of being out of control, because it is a big factor in my life now, and something I never expected.

The delights of spending time in the bedroom with this man—and on a couple of occasions in the living room, and on one amusing time in the woods at the back of the house —are not getting old. In fact it's all just getting better and better. As we learn the landscape of each other's bodies, and discover what we like, I have a genuine sense of astonishment. It's like someone has turned the lights on, and I suddenly understand why people are so obsessed with sex.

In truth, once I was past the age of youthful exuberance, I sometimes found myself wondering what all the fuss was about, because in my experience, sex was never like it is in the books and movies. There were no kisses that made my knees buckle, and I suspected most men couldn't find a G-spot with Google Maps and a Sherpa guide. I love watching romcoms, and I'm a sucker for a love story, but the sex part … well, it's only like that in fiction, right?

Now, though, I get it. Gabriel can literally look at me a certain way, in fact the way he is looking at me right now, and make me tremble. Because I know that the look will be followed by a touch, and the touch will be followed by fireworks. It's a revelation, and I suspect I have become an overnight nymphomaniac. Luckily he seems to feel the same way, and we can barely keep our hands off each other.

Today, we have snuck away, pretending we are attending an antiques auction in Cornwall when in fact we are actually in Devon for a day and night of illicit bonking. Well, not illicit I don't suppose—just secret. Just yummy. Just … perfect.

We've had dinner and drinks, and walked on the beach, and enjoyed the freedom to hold hands and kiss in public. And now we are back here, and he has that look in his eyes. I feel my heart rate speed up, and for a second I feel like a trapped animal as he closes the distance between us.

He is there, right in front of me, his body inches from mine but not quite touching. I look up, meet his gaze, and sigh as he runs his fingers down the side of my face. It's a gentle caress, a flutter of contact, but then his hand is on my neck, his thumb tracing lazy circles on my collarbone. He lifts my hair, pulling my head back slightly, then leans forward and kisses his way from my throat to the side of my neck, to a tender spot just beneath my ears that I never knew existed.

I murmur out loud, and feel his lips curve into a smile against my skin. Even this, I think—even this lightest of touches—is enough to make me crumble. I let my hand graze the side of his jean-clad hip, tug him even closer. It's my turn to smile when I feel him hard against me. At least the feeling is mutual.

He whispers into my ear: 'Want to try something new?'

'Maybe. What do we have left? Is it illegal?'

He laughs, and takes me by the hand, leading me away from the window and around the bed. Which is weird, because I thought we'd be going to bed. Instead, he takes us through into our huge en suite bathroom, and the massive walk-in shower. The shower that is easily big enough for two.

I feel a flicker of nerves, because my confidence levels still haven't quite caught up with events. Obviously Gabriel has seen me naked before, but this feels different. Being naked and rolling around in bed, with covers that can be used to disguise the bits I don't like, is one thing. Being this exposed is another.

He places his hands on my shoulders, and pushes me gently back against the tile wall. He smiles at me, that half-quirk of his lips that has always melted me, and says: 'You're beautiful, Max. Every inch of you is beautiful to me. There isn't a single part of you and your body that I don't find attractive. I can tell you've just tensed up...'

'I have. I'm sorry. I just feel a bit, um, well—'

'Worried that if I see you standing upright, naked, with the lights on, that I'll suddenly run screaming from the room?'

'Yes, something like that. Look, I never claimed to be sane!'

He laughs, and strokes my hair back from my face, and looks at me intently.

'Can you feel my body against yours?' he says, leaning

into me. Oh. I really, really can. I nod, and possibly purr a little.

'Does that feel like the body of a man who is going to run screaming from the room, or the body of a man who wants you?'

His hands go to my shoulders, and then to the front of my blouse. Slowly, steadily, in no hurry at all, he starts to unbutton my top, dropping light kisses on every bit of flesh he exposes.

I sigh, and bury my hands in the thick silk of his hair, and reply: 'It feels like the body of a man who wants me.'

He finishes on the buttons, and comes back up to eye level.

'Exactly,' he says, easing my top away from my body, and unhooking my bra strap with ease. 'Just trust me, okay? Relax. If you just relax, you will enjoy this.'

I let him undress me one item at a time, and the urge to hide or to cover myself up with my arms decreases with every second. His hands move deftly, confidently, stripping me of jeans, socks, underwear, all the time stroking and caressing whatever he reveals. I am a quivering mess by the time I am naked, and realise that I really don't care anymore, because this man—this glorious, sexy man—clearly wants me as much as I want him.

'Go and get the temperature right,' he says, his voice deep and husky. 'I'll be right there.'

I do as I am told, not even flummoxed by the usual battle with an unfamiliar shower, and look on as he tears off his clothes and leaves them in a heap by mine. He is gorgeous, long, lean, lined with muscle. There's a scar on his right side that he doesn't talk about, and his chest hair runs in a dark plume down to his groin. He is not pretty, he is not manicured or overly groomed—but in his own way, he is beautiful too.

He closes the door behind him, and the steam starts to build in all kinds of ways. He leans me against the wall, and kisses me with his usual skill. I feel his hands slide along my skin, and his lips on mine, and when I open my eyes I see the water hitting his shoulders, rippling down his arms and torso. He grins at me, obviously knowing that I like what I see, and then inch by inch he works his way down my body.

He kisses my breasts and takes my nipples into his mouth, making me sigh as he exerts just the right amount of pressure. Then he trails his way even further down, his lips soft but demanding against my skin, until he is on his knees. His hands stroke my inner thighs, and he is a glorious sight before me, the water flowing over his back as he spreads my legs and continues with his kiss.

He was right, I think, as the heat starts to pulsate through me and my knees start to tremble. I just needed to relax.

Chapter Fourteen

A few days later, when Sophie finally confesses that she is in a relationship with James, the farming apprentice, I am pleased for all kinds of reasons.

She makes this announcement as we sit at the kitchen table one evening, and does it so amusingly I spit out my tea.

'So, yeah, me and James had the talk—please give The Talk capital letters in your mind—and we've decided that we're exclusive. Before, it was just a situationship.'

'A what?' I say, after I've finished spluttering.

'You know, where you're seeing each other but it's not official? But now, we've had The Talk, and it's an actual relationship. Bearing that in mind, I was wondering if you could maybe explain how babies are made, because he seems to think there's some connection?'

Sophie is way beyond needing instruction on the birds and the bees. She had a long-term boyfriend for over a year, and I know she was active on that front because I went with her to the family planning clinic to discuss contraception. I had to try really hard not to cry as my baby was prescribed the pill and given free condoms, but I was glad she trusted me and was being sensible. I'd love grandchildren one day, but not for a while yet, thank you.

'Right,' I say, wiping up the tea and recovering myself. 'Well, that's good to know. I really like James, and if you're happy, I'm happy. You know where I am if you need me, for anything. It's always awkward isn't it, The Talk?'

'Yeah. Mainly because both of you are a bit worried the other one doesn't feel the same, and nobody wants to go first and look like a tit. Is that what's happening with you and Gabriel?'

I lose another mouthful of tea at that, and decide to abandon it all together.

'Don't look so shocked, Mum, I'm not an idiot. I can see the signs. You didn't really need to stay overnight in Cornwall, did you? Plus I came home early last week without you knowing, and I had to put my headphones on to drown you out. I was traumatised. Scarred for life.'

My mouth drops open, and I shake my head in a combination of shock and shame. I have no idea how to respond to this, but luckily Sophie doesn't seem to need me to.

'It's okay. I think it's a good thing, Mum. I don't want the gory details or anything—we've got to have healthy boundaries and obviously, *yuk*—but why shouldn't you have a bit of fun? Assuming that's all it is?'

'I don't know what it is,' I say, deciding that there's no point in trying to deny it. 'And unlike you and James, we haven't had The Talk.'

'How immature of you. I hope you're being safe at least!'

She's clearly enjoying herself, and I assure her that we are. I refuse to discuss that particular topic any further—healthy boundaries and yuk are both good reasons not to—and instead turn the conversation towards our impending move.

That, as well as the work and the sex and the fun, is the other main development in our lives. Hyacinth has a brand new roof, her ceilings have been plastered, her attic boarded for storage and the whole upper floor has been given a clean bill of health. Cherie has kept it plain and bare, and given me a very generous budget to do the refurb.

It is now the end of November, and the work has taken a lot longer than we'd expected. These things always do; once you start one repair, you tend to find other things that need doing. The bathroom initially looked like it was okay other than some smashed glass and a broken toilet lid, but nothing worked properly after the chimney crash. Nobody could figure out why, but the plumbing had turned into a game of chance, and Cherie decided to simply replace it all. She let me choose the suite and the fittings, which was nice. Who doesn't love a spa bath?

They also discovered during the work that the electrics were playing up, which may or may not have been related to the storm, so that needed sorting as well. Then, of course, there was the weather. We've had some blissful days, all sunshine and crisp cool air, but we've also had a lot of wind and rain, which delayed everything. The workmen kept disappearing to deal with other people's emergencies, and basically everything dragged on and on.

Cherie and Laura were constantly apologising for this, assuming I was desperate to get into my new home. It's a logical assumption, but in reality, part of me is dreading tomorrow when we finally move in.

It's not just the sex. It's everything; I'll miss it all. I'll miss the badgers, who are becoming harder to spot now—they've been in a feeding frenzy stuffing themselves with all the autumn berries and lining their nests, building up fat to survive the lean times in deep winter. They don't hibernate, but will retreat to their little hobbit hole in a state of torpor when it's cold. I can definitely identify with that.

I'll miss Belle, and all of her weird noises. We've become friends over the last couple of months. She only tries to bite me maybe one out of three times these days.

I'll miss the quiet solitude of this place, the way the autumn shades have transformed it into a landscape of gold and red and bronze. A few days ago I went into the woods on a windy day, and the leaves were blowing off the trees and whistling around, surrounding me in a whirlwind of crinkling russet and amber while I danced and laughed.

I'll miss the nighttime sounds, the owls hooting, Belle braying, the rustle of passing foxes and the many tiny creatures that make the countryside their home.

I'll miss the house itself, with its beams and its uneven stone floors and quirky layout. I'll miss the way the Aga radiates so much warmth that when you walk through the kitchen door, no matter what the weather is like outside, you immediately feel warm and cosy.

I'll miss all of it, but mainly, I suspect, I will miss *him*. Gabriel. He has as many shades and subtleties as the falling leaves, as many nuances as the stars in the clear night sky above us.

I realise, as I ponder this, that Sophie is still talking. Something about a trip to Bristol and a sex dungeon.

'Wait? What? A sex dungeon?'

'I thought that might get your attention! You're distracted. I hope you're not just thinking about boys. There's more to life than boys you know. Friends, work, hobbies…'

This is, of course, a mashed up version of conversations I have had with her, and she is clearly thrilled to be turning the tables on me.

'When's Ben coming?' I ask, ignoring her sarcasm. I was thrilled when he said he'd be joining us in Budbury, and am so looking forward to seeing him again. He'll be going to his dad's for New Year, but we get him for Christmas, which is a compromise I can live with.

'Term finishes on the 9th so he'll be here on the 10th. It's going to suck balls.'

'Sophie! What a horrible thing to say! And I know you don't mean it anyway. Okay, so we've got time to sort his room out.'

'What's the point? He'll just cover everything in crusty socks and man sweat. Not like me, I'm a fragrant princess.'

'You'll just cover yours in charger cables and video games.'

'True. So, what do you think we'll do next? I mean, I know it was a three-month trial, which takes us up to the end of December. What do you think? For what it's worth, I like it here, but I'm also aware that I'll possibly be heading to uni next year so my opinion should probably carry less weight.'

My heart does a little shudder at the thought of her leaving—of both my babies flying the nest—but I make sure to hide it. It's a good thing, Sophie moving on with her life, and I don't want to hold her back in any way. If her resits go well and she gets a place at a uni she likes, there's no reason for her not to leave.

It will hurt, but I realise that if we were still at home, still in Birmingham, it would hurt even more. Here, at least, I have my own life. And I don't just mean Gabriel. What we have is undefined and possibly transient, both terrifying and wonderful. What I'm building with my work, with my new friends here, is less spectacular but maybe more reliable. I don't know, it's all a bit of a conundrum.

'I'm not sure, Soph. I really like it here. When I think about leaving and going back to my old life, I feel sad. I enjoy working at the café. I'm interested in seeing if this interior design thing has any legs. I have friends, and cake, and Gary's happy. It's beautiful, isn't it? Even in the wind and the rain when the sky is grey, it's beautiful. I like the idea of seeing the seasons change here, and getting to know everyone better. I suppose my life has just been more … full, since we got here.'

'I note you're not mentioning Gabriel at all?'

'Well, that's new, and I have no clue where it's going, and I don't want to factor it into my decision in case it goes wrong.'

'That's very defeatist of you.'

'Maybe, love, maybe, but life hasn't exactly taught me to expect hearts and roses, you know? The thing with your dad did some damage, and I'm not sure how long that will take to repair. Or even if it can be repaired. I'm not trying to be mysterious or hide stuff from you. I just don't really know what's going to happen, or how I might feel about it. But, as you say so wisely, there's more to life than boys, and that's how I have to think about it. All of this, of course, is also dependent on whether Laura and Cherie want me to stay on at all.'

'I think that's a given. They love you. What's the score with the tenants?'

'They've said they'd like to renew the contract.'

'Bob's your uncle then, whatever that means. Anyway. Can I use the car? We're having a movie night at James's. Ghostbusters marathon.'

I laugh out loud at this. For all their tech-dominated lives, the younger generation still cling to the old-school classics.

'Are you packed and ready for tomorrow?'

'Scout's honour, yes. Can I take Gary?'

'All right then. Just make sure you're not back too late. And don't let him eat popcorn or chocolate!'

She agrees and scoots away to grab her stuff. Gary looks confused when she hooks him up to his lead, but follows her out happily enough. She gives a farewell toot on her horn, and she's away.

That leaves me alone with my thoughts, and my cold tea. I decide that neither of those is a good thing, and go to see where Gabriel is. I find him outside, welding something by the barn. It's only five but already dark, and the sparks fly around him like bright orange glitter. He has a little floodlight set up, so bright it could signal Batman, and is wearing a big plastic mask to protect his eyes.

There is something almost unbearably sexy about a man doing manual labour. I have no idea why—maybe some biological throwback to the times us ladies were programmed to seek out strong hunter-gatherer mates—but the sight of him working always gives me a little thrill.

It's a lovely evening, cold but calm, and he's wearing the chunky fisherman's sweater he had on the day we arrived. Now, though, I know exactly what's beneath it, which makes it a lot more interesting.

When he notices me, he stops what he's doing, and takes his mask off. His hair cascades around his face, and my insides go all gooey. He picks up a drill instead, and starts messing with the bit attachment.

'What are you doing?' I ask, genuinely curious.

'I found an old fire pit— Well, no idea if it was that originally, maybe it was some kind of feeding trough? But I used the angle grinder on some scrap metal to make some legs, and now I'm attaching them. If I make a grid for the top, might even be a barbecue. You stopped listening at angle grinder, didn't you?'

'Yeah. I'm too flustered now. Sophie's gone over to see James. I'm as sorted as I can be for tomorrow. Do you want to do something?'

He grins at me, and replies: 'Shall I keep my tool belt on? Shall I chase you around with my drill?'

'Don't be silly,' I reply dismissively, already turning back towards the house. 'There's no way you could catch me!'

I glance over my shoulder in time to see him start running, just like I thought he would. I half-screech, half-laugh, and take off as fast as I can. He pursues me round to the front of the building, Belle braying loudly at our stupid antics, and I manage to evade him by throwing a handful of hay at his head.

I make it inside the kitchen, and try to slam the door behind me, but he's already got one of his steel toe caps inside, and instead I sprint away, by this point just laughing.

I dash away from him, but he corners me in the living room—quite literally. I am crammed up in one corner, alternating between sucking in air and giggling and finding that I'm quite out of breath. Gabriel presses the button on the drill and it revs up, filling the room with its aggressive zzzzzz noise and making me laugh even more as he brandishes it in the air.

'Admit it, woman!' he cries. 'You can't escape me!'

I have tears streaming down my cheeks by this stage, and hold my hands up in front of me, saying, 'Okay, okay! You win! You're the biggest and strongest of them all, Gabriel!'

He drops the drill, and hammers his own chest like Tarzan, roaring in approval. He picks me up and slings me over his shoulder, my head dangling down behind his back like I'm in a fireman's lift. I yell for him to put me down, and start hammering on his back with my fists, but he completely ignores me. He gallops up the stone stairs, through the door to my room, and slings me roughly onto the bed.

I bounce a couple of times, and literally can't stop tittering as he stares down at me, trying to look menacing and almost succeeding. He could look menacing, with his broody looks and dark eyes, but I can tell his heart isn't in it. He's having too much fun.

'Did you put your back out?' I say innocently. 'Is that why you're just standing there?'

He narrows his eyes at me, and suddenly he does look a bit on the menacing side. In a split second, he's climbed onto the bed and is straddling me, grabbing my hands and holding them down onto the mattress. I squirm around a little, give him a half-hearted kick, and eventually settle for simply enjoying the experience.

'Aren't you going to try and escape?' he says, grinning at me and raising his eyebrows.

'I don't think I am,' I reply, arching up to meet him and enjoying the way it makes his nostrils flare. 'Why would I want to escape? I've got you exactly where I want you!'

'*Exactly* where you want me?' he answers, leaning down to nuzzle my neck, making me sigh out loud in a way that now feels deliciously familiar.

'Well, maybe not *exactly*…'

It doesn't takes us long to get naked, and there is little preamble. I suspect the thrill of the chase was our foreplay, and we're both more than ready to go a little crazy. I throw my legs around him, and he holds my hands over my head, and when he slides inside me I gasp with the thrill of it.

Our hands and mouths work their magic on each other, and things definitely get wilder than usual. We test the bed out to its absolute limits; we spend some time on the chair, and eventually end up on the floor.

By the time we collapse, exhausted and coated in sweat, I am practically floating, having some kind of out-of-body experience. I have been well and truly seen to, and all my womanly needs have been extremely well met. Now I feel both exhausted and exhilarated.

His head falls down onto my shoulder, and I wrap my arms around his waist to squeeze him close. Even the afterglow feels exciting with this man, and I don't want the contact to end. My skin feels sad when it's not touching his.

He laughs, and says: 'I'd like to scoop you up and throw you on the bed again, but I don't know if I have the energy. I think you might have finally finished me.'

He clambers upright, and I stare up at him. I don't think

I'll ever get tired of the sight of this man's body, and I hold my hands out to him. He pulls me up, and peels back the duvet. I climb in next to him, and cuddle up in his arms.

We're both silent for a few minutes, recovering from our efforts, and I find myself feeling almost sad about the fact that this is my last night here, in this house. With him. I know it's a new beginning, moving into Hyacinth, but it is also an ending.

'You okay?' he asks, kissing my forehead and holding me tight. 'Your silence has changed.'

'What?'

'Well, to start with, your silence was all content and happy, the kind of silence that says, "That was the shag of my life, I am such a lucky woman." But now your silence is a bit more pensive, like it might want to sneak off and have a cry while it listens to an Adele album.'

'You could be right. I should probably get up and finish packing. It's not late enough to go to bed. Not to sleep, anyway.'

'I know you've already finished your packing, Max. What about if we go out? Are you up for a little trip? And if so, can you get us a flask of something hot, and wrap up warm? There's somewhere I'd like to show you if you're up for it.'

I grasp the suggestion with both hands, knowing that my mood might sink if I lie around here worrying about what the next day might hold, and whether this might be the last time I lie here with him in this bed.

Before long, I'm up and dressed, and have gathered a

flask of hot chocolate and a can of squirty cream. I add on a few layers as well as my walking boots while I'm at it.

He meets me outside, and he's driven his ancient Land Rover out of the garage and loaded sleeping bags in the back. He's wearing a beanie hat, his hair flowing out from underneath it, and passes me one to wear as well. Maybe we're going to Alaska.

We drive for almost an hour, down the winding lanes that I am now familiar with, the headlights picking out scurrying mice and one very surprised fox that runs in front of us. We stop to let it pass, and it turns towards us, the beams reflecting back at us from its eyes. Gorgeous.

Eventually we park in a lay-by next to a hill, and even though it is not late, there's no one else around. This is understandable, as it is an insane thing to be doing in the dark. We both have torches and he leads the way, climbing a path that winds around the hill like a ribbon, until eventually we reach the top. There's a kind of plateau here, and he zips the sleeping bags together to make one big one, laying it on the ground and adding pillows.

He holds it open for me to clamber inside, and before long we are snug as two bugs in a rug. I lie with his arms around me and my head against his chest, and he says: 'This is an old Iron Age fort. It's been here since about 400 BC, they reckon. There are a few of them around here, hence my granddad's visit all those years ago I suppose. This is my favourite, because it's more remote, and you don't see many people here. And because of that.'

As he speaks, he points up at the sky, and I turn to gaze at it. The whole vista is painted in shades of indigo and black, streaked with clusters of gold and silver. Some sparkle in solitary beauty, others are lined up together like a glittering string of jewels. It's a cloudless night, and it feels like we are lying together beneath a blanket made entirely of stars.

'Wow,' I murmur, because that's really the only word. The night skies in this part of the world are sensational, given the lack of light pollution, but this is in a different class. 'It's beautiful.'

'It is. It's my favourite thinking place. I've been out here, doing exactly this, quite a few times.'

'But without me and the squirty cream?'

He laughs and drops a kiss onto the top of my head, holding me so close the warmth of his body seeps into mine.

'You and squirty cream could be quite a tempting combination, Max, but it's a bit too cold for that.'

'You're right. I'll save some for later. Do you know their names? The constellations?'

'Well, it changes according to the season, but tonight we have Orion, and Taurus, and over there is Bob the Builder.'

'You made the last one up!'

'What gave it away?' he asks, tugging the sleeping bag up to our chins. If any passing space satellites are watching, they'll just see two beanie hats sticking out at the top.

We lie contentedly together for a while, watching the

stars journey across the sky, listening to the sounds of the night birds and the cows in a distant field. We could be the only two people on earth, caught out of time. Suspended in space, floating in our own glimmering reality.

'I'll miss you when you're gone,' he says quietly, turning on his side to face me. I reach out and stroke his hair, trail my fingers around his jaw.

'I'll miss you, too. But I'm only in Hyacinth. You can come and visit me; I'll come and visit you. If you want that, I mean. No pressure. If this was just a fling that's come to its natural end, that's okay too.'

I wouldn't be thrilled about it, but I suppose I'd cope. He is silent in response, which of course makes me nervous.

'Is that what it is? I don't mind, honest, but I'd rather know.'

I see his lips curve into a smile, the moonlight shining in his deep brown eyes, and he replies, 'Ah. Are we finally going to have The Talk?'

Obviously, I give it capital letters in my head, and say, 'I suppose we probably should. My nineteen-year-old daughter has kind of shamed me into it. She says it's always scary because one of you has to go first, and you're scared you'll look like a tit.'

'She has a way with words … and she's not wrong, is she? So, I'll go first, and be totally honest. I don't want this to end. I really will miss you, and that worries me a little. I've been so used to getting by on my own, for years now, and suddenly I'm wondering how I'm going to cope with the solitude. When you two first arrived, I was concerned by all the noise and the chatter and the stuff. Now, I'm concerned that it's going to be too quiet. Too empty. And that feels strange and a bit unsettling. I don't want this to end, but I also don't know if I'm ready for it to be any more serious than it already is.'

'Wow,' I say, grinning. 'You've actually been thinking about The Talk, haven't you?'

'Yeah. I practised it in front of the mirror in the bathroom. How did it go?'

'It went fine, and mine is pretty much the same. You know my history. You know that it was only just over a year ago that Richie walked out. A lot might have happened since then, but I'm still sore. This has helped—you have helped—but like you say, it also feels unsettling. I hate the thought of being apart from you, but maybe the only way we'll see things clearly is if I move out.'

'Is that because you're going blind with all the orgasms?'

'Exactly that! Maybe, once I'm gone, we can … start again? Maybe do some normal things, like go on dates, and have dinner together without the dog and the teenager? Feel our way through it all? Maybe you'll just get used to us not being here, and decide you like it that way. Maybe I'll get my independence back and like that. Or maybe we'll just … I don't know, take our time and see?'

'What about the sex?'

'Oh, we'll still be having that, don't worry. I'm not suggesting we go through some long-winded courtship ritual, Gabriel. We've come too far for that, and I still have a few ideas about that squirty cream.'

He goes quiet, and I don't know if he's reassessing our entire relationship, or just thinking about the squirty cream.

He rolls on top of me and kisses me so well and so thoroughly that I start to see stars in all kinds of ways. I guess it must have been the latter.

Chapter Fifteen

The second week in December sees an influx of two things in Budbury: the first flurries of snow, and the Great Return of the Young Folk.

Nate and Lizzie, Laura's older children, come home from Liverpool and London, along with a lad called Josh, the son of Scrumpy Joe who runs the cider cave. Most importantly for me, Ben arrives from Manchester, landing at the nearest train station with his bike and his big rucksack full of laundry.

It's an absolute joy to have him back with me, right up until the point where he and Sophie start bickering. It starts gently with a bit of banter, warms up into some light mockery, and inevitably escalates to all-out warfare. I always forget, when they're apart, exactly how bad it can be.

I'm an only child so I have nothing to compare it to, and I find it genuinely upsetting when they fight so much.

Sometimes it's funny, but sometimes it's upsetting. Not for them—they bounce back from the insults and the threats immediately—but as a spectator, I find it troubling.

Laura tells me this is all completely normal, that she and her sister Becca were total opposites as children and constantly fought.

'This is true,' Becca had confirmed. 'She was vile. I was walking home from school one day, minding my own business, and she threw a full dog poo bag in my face in front of all my friends.'

'That was the other way round!' Laura had spluttered, and I could tell from the evil look on Becca's face which one was telling the truth. Maybe there's still a bit of that sibling dynamic left today.

I think part of the issue with my kids is Sophie feeling like Ben is intruding on her turf. She feels like she basically owns Budbury, or possibly actually invented it, and then he turns up, all handsome and flirty and funny, distracting her friends. It sounds childish, and it is, but most of us are childish, aren't we? We just hide it better when we get older.

The Young People gang is now much bigger, with the influx of new blood, and they roam like a pack of feral animals. You'll come across them in the café, in the pub, on the beach, here at the Rockery. They range in age from eighteen to twenty-four, and in the city that would be a huge age gap, but here they band together. I'm sure there are all kinds of interpersonal dynamics I don't know about —I recently discovered that Lizzie and Josh were together for years, and only split up when he went to uni—but they seem to rub along well enough.

Ben, who has had both boyfriends and girlfriends in the past, seems to see it all as a huge dating game. On his third night here, he sprawled across the sofa and announced, 'It's been a hard decision, but I think I'll choose Josh. He's super-cute and his dad owns a cider cave.'

'He's not a Pokemon!' Sophie had objected. 'You can't just choose him, plus he's straight!'

'I bet I can turn him. I'll get ten points for that,' Ben had said confidently. He's tall and sporty, and has floppy sandy hair that gives him a young Hugh Grant vibe. He's very, very sure of himself.

'It's not a competition!' she'd shrieked, hitting him on the head with a cushion.

'Yes, it is, there's a rewards scheme, didn't you know? Turn twenty and you get a VIP pass to a Sea Life Centre. Fifty and it's an air fryer. I'm aiming for a hundred, and a free weekend at the Premier Inn of my choice.'

He's also very, very funny, and even Sophie has to giggle at a lot of his outrageous comments, almost against her will. You can see her trying to keep it in, her lips clamped together. Sometimes she has to walk out of the room just so he doesn't get the satisfaction of seeing her laugh.

Today, as I walk down the stairs rubbing my eyes and feeling the siren call of coffee, they're both already up. There's a trip to Bristol being planned, allegedly for Christmas shopping but I suspect more likely for Christmas drinking.

I pause on the stairs when I hear their voices, because if they're already fighting, I might just turn around and go back to my room. Instead, I am surprised to hear them actually talking like normal humans, in a slightly lowered tone that suggests they don't want to wake me up. I smile, and enjoy the moment of peace, the moment of gratitude at having them both safe and home with me. That moment evaporates when I hear what they're talking about.

'It's not that I don't like Gabriel,' says Ben quietly. 'He's really cool. Like, countryside John Wick level cool. But I suppose … maybe I just thought that one day, they'd get back together, you know? Mum and Dad?'

My eyes pop wide open, and I consider creeping back up the stairs. Eavesdropping is rude, and you never hear anything good about yourself. But they're talking about me, and Gabriel, and I find it impossible to move.

'What?' says Sophie, trying to whisper but so exasperated it comes out sharply. 'Really? After everything he did?'

'I know, I know; it was bad! I just thought he was going through some kind of mid-life bloke crisis, and he'd end up coming home.'

'I get that. So did I to start with. But he didn't, and there's no use holding on to that fantasy. You don't even live at home anymore. You didn't see how bad things got.'

'With Mum?'

'No, with Taylor Swift, who the fuck do you think I mean? She was a mess, Ben. She tried to hide it, especially from you, but it was not good. She felt like everything had been a lie, like everything they'd ever had together was fake. That he'd never loved her, that she'd never been good enough, that she never would be.'

'She said that?'

'Not directly, but unlike you, I'm actually aware of other people's feelings, you dickhead.'

'Okay, okay, calm down, I'm sorry, and you're right. You were there and I wasn't, and I get it. But she seems better now.'

'She is. It suits her here. She's happy, and Gabriel's been part of that. He makes her feel a gazillion times better than Dad ever did.'

'But he's our dad! Don't you sometimes wish they would get back together? That things could go back the way they were?'

'Maybe, sometimes,' she answers, 'but then I remind myself that he's the world's biggest twat, and I get over it.'

It makes me sad to listen to them talking about this, to realise how much my decline affected Sophie, to hear that Ben still yearns for the days when our family was whole. I suppose since coming to Budbury, I've managed to escape some of that sadness, and now it's reared its ugly head again.

She is right, though, that is exactly how I felt. And because his affair had been going on for so long, everything felt especially painful. Every time I remembered something we'd done together in the previous years—our holiday to Cyprus, Christmas, birthday celebrations—I'd find myself thinking, *well, I thought we were happy then, but actually none of it was real.* I'd randomly remember something—like us all going out for lunch on Father's Day—and then convince myself that he'd hated every moment, and as soon as he was alone he'd been having hot phone sex with his lover.

It soiled all my memories, made a mockery of our lives together. I felt like I couldn't rely on anything anymore, not even my own recollections.

Richie had told me, once it all came out, that I shouldn't think like that, that he had been happy, in lots of ways, that the good times had been real. He was trying to console me, but it's hard to accept the word of a man who has proved how good he is at deception. He'd managed to live a double life for so long that nothing he said felt genuine.

That was the real damage: the undoing of everything I once believed, of everything I once felt confident about. He unravelled our past, and I suddenly felt like I was on a trapeze with no safety net beneath me.

Here, I've gradually started to feel differently, not about him, or that pain, but about myself. I've not just put the pieces of me back together; I've found new ones. Hearing the kids talk like this is unsettling, and I decide that enough is enough. I deliberately cough, very loudly, and stamp on the stairs so hard nobody could fail to notice me.

The voices immediately stop, and Gary rushes out to greet me. I plaster a smile on my face, and walk into the room. Both of them are sprawled on the couch.

'Morning!' I say brightly, seeing them exchange 'phew that was close' looks. 'Looking forward to your day out?'

'It'd be better if this ball-bag wasn't coming,' says

Sophie, gesturing at Ben. Her language takes a significant swan dive when her brother is around.

'What are your plans, Mum?' he asks, kicking her in the ribs as he speaks. 'Got an exciting trip to a junk shop planned? Painting seashells? Searching for that perfect ship in a bottle?'

These are all possible, especially the ship in a bottle—I really want one for the mantlepiece. The refurb in Hyacinth is going well, and is a huge amount of fun. I've kept the décor all white and light blue, and Gabriel and I laid beautiful pale pine wood flooring on the upstairs landing and in the bedrooms. Each bedroom has a big shagpile rug in the same shade of blue as the bed linens, so deep your bare feet sink into it. Lush. The bathroom is fab and fun, complete with a collection of rubber ducks and little boats to sail in the tub—allegedly for visiting children, but let's be frank, mainly for me.

We've replaced the damaged stair banister, and I've painted it a glossy white and added little stencils of seashells and starfish on some of the spindles. It looks beautiful, fresh and clean but also quirky.

Downstairs is still a bit of a work-in-progress. It all needs redecorating, and the carpet was ruined by the storm, but I'm holding fire for the time being because Cherie is getting a new kitchen fitted, and that will be messy. For now, I'm gathering a few items together: a coffee table I found in a charity shop that needs sanding down and painting, an old ship's compass to install on the living room wall, some gorgeous pine bookshelves for the alcoves that I will fill not only with books, but with seashells and fossils and maritime treasures. I want it to look modern and stylish, but also welcoming, and that means I'm allowed a bit of clutter.

Cherie is delighted with it all, and Laura is emotional at seeing her former home changed. I promise that the framed photo of Jim Morrison in the downstairs loo—there in honour of the fact that the cottage is named after a Doors song—will always remain.

Sophie has been doing a few of my shifts at the café to cover for me, and Cherie is already making noises about me looking at some of her other little holiday homes when I'm done. I've so far point blank refused to be paid for anything, but if this extends into the rest of the Rockery, I've agreed to rethink.

I'm loving the whole experience, and I know that the perfect ship in a bottle is out there waiting for me. I just have to find it.

After I'm dressed, I drop Ben and Sophie in town to meet their friends, making them promise to stay in touch now the weather is turning. They might be technically adults, but I don't know a mum alive who wouldn't worry about their babies setting off on an adventure when there's snow falling.

It's a Monday and the café is closed, so Gary and I decide to take a spontaneous trip to see Belle. And the hot guy who allegedly owns her, though I don't think anyone actually does. She's a force of nature and will probably outlive us all. She'll be there at our funerals, scream-braying and biting the pallbearers.

Gabriel and I have done as we planned, and carried on seeing each other. We have been on dates, and we have worked on Hyacinth, and we have had some spectacular sexy times.

I do miss sharing a home with him, but I'm also busy with two squabbling offspring and an adorable dog. They go some way to filling the gap, and certainly make the place a lot louder and messier. Gabriel seems to have settled back into his natural rhythms, but I know he doesn't like it as much as he used to. Part of me is a bit worried that I've disrupted him—like when humans feed badgers and make them too domesticated—but part of me is thrilled. I want him to miss me. I want him to want me. I want this to work.

When this is working, it's simple and straightforward, and I am happy. Of course, I know that how happy I am when it's working directly correlates to how unhappy I might be if it stopped working. Listening to the kids talk about how broken I was after Richie left has rubbed up a few sore spots, and I know I am risking a lot. I hate the thought of falling into the black hole of despair ever again, but at the same time, I can't just cut myself off from life to keep myself safe. Because that's a black hole of a different kind.

I toot my horn as we pull in, and then make my traditional visit to my spirit animal. I am now at the stage where I can risk offering her an apple, and she even gives me a little nuzzle with her head after she takes it. On Matt's advice, she's wearing a nice jacket, because she is an old lady and needs a bit of extra protection from the cold. She'd look cute if she wasn't so ugly.

I gaze around as I walk towards the house, and sigh at how beautiful it is. The snow has settled out here in the wilderness, a pristine layer of white coating the rooftops and the trees. Gary runs around sniffing at it, burying his head in deeper drifts and emerging with a snowy nose. Dogs are like children that never grow up.

The warmth of the Aga is welcome as I slip inside, taking off my coat and gloves and enjoying the familiar sensations. I glance at the sink, see the traditional one mug and one plate on the drainer. A quick look in the fridge shows me his rations, alongside a moussaka I made him and the remains of a Red Velvet cake Cherie dropped off. Almost against his will, Gabriel is being sucked into the black hole of kindness that is Budbury.

I shout his name and he replies: 'I'm upstairs!'

That'll save time, I think, grinning an evil grin. I'm actually quite surprised when I find him in his own bedroom, with a duvet in his hands. We've always spent time in my old room, and his has remained untouched by the renovation work. His sad-sack sleeping bag was always a constant presence, and I'm shocked to see it rolled up and tied on the floor.

'Are you feeling okay?' I ask. 'Do I need to call a paramedic?'

He smiles at me, and tucks a thick wave of hair behind his ear. My tummy does a little tap dance, because my reaction to this man never seems to change, no matter how much I see of him.

'I thought it was time to join the human race,' he says. 'And make a few changes. I painted.'

'I see that,' I reply, looking around at the walls. Okay, so they're painted a dull shade of mid-blue, but it's an improvement on the half-stripped paper vibe. There's a shade on the dangling light bulb, and a small reading lamp on the table by his bed. By Gabriel standards, this is giving off luxury boutique hotel energy. 'It looks great. What brought this on?'

'Not sure. When it started snowing the other day, I spent ages walking around the woods. I found a new pond, never even knew it was there, all frozen up and really pretty. And Belle actually let me scratch her ears. And I ate Red Velvet cake while I read in front of the fire. It felt … nice. Can you help me with this? I've never quite mastered the skill …'

He holds up the duvet and a navy blue cover as he speaks, and I automatically take one end and start working on it.

'It felt nice?' I repeat, smiling. 'Gabriel, did it feel … Christmassy? Did it thaw your heart? Can I expect you to start carolling and making your own mulled wine?'

Christmas is less than two weeks away now. In Hyacinth, we have a large and very badly decorated tree, covered in random items I've picked up on my travels. Our own decorations are still in the attic in Solihull, and I'm glad—they are laden with the ghosts of Christmas past, and I'm happy to start some new traditions. And while I might have some flair for making a home look lovely, when it comes to Christmas trees, there are no design rules at all. Sling everything all over it is my motto.

'I wouldn't go that far,' he says, looking astonished at how quickly the duvet cover goes on. 'But I might not be entirely averse to getting a little tree. Maybe some mistletoe.'

'Excellent idea. But how did this reverse-Grinch revelation translate into doing your bedroom up?'

'Well, when it felt nice, seeing how beautiful this place was in the snow, I thought about how much I was enjoying stuff at the moment. How much has changed. I'd have expected that to scare the shit out of me, to be honest, but it didn't. And I realised I was ready to finally get rid of the sleeping bag. I've admitted defeat. This is my home, and I might as well accept it.'

'You say that like it's a bad thing!'

'I know I do. Old habits. Since me and Helen split up, I've moved around a lot. Travelled, doing work where I found it. In France I lived in a place so run down it makes this look like paradise. I was doing it up for the English owners. There was no electricity, no heating, an outside toilet. I got used to sleeping on the floor, in that bag, and I didn't mind it. I suppose, not to get all deep and meaningful, that maybe I thought it was all I deserved. I felt like I'd made a huge mess of everything in my life. I missed being in the Army, despite the toll that had taken on me, and my marriage was over, and sleeping on a stone floor in a country where nobody knew me seemed like the best option.'

I finish buttoning up the cover, and try to hide the flood of sympathy I have for him. He won't appreciate it.

'And now?' I ask simply.

'And now I don't feel like that.'

He has a certain look on his face by this point, one that tells me he's reached his limit on sharing, and I know from experience that I won't get anything more from him on the touchy-feely front. We have made progress but I can't expect miracles, even if it is nearly Christmas.

We are both taking baby steps away from our pain, and towards each other. We are tiptoeing over our tender spots, and our time together feels like a mutual balm. Yes, of course I have doubts—I know what it will cost me if this implodes—but again, I also know that doubts are healthy. They're human. Nobody could go through what I've been through and not have doubts. But letting your whole life be dictated by those doubts? Not something I am going to let happen.

We smooth the duvet down and add the pillows, and stand back to admire our work. The bed is huge and gorgeous, and he's even polished the brass bedstead.

'That', he says, giving me The Look, 'is a bed that needs christening...'

'I couldn't agree more,' I reply. 'Quick, take off all your clothes!'

I get there first, kicking my leggings flying to the other

side of the room as he's still wearing his boxers. He's just out of them when I give him a sudden shove so he falls back onto the mattress. He's a lot bigger than me, and it's only the element of surprise that allows me to take the advantage. He grins up at me in surprise, and I climb on top of him. This has never been my most confident position, but Gabriel has made me feel like a goddess, and for once I'm not worried about whether I'm too heavy, or if my jiggly bits are showing.

I place my hands against his body, running my fingers over the flat planes of his belly, across the ridges of his abs. I will never tire of this soft skin over tough muscle, or the way it feels to run my nails through the silky hair on his chest. I lean forward to drop kisses onto his shoulders and neck, nip at the golden column of his throat, enjoying the way he sighs and moans my name as I move against him. I sit up, glorying in the sight of him beneath me, seeing the need in his dark eyes.

I wriggle my hips a little, and smile in satisfaction. He is already hard, pressed up against me and hitting the sweet spot in a way that makes me rub against him. I'm already starting to feel breathless at the way our bodies connect, feeling a curl of heat that I know will only build and build until it's a raging inferno that burns me up from the inside out. I know how this story ends, and it goes way beyond happy.

He sits up, unexpectedly, grabbing hold of my shoulders and spinning me around in his arms. Suddenly, I'm the one lying flat on the bed, looking surprised. He's turned the tables, and he grins as he hovers above me.

He leans down, sucks one nipple into his mouth, then lets his hand run down my body. His fingers find the very same sweet spot, and work it until I am unravelled and delirious, flooded with the sensation of it all. Only then does he seek his own pleasure, sliding inside me while I'm still quivering and shaking. I wrap my legs around him, urging him closer, deeper, harder. I whisper his name, my fingers twined in his hair then roaming the rippling movements of his back, trying to touch him everywhere at once as he loses himself in me the same way I lost myself in him.

Yes, I have doubts. But at moments like this, they are a million miles away.

Chapter Sixteen

There is much excitement in the Comfort Food Café, because Katie has actually gone into labour, six days before her due date.

To celebrate, all the village ladies have congregated here in the late afternoon to drink coffee, eat cake, and quiz me about my sex life.

'Oh come on!' says Auburn, sounding frustrated. 'You can't do this to us! You can't come over here and steal our jobs and steal our men and then not even tell us about it!'

'I can do that,' I reply, grinning at her over the steam of my cappuccino. 'In fact I already have.'

'But I was friends with Mr Pumpwell. At the very least I deserve to know what his great-nephew is like in the sack!'

This all started innocently enough. We gathered around one of the big round tables, a lemon drizzle cake and warm fudge brownies in the middle.

The café is dressed for Christmas, and looks like every

single decoration available in the entire world was put into a giant box, then tipped over the existing clutter. It's shiny and messy and festive and wonderful.

Cherie is here, looking a little tired, along with Laura, Becca, Auburn, and Zoe. Edie is sadly absent, as her niece has taken her out for afternoon tea. We officially opened the meeting with a video call to Willow, who is currently in Seville. I barely know her but it's lovely to see how happy she is, and how happy they all are for her. After that, the talking began.

We covered topics as diverse as Zoe's new stock of crime thrillers in the book shop, Auburn's plans to visit her husband's family in Denmark for Christmas, and the fact that Midgebo recently managed to eat a Sonic the Hedgehog cake Laura had made for the girls.

'You should have seen what came out of him,' she said, aghast. 'All that food colouring! Actually, I took some photos… It was quite a nice shade of teal, thought you might consider it for your next refurb project, Max!'

We all admired the pictures—because that's what friendship is all about, admiring your pal's snaps of dog poo—and then, somehow, things moved on to me. It began with Becca asking me—to many shocked noises—what I'd do if I was tasked with redesigning the Comfort Food Café.

I looked around, at the streamer-coated mobiles and the crammed bookcases and the giant ammonite now draped in gold tinsel, and replied: 'Nothing. I wouldn't change a thing about this place. It's already perfect.'

Cherie smiled, patted my hand, and said: 'That's exactly right, my love. Now, tell us all about you and Gabriel!'

It's not a secret anymore, because neither of us thought it needed to be. Once my kids knew, the rest didn't matter. Laura has, obviously, made a few forays into interrogation, but I've fended her off. This, though, is different. This is an en-masse assault from the Budbury Ladies' Coffee and Cake Club. Cherie, Becca, and now Auburn have all piled in with the questions.

When I refuse to answer, Auburn throws a sugar sachet at me, and Zoe cackles in amusement.

'You keep up the resistance, Max,' she says. 'When I got together with Cal, I thought Laura was going to start pulling my fingernails out to get the racy details.'

'Well, Cal is gorgeous!' Laura bleats, as though that excuses everything. 'Why wouldn't I want to know? I'll tell you anything about Matt!'

'Poor Matt,' says her sister. 'Pimped out for cheap thrills. But seriously, Max, we're all desperate to know. Is he as good as he looks?'

I stay silent, but feel a blush spread across my cheeks. I concentrate on the coffee, because it's less dangerous.

'She doesn't need to say anything, does she?' Cherie pipes up, nodding at me knowingly. 'Of course he is! Look at her, she's glowing! That is the face of a woman who is getting an extremely good seeing to on a regular basis…'

They all burst out laughing, and I have to join in. I say nothing, but I do allow them a very small nod of agreement. Because it really is that face.

'You'd better all get your minds out of the gutter,' I say, glancing at the clock. 'Because he'll be here later. We've got a hot date.'

'Oooh,' says Laura, leaning forward curiously. 'Where? Will there be a hot tub? And Prosecco? You need to be careful with that; it got me pregnant with twins!'

'I'm pretty sure that was Matt, not the Prosecco, but I take your point. Anyway. We're going to Lyme Regis so we can walk along the promenade in the snow and look at all the Christmas lights.'

There's a collective sigh at this, and it makes me smile. It is pretty dreamy, now I come to think about it.

'Anyway,' Cherie announces, raising her mug of hot chocolate, 'here's to Katie, our poor friend, who is probably going through agony as we sit here and act like a load of old perverts!'

We all raise our various glasses and mugs and cups, and clink carefully against each other. It's exciting, Katie having the baby. I love babies. I'm one of those women who stops to admire them in shops, and always wants to hold them and sniff their heads. Despite all of that, my overriding thought is still 'rather her than me'.

We all stand up in a screech of scraping chair legs, and I help Laura take the trays back through to the kitchen. She automatically puts some of the remaining brownies aside for Edie, and tells me she's going to stay on and make up some 'home-made ready meals' for Katie and Van. I offer to chip in, but she's clearly in her happy place, in much the

237

same way as me when I'm looking at my Farrow & Ball colour card.

Gabriel said he'd be here at about four, when he's finished his latest project: while the badgers are more dormant, he's fitting padded seats in the viewing hide. He's wild and crazy like that.

I have plenty of time before then, so I make myself useful doing some cleaning as the others depart. I'm elbow deep in the blender, scraping it clean of Bounty bars, when Cherie shouts from the front: 'Prepare yourselves ladies! Looks like we have an actual paying customer!'

Laura and I both look comically surprised by this, even though we work in a café. It's been so quiet today I think we'd forgotten that customers exist.

'I'll take it,' I tell her, wiping my hands on a tea towel and walking over towards the counter.

My welcoming smile fades the minute I see who it is. Standing there, his hands shoved in his pockets, looking predictably nervous, is Richie. I stare at him, and stare at him some more, and eventually shake my head in confusion. I close my eyes and open them again, hoping he might disappear.

Nope. He's still there, shifting from foot to foot, attempting a smile.

'Surprise!' he says lamely, waving his hands in the air.

'Um … yes, it is. Why are you here?'

'I wanted to see where the kids are living. Seen pictures, but if this is a permanent move, thought it'd be nice to see it for myself. Plus I wanted to talk to you.'

'About what? And why didn't you call or message to arrange this? Why the ambush? I'm at work!'

He gazes around at the completely empty café, and raises one eyebrow. Fair point.

'I didn't call to arrange it because I knew you'd keep putting it off. Or you'd be busy the day I came and I'd only get to see Sophie and Ben.'

'And what's wrong with that?' I ask, my voice going up in pitch. This is weird, and I don't like it. I don't like having him here, in my café, making me feel odd. He is the father of my children, and we will always be connected by them, but I don't think I'll ever be able to see him without it hurting. I'd almost forgotten how much.

'I wanted to see you as well. You look great, Max. Country life must be suiting you.'

He's a good-looking man, Richie, but I no longer see that when I look at him. I don't see the bright blue eyes and the sandy hair that I used to admire. Now, I see the changes: the neatly-trimmed beard, the stylish haircut. The polished Chelsea boots that would look good in the city, but feel out of place here. The changes that signify he is living a different life now, in a different world, with a different woman, which makes his unexpected presence here even more confusing.

I'm suddenly aware of my appearance in a way I haven't been since settling into life in Budbury, and I don't like it. One of the reasons I left Birmingham was to avoid having to bump into him, and now he's travelled halfway across the country and tracked me down.

I hear Laura in the background, pretending to work but hovering ever closer, and see Cherie eyeing us up from across the room. They're like very nosy guard dogs, and I know that with one twitch of my fingers, they'll be over at my side, ready to either offer him cake or tear him to pieces.

'I don't really have time for this, Richie,' I say firmly. There's still over half an hour until Gabriel is due, but I don't really want to spend it talking to my ex. 'I have things to do.'

'Look, I get it,' he says placatingly. 'Like you said, I've ambushed you. The kids don't know I'm here either, but I'll message them when we've had a chat. Maybe I can meet them for a drink, maybe stay the night?'

I turn this over in my mind, and come to the conclusion that I have no idea how I feel about it. Or, more accurately, I feel too much about it. I want him to stay in their lives, and I'd like it if I could become calmer around him. I hate the fact that he can still derail me like this, that even here, he has that power.

'Come on,' I say, waving goodbye to Laura and Cherie and grabbing my coat and hat. 'We'll go for a walk.'

I lead him down the hill and onto the beach. The snow is layered over the sand, crunchy beneath my feet, and the waves make a funny little crackling noise as the water meets the ice. It's a crisp, clear day, and the sun is hovering over the horizon, a dull orange ball reflecting against the sea.

'Wow, it's really pretty here!' he says, as we make our way a little further along. I swipe the snow off one of the boulders with my gloved hand, and we sit. He's only wearing a lightweight pea jacket, and I can tell he's cold and uncomfortable.

'It is, yes. I like it a lot. So, um, how are you?' I ask, trying to be civil. Part of me wants to tell him to eff off, but again, he is the father of my children. We shared decades of our lives, and even if I don't look back on them as kindly as I once did, they still happened.

'I'm fine, yeah. Wow. I know I've already said that once, but that view is gorgeous. Sophie and Ben seem really happy here, too.'

'I think so, though Ben will be coming up to yours soon.'

He nods, and there is an awkward silence. Sophie was invited to stay with him for New Year, but she declined. I know she loves her dad, but she's struggling to forgive him.

'Sophie's applying to university,' I say. 'I'm sure she's told you, or Ben has. She did really well in her mocks.'

'Yeah?' he asks, grinning. 'What did she get?'

'Two As and a B.'

'That's fantastic! Where's she applying to?'

He sounds genuinely interested, and I remind myself that he loves his kids. He was a good dad, even if he was a rotten husband towards the end. I tell him about her potential uni choices, and the personal statement she's been working on for her UCAS form, and before long we are on safer ground. Talking about Sophie is okay. It's normal. It's almost comforting, in fact, discussing all of it with him … because he has known her since before she was born, and understands every reference I make.

We move on to Ben, and how he's doing, and then even Gary. It's utterly odd and disconcerting, like we're two old friends catching up on what we've missed. Truthfully, it's not unpleasant once I've got over the shock, and it's easier when Valerie isn't around, obviously. Even thinking her name reminds me of reality, and I ask: 'Richie, why are you really here?'

He looks at me intensely for a moment, and just for one brief second, I remember the spark we used to share. His bright eyes, his easy laughter, his collection of terrible knock-knock jokes. He takes my hand in his, squeezing my fingers in a way that feels both alien and familiar, and I gasp in shock.

What the hell is going on? Has he finished with her? Does he want me back? Was this all like Ben said, just a middle-aged man crisis that's now been worked out of his system? And if that's the case, how do I react? We can't turn back time, or rewind our emotions—the damage is done.

'I wanted to see you in person,' he says slowly, obviously as edgy as I am, 'to tell you that Valerie is pregnant. I know this is a biggie, and that it might upset you, and I didn't want you to hear it from the kids.'

Right. Well, so much for the mid-life crisis resolving itself. I stare at him, pulling my hand away from his, completely taken aback. I have to admit I didn't see this one coming—Valerie is only a couple of years younger than me and never seemed the maternal type—and the notion makes my stomach churn. I don't know why—it's over between us, and has been for a long time. I've moved on, and this shouldn't bother me.

And yet, it does. It's unexpectedly unsettling news, and I don't have time to unpack it all now, because he is sitting there waiting for me to respond.

'Oh. I see. When is she due?'

'June. It was a bit of a surprise, to be honest, but once I got used to the idea I was really happy.'

'Congratulations,' I manage to murmur, as all of the ramifications start to run through my mind. The complicated set of relationships that we will all have to navigate; the politics of a blended family; the one hundred per cent proof that the thing that used to be Max and Richie is over.

I mean, I knew that, obviously, and it's not like I've been sitting around pining after him, most certainly not since Halloween. But it's still strange, and I can't quite get my head around it. He hasn't just moved in with Valerie; he's created a whole new life with her.

'How do you think Ben and Sophie will react?' he asks, looking petrified at the concept.

'I'd say there'll be a process,' I reply, pondering it. 'Shock, possibly horror, and then a gradual build up to jokes about old people being crap with contraception. And after that, they'll be pleased.'

I realise as I say it that it's true. This has been the emotional equivalent of a mallet to the skull for me, but once the dust has settled, it will be lovely. There will be a baby, and all the chaos and joy that a baby brings. Ben and

Sophie will have a little brother or sister, and that will be a wonderful thing to watch develop over time.

'You think so?'

'I do. I really do. Just don't expect it to happen straight away. You've had ages to get used to the idea, so give them a grace period, okay?'

'I will, I promise. And I'm sorry, Max. For everything. The way I behaved, the way I went about things ... well, it was horrible. I treated you badly, and I was so wrapped up in what I needed that I managed to convince myself it was excusable. Marriages end, but the way I did it ... well, I'm ashamed, and I'm sorry. I should have told you earlier, and I shouldn't have made you feel so bad about yourself. You deserved better.'

He sounds genuine, and I realise that this is the first time he has sounded that way. During the hellscape that was life when he first told me about Valerie, we were both a mess. I was shocked and desperate to cling on to him, refusing to believe the truths he was finally telling me. Maybe I was an idiot for not spotting the signs earlier, but I'd been busy with my mum and the kids, and I simply didn't have a clue. It hit me so hard it almost broke me. The one thing I thought I could count on had been taken away from me.

At the time he said the right things—that it was him not me, that he still loved me in his own way, that he'd never planned to hurt me—but he also said the wrong things. Like I'd let myself go, like our sex life was dead, like I'd never made time for him. Looking back there was a grain of truth in all of it, which was enough for me to hate myself entirely.

He'd veer between passively aggressively blaming me for what he'd done, and apologising for it. But I could tell that he didn't really mean it. I could tell he could barely wait to get out of the door.

I'll always remember how he looked at me the day he finally did leave, with a mix of pity and contempt, muttering hollow 'sorries' as I followed him down the drive begging him not to go. I thought my life was ending, that I would never be happy again. I shudder at the thought, and feel grateful for the fact that I was wrong.

Now, sitting here on a snow-swept beach that feels a million miles away from those gut-punch days of tears and recriminations, he actually does sound sorry. Truly regretful. Not for leaving—he is clearly where he wants to be—but for the way he handled it. It unravels something in me, untangles a knot maybe, and I find myself feeling slightly better about everything. Lighter somehow, now he has finally acknowledged it. Like the emotional blockage I've carried with me for so long can finally start to dissolve.

'It *was* horrible,' I reply, leaning into him. 'And I did deserve better. But it's in the past, and nothing we say can change it. We just have to try and move on. And a baby is always good news. I'm pleased for you, Richie. You were always so great with the kids.'

'Is this the part where you say that's because I was always a big baby myself?'

'I can neither confirm nor deny that. But it'll be okay. You'll remember how to change nappies, and you'll be a dab hand at bath time, and eventually you'll do all the stuff you did with our kids: teach them to ride a bike, and cheat at Snap, and take them to swimming lessons. You've got a whole new adventure ahead of you.'

'I know,' he says, wiping his face with his hands and looking exhausted at the thought. 'Val has no clue what we're in for! But yeah, like you say, it's an adventure. Thank you. For being so nice about it. I was shitting myself the whole drive down here.'

'I bet you were! Now, look, I really did mean it when I said I had things to do, Richie.'

I stand up, keen for him to be gone. This has been a lot to take in, a lot to digest, and I'm still much more rattled than I am letting on. I need to think about it all in a place that doesn't also contain him, where I can be honest with myself, and possibly have a little cry. It is the end of one era, and the beginning of another … and that is fine. It will be all right. But it is new, and I have to get used to the way it feels.

'Hot date?' he says jokingly as he stands to join me, and I can tell he is surprised when I reply, 'Yes, actually. His name's Gabriel.'

'Oh! Well. Good. Great. That's nice. Maybe I'll meet him one day.'

'Maybe, but not today, and he'll be turning up soon. He's the jealous type, and he has a chainsaw.'

'Really?'

'No to the jealous type, yes to the chainsaw. But I do need to get moving, Richie. Call the kids and ask them to meet you at the Horse and Rider—that's the pub in the village. If you ask nicely I'm sure they'll bring Gary too.

Buy them a drink, and tell them your news, and don't expect perfection, okay?'

'Okay. I need a drink myself. Thanks again, and … erm … stay in touch, all right?'

He opens his arms for a hug, and I step into it. It's tentative and awkward to start with, but eventually we both relax. There's a moment where I feel the tension poof out of me, and I wrap my arms around his back as he holds me close. It feels understandably familiar. It feels safe and nice and a tiny bit like home. The kind of history we share isn't easily erased, and my body still remembers its place next to him. I nestle into his chest, and he rests his head on top of my hair like he always used to, and we cling to each other for way longer than is necessary.

I think we both know that this is a kind of goodbye. Our lives ran on parallel tracks for a very long time, but now they have diverged.

I look up at him and we share a smile, and I can tell I'm not the only one feeling emotional. He swipes at his eyes as we finally pull apart, both maybe a little embarrassed now. We walk together up to the car park, and I point him towards the pub. I watch him disappear up the road, slipping and sliding in his stupid boots, his phone to his ear.

I give him a final wave, and climb into the car. I actually still have a while before I meet Gabriel, but I can't face going back into the café.

I turn the heating on and rub my hands in front of the vents, and soon start to feel cosy and cocooned. I can't risk putting the radio on. One mournful Motown ballad or even a bit of Adele, and I'll be done for. Instead, I simply sit, and think, and yes, have a little cry. I feel sad and relieved and nostalgic for the past and hopeful for the future, all at the same time. I allow myself that, because as you get older and life becomes more complicated, you start to realise that we're all capable of feeling many things at once.

As usual, though, once I start crying, I find it hard to stop. I cry about my mum, and I cry about the memories of our now-dead family life that flood my mind. I cry about the fact that my kids are grown-up, and I will never again sit in a dark room at night holding a baby so small its whole head fits into the palm of my hand, overwhelmed with love and wonder. I cry about Cherie and her grief, and Gabriel and his hidden suffering, and I cry about the old people in the shop having to use self-service tills to pay for their microwave meals. I even cry about the fact that yesterday I saw a seagull hopping along with only one leg.

All of this takes some time, but is deeply cathartic. I feel better afterwards, but I notice as I glance in the mirror that I look terrible. I am a bundle of snot and tears, and my eyes are red and swollen. This is not how I wanted to look for my hot date.

I root around in the glove box for some tissues, and wipe my eyes. I add a bit of tinted moisturiser to cheer my face up, and then get out my phone to message the kids. No spoilers—it's up to their dad to break the news that they're getting a brand new sibling—but just to say I'll see them later. I'll keep an eye on my phone in case they need me, and hopefully by the time I see them again in person, I won't look like someone has punched me in the face.

By then, I will have spent an evening with Gabriel, and everything will feel better. I decide that I will tell him all about Richie's visit, because there's no reason not to. He'll be able to tell I'm upset anyway, and I know it will feel good to talk to him about it all. He is an excellent listener, and he always brings a slightly different perspective to things—beneath the grumpy exterior beats a very kind heart. Even the thought of being near him makes me smile, and that helps. There is so much that is good about my life now, and this is just a blip, a new situation to adapt to.

It's only when I'm about to turn the phone off that I see what time it is, and realise it's later than I thought. It's twenty past four, and I have been sitting in my car melting into a puddle for way too long. For almost forty minutes in fact.

I frown as I realise that Gabriel should be here by now. I give it another ten minutes, keeping an eye out for his truck pulling into the car park, sure that he will turn up soon. I message him, but with little hope of it landing or him seeing it.

When he's half an hour late, my brain does a fun thing where it decides to fill me with sudden irrational fear. Gabriel is the most capable man I've ever met, but even he could trip over a tree root and bang his head. What if he's lying hurt and unconscious in the woods? What if he's dying of hypothermia? What if he's being eaten alive by hungry badgers? What if Belle has killed him?

I call, but predictably enough it goes straight to voicemail. The reception isn't great at the farmhouse, and he's equally not great at answering. I try Laura and ask if he's in the café, but she says no. I get off the line as quickly as I can, before she can ask questions about Richie.

Still tormenting myself with the hungry badger scenario, I decide to drive over and check. Just as he is capable of tripping over a tree root, he's also capable of losing track of time, or falling asleep after a hard day's work. If that's the case I'll just make some tea and chill for while. We can do Lyme Regis another day, and the kids might need me at home in the aftermath of baby-gate anyway.

The snow has started to fall again, and is tumbling down in thick flurries this time. Big, fat flakes plop onto my windscreen, momentarily dazzling before they get wiped off. The lanes between the village and Gabriel's place are both beautiful and slightly terrifying. The hedgerows are white and heavy, and I spy a little robin perched atop a branch, its red breast shining as it watches me drive slowly by. The fresh snow is settling on frozen ice, and it takes me about twice as long as normal to get there.

I toot the horn and go to see Belle, but she's nowhere to be found. Gabriel recently installed a heat lamp in her stable, and she's no fool.

I crunch over the snow in the courtyard, pulling my hat down around my ears, and am about to head inside when I hear a loud crashing noise. I stop, my head tilted to one side just like the robin, and track the sound. It's coming from the barn.

As I round the corner, I stop and stare at the scene in front of me. Gabriel is standing there in the snow, not even wearing a coat, hefting a sledgehammer over his shoulder. Around him I see the scattered remains of the discarded kitchen cupboards from the skip, and the shattered carcass of Mr Pumpwell's old bath. The fire pit that he'd made is lying on its side, the metal all bashed in and two of the legs detached. I spot pale blue shards of pottery embedded in the snow, and realise that the Wedgwood plates have gone, as well as an entire set of old kilner jars we'd found in storage.

He raises the sledgehammer over his head, and slams it down on an already splintered wooden door. He's so intent on what he's doing that he hasn't even noticed me, and he's only wearing a T-shirt and jeans. He must be freezing.

I frown and run towards him, shouting: 'Gabriel! What are you doing?'

He glances over at me in surprise, his face cold in every way.

'I'm smashing things.'

'I see that. But why? And where's your coat? Come on, let's go inside. You're turning blue!'

He stares at me for a few seconds, and I'm genuinely not sure if he's even hearing me. He seems to be in some kind of fugue state, distant and faraway. His nostrils flare in distress, and his hair is coated in thick snowflakes. Eventually, he nods once, and drops the sledgehammer. He strides past me without a word, and heads inside.

The warmth of the Aga works its magic, and I put the

kettle on as he disappears upstairs. I feel awkward and uncomfortable, not sure if I should follow him or not. I've got so used to the new Gabriel that I'd forgotten how intimidating the old Gabriel could be.

By the time he comes back down, he's added a few layers of clothing, and has a plaster wrapped around one of his fingers.

'Are you okay?' I ask, nodding at his hand and passing him his tea. He sits at the opposite side of the table to me, and replies: 'Splinter.'

Right. Well, I suppose that might happen when you're busy smashing things. He's normally safety-conscious, uses thick gloves and sometimes eye protectors, always aware of what he's doing, always controlled. What I just witnessed outside was the very opposite of controlled.

'What's wrong?' I ask simply, sipping my tea. He stares into his mug for a while, not meeting my eyes, then looks up.

'I saw you,' he says. 'With him. I recognised him from the photo you have in the living room at Hyacinth. Why do you still have that anyway?'

Gabriel has never spoken to me like this before, and it shocks me. This isn't just curt; it's nasty. I blink a few times, and say: 'Because he is the father of my children, who live there, and I don't want them to think their dad is something they can't discuss when they're around me. And what do you think you saw?'

Inside, I am crumbling. I feel like the floor has turned to quicksand, and I am swamped with sudden nausea. On the outside, I manage to sound calm. Gabriel is upset enough for the two of us right now, and I don't want to fan the flames.

'I finished work early. Thought I'd go for a walk on the beach before we set off. And I saw you. In his arms, looking like you were enjoying it. Are you getting back together? Were you ever even apart? Was all of this just a distraction while you waited for him to come back to you? Or did you get with me to make him jealous?'

He is speaking in jagged bursts, and his fists are clenched on the table. I've seen him distant, and aloof, and even rude. But I've never seen him angry, and it is not nice. It's also not fair, and part of me wants to scream at him, to yell and shout and do some smashing of my own. I take a deep breath, and choose my words.

'Gabriel, there is so much there that's insulting, I don't know where to start. I don't know if you're even capable of listening right now. You're actually scaring me.'

His eyes widen slightly, and I see him physically react. He does his own deep breathing, and leans back away from me as he nods, slowly. Some of the furious fire goes out of his eyes, and he starts to look like himself again, albeit a very unhappy version of himself.

'I'm sorry for that. I know how I can be. But I need answers, Max. And I am listening.'

'Right. Well, first of all then, fuck off with your accusations! I apologise for the language, but really? How dare you! Have I ever given you any reason to think I'm the kind of woman who would sneak around behind your back? The kind of woman who would sleep with someone as a distraction? No, I can answer that one straight away: I bloody well haven't!'

My tone kicks up a notch there, and I tell myself that there is nothing to be gained by us both losing it.

'But I saw you, Max. That wasn't a quick goodbye hug. That was something more. That was real. You looked up into his eyes and I thought you were about to kiss him. And that… Well, that hurt a lot more than I thought it would.'

Something seems to deflate in him as he says this, and I see his tense shoulders drop a little. *Ah*, I think, *now we're at the crux of it.* Mr I-Am-An-Island has finally realised that he is human after all, and that must be terrifying for him. He is damaged. He is in pain. He is lashing out, like a wounded animal. I understand all of that, but it is still unfair. And if there's anything my experience with Richie taught me, it's that I won't allow myself to be badly treated ever again.

'So, after you saw what you thought you saw, you just left?'

'I don't think I saw it, I *did* see it! And yes, I left. What did you expect me to do?'

'I don't know, Gabriel. Talk to me about it? Give me the chance to explain instead of jumping to conclusions? Ask me what was going on instead of making judgements? Maybe it was just easier for you to go off at the deep end, run back here and decide I was the bad guy? That's a lot simpler and cleaner isn't it?'

'Maybe. Maybe you're right. But I was shocked, and

upset, and I didn't want to be near you. I'm still not sure I want to be near you.'

That hurts, of course. It digs deep inside me and lodges there like a bone stuck in my throat. Today has been an absolute bastard, and I was already emotionally strung out by the time I got here. I'm not sure I have the energy for this, and am tempted to simply walk out. Leave him to his smashing.

Except there is a look on his face, in his eyes, that is so sad, so distraught, that I know I can't. He's told me what happened with his ex-wife, and I of all people understand how someone cheating takes a wrecking ball to your capacity to trust. You always expect the worst, and he is convinced that he's just witnessed it.

Maybe I'd overreact in exactly the same way if I saw him and his gorgeous blonde ex having a cuddle, I don't know. If I did, it would come from a place of pain and bitter past experience, and whatever happens between us, I don't want to contribute to that pain. I have to make him understand that I am not the same as her, that history is not repeating himself.

'What you saw, Gabriel, was perfectly innocent. Richie turned up unannounced because he wanted to tell me that he's having a baby. That his new partner is pregnant. He wanted to tell me in person, which was one of the first decent things he's done in years.

'We talked, more openly than we have for a very long time. It was weird and emotional and intense. Yes, we hugged, and if I looked like I was enjoying it, then maybe I was. It felt like closure. It felt like I was finally saying goodbye to him, and to our past—to the last twenty years-plus of my life. And to give you your answers, no, we are not getting back together. Yes, we really were apart. I definitely didn't sleep with you to make him jealous, and no, you were not just a distraction. You were much more than that.'

He stares at me seriously, like he's trying to read my mind. Like he's trying to figure out if I'm lying, if he can take a risk and believe me. This man is really messed up.

'I was going to tell you,' I say. 'After he left, I sat alone in my car and cried about a one-legged seagull, amongst other things. I was upset, and concerned about my kids, and knocked off balance. But underneath all of that, I was looking forward to talking to you about it, because you're not just someone I sleep with, Gabriel. You're pretty much my best friend. I would never lie to you, and I would never cheat on you, and I would never keep secrets from you.'

He leans his elbows on the table, and rests his face in his hands so I can't see him. His hair falls around his head, and I want nothing more than to reach out and comfort him. But I need to know that he has listened. I need to know that he understands how wrong he was, and how much he has hurt me.

He finally looks up, and there is a shimmer of tears in the liquid brown of his eyes.

'I've really messed up, haven't I?' he says, his voice gravelly with emotion.

'Yeah, you have. Gabriel, I would never do something

like that to you. To anyone! I've been on the receiving end and I just wouldn't. I wish you'd trusted me enough to give me the benefit of the doubt.'

'You're right; I should have. Instead I came back here and started smashing things. I'm an idiot, and there's no hope for me.'

I want to argue with that, tell him there is hope. Simply reassure him and point out how far we've come together. When we first met, we didn't even like each other. We were both hurting, both hiding. A lot has changed since then, but now I fear we are almost back at square one. I want to make him feel better, but I don't know if I can. I am still too fragile myself. This whole conversation has felt like playing cricket with live hand grenades.

'What happened with Helen was traumatic,' I say, quietly. 'And I know you never talk about it, but your time in the Army was too. Maybe your mum dying when you were young, all of it. It's a lot, and it's all left its mark. It's natural that it's affected you, in all kinds of ways—you're only human, Gabriel, much as you like to think otherwise. That comment you made earlier, about this whole thing hurting a lot more than you expected? I don't necessarily think that's a bad thing.'

'It felt pretty bloody bad!'

'Yeah, I know. But it also means that you've opened up, doesn't it? We both have, in our own ways. We've kind of … blossomed?'

He smiles, and reaches out to hold both my hands in his.

'You might be right, Max. And I know you're trying to

make me feel better, because that's your nature. But look at me; look at how I behaved. The things I said, just because I felt hurt. You came here after a difficult day thinking you could rely on me, trusting me to be someone you could turn to, and instead I scared you. I scared myself to be honest. Even Belle got a fright. She took one look at my face and ran back into her stable.'

I twine my fingers into his, and feel such a strong rush of affection for this man that I'm not sure I'll ever let go.

'It's okay,' I say. 'You're not perfect. I'm not either. And that's all right. Look, we're both upset right now. Everything is heightened. It's all been very dramatic, and we're not thinking straight. Plus you have a splinter.'

He laughs bitterly, and thinks about what I've said. I can almost see his thought processes, and feel my stomach clench and tighten. The sense of dread is so strong it's making me physically ill.

He pulls his hands from mine, and gives me a sweet, sad smile.

'You're right, about everything. And I'm sorry—really sorry—that I judged you like that. Obviously it says more about me than you, Max. But I am what I am, and I can't even promise that it will never happen again. I think I have a touch of the psycho to me, to be honest, and I'm not sure that will ever go away. I'm worried about it, about how I reacted, and I'm worried that I might drag you down with me.'

'What are you saying?'

'I'm saying I think I need a break, Max. I'm sorry.'

Chapter Seventeen

W hen I let myself back into Hyacinth later that evening, it feels cold and empty. Not even Gary is there to greet me, and I miss the warmth of the Aga.

I walk around, touching the radiators and finding that they are all working fine. I guess it's just me, then.

I close the curtains, and switch on the lamps, and try to make it as cosy as it can possibly be. It doesn't work, and I slump onto the sofa feeling miserable and lonely.

Gabriel and I have decided to just be friends, but I can tell from the way he is acting that we might not be close friends. He will keep me at arm's length, and retreat back into his closed-off little world. His emotional sleeping bag. I know him well enough to predict that he will rarely be seen in the village, that he will be too busy to socialise, that he will isolate himself in every possible way. He will become his great-uncle, despite his best efforts.

It broke my heart to leave him there, but I had to accept

his decision. Part of me even thinks he's right. That whole scene was so draining I have nothing left in me, other than sadness. We came close to something special, me and Gabriel, but in the end we were both too broken to grasp hold of it and keep it safe.

He is the more obviously broken one. He carries his traumas and his scars around with him wherever he goes, and clearly feels safer alone. But I'm not without bruises myself, and it's been hard to trust another man again. Gabriel hasn't betrayed me in the same way that Richie did, but the sense of desolation I am feeling now comes close. My whole life here in Budbury is tied up with him, and I can't imagine it any other way.

I drag myself up and switch on the Christmas tree lights. As I sit down again, I realise that their insufferably cute festive energy seems to mock me.

'You can shut up as well,' I say, considering throwing my boot at the tree.

I am all cried out after my meltdown in the car, but I am hurting so much that I feel paralysed by it. I'm glad the kids are still out with their dad, because I don't want them to see me like this. I have vowed to myself that they will never have to suffer because of my feelings ever again. I am the mother, and they are the children, and from now on, Sophie will be able to live her life fully and without concerns for the mad woman back home. Even if I'm down, I will not show it.

And maybe, I tell myself, I won't be as down as I think,

for as long as I think. I'm not sure I actually believe that, but I need to have some hope.

I decide to give myself a pep talk, out loud, because perhaps if I say these things out loud, I *will* believe them, perhaps they will feel more real, and less like a big fat lie.

'I have a life here,' I announce to the Christmas tree. 'I have a job and friends and a potential new career. I will learn to fill my days without Gabriel, even if it doesn't feel like it right now. My heart will go on, and I will survive.'

I've slipped two very appropriate songs into that pep talk, and I decide to sing them both. I think maybe I need some sleep, or possibly a month in a sensory deprivation tank.

I'm still working my way through Gloria Gaynor's classic when the kids get home, and Sophie immediately joins in with the chorus. Ben starts doing the actions and walking out the door when we point at it, and Gary jumps around in delight at all the fun. Before long we are all laughing, and then Sophie goes to the kitchen and brings through the biscuit barrel and a multi-pack of Monster Munch. I still have a lead weight in my guts where happiness used to live, but everything feels a shade lighter.

'So, how did it go?' I ask, glad that Richie decided to just drop them off and run for it. We've said as much as we needed to to each other earlier, and it's not his fault that it indirectly led to my whole world being smashed in with a sledgehammer.

'Okay,' says Sophie, perched next to me, slightly tipsy. 'I mean, it was a bit weird, but once I got my head around it, I was happy. We were coming up with baby names. I suggested Velma for a girl, 'cause she's the coolest of the Scooby Doo gang, and Velma for a boy, 'cause she's the coolest of the Scooby Doo gang.'

'Interesting. I'm sure Valerie will be delighted with that idea. Ben? Are you all right?'

Once the dancing stopped he became quieter, more subdued, and I remember the conversation I overheard. About him still harbouring hope that his dad and I would get back together. That was never going to happen anyway, but it's most definitely not going to happen now.

'Yeah, it was just a surprise is all. I don't know Valerie very well, but she always comes off as one of those women who don't shit, you know?'

'No, I don't know!'

'You know, those women who are so pristine and so perfect you can't ever imagine her having anything as messy as a bowel movement? And I know you've not been to her house, but it's like a show home: everything is silver and grey and chrome, and one of the new chairs still has the plastic wrapping on it! I just can't picture her dealing with a baby.'

'Well,' I reply, secretly laughing inside at his scathing description, 'I'm sure she'll be fine. And your dad knows what he's doing.'

'Does he, though? Didn't you say he almost let me drown in the bath once because he was checking the Aston Villa results on his phone? And didn't he drop Sophie on her head, which explains a lot?'

She punches him in the kidneys, and I say: 'Well, you didn't drown, did you? And Sophie just bounced, so that was all right. Anyway. You two will be fantastic siblings.'

'This is true,' he says, gazing theatrically into the distance. 'I have so much to teach them.'

'Like what?'

'Like this!' he announces. He pulls off his socks, and inserts a fragment of beef Monster Munch between each toe. He holds his foot out, and Gary obligingly starts licking and nibbling to get at them.

I laugh, and say: 'Well, that's something you don't see every day! But stop now, because crisps aren't good for him. Or us.'

I shove one in my mouth as soon as I say this, which spoils the effect. We chat some more, and eventually they go off up to their rooms.

I stay downstairs for a while afterwards, tidying up and letting Gary out into the garden. I join him out there, shivering, looking at the snow collecting on the tops of the trees, the hazy outline of the hills bathed in starlight. It is peaceful and calm and pure, and it helps.

I sit on the sofa again, and realise that I don't want to go to bed. I can give myself as many pep talks as I like, but the loss is still jagged and sharp. I have a Gabriel-shaped hole in my life, and it makes my heart ache.

Chapter Eighteen

I wake up the next day with a sore head, and a sense of doom that descends on me approximately ten seconds after I open my eyes.

I am momentarily cheered by the news on the village group chat that Katie has delivered a healthy baby boy called Oliver, weighing in at seven pound ten. Mother and baby are doing well, and predictably enough, a rota is being set up to help them out with childcare for the other two boys. I offer my services and received a huge smiley face from Laura.

My own face is significantly less smiley. I stagger into the bathroom, and see red eyes, crusted lashes, and pale skin. Delightful.

Disgusting as the view in the mirror is, I feel even worse on the inside. I had a bad night, full of fractured and tormented dreams as my subconscious presumably tried to deal with the double whammy of the day before. My subconscious clearly sucks at it, because as I make my way downstairs to get caffeine, I still feel sick.

The kids are both in bed, and I'm glad—at least I don't have to fake it for their sake. Gary doesn't mind if I'm a grouch. The poor dog has had so many tears shed on his fur I'm surprised he hasn't turned into a fish. I feed him and let him out, and he turns the snow in the garden yellow in a big zig-zaggy line before running back in.

I make my coffee, and a bowl of cereal I know I probably won't be able to eat. Everything feels heavy, my heart, my mind, my arms. Every small task I have to complete—kettle, mug, Crunchy Nut Cornflakes—seems to take maximum effort. It's like I'm wading through treacle. I'm due in at work before too long and I'm worried about how I'll manage.

I've never thrown a sickie in my life, and I'm not about to start, but that doesn't mean it will be easy. Everything feels different today, greyer, tougher, more of a challenge. I tell myself that it will get better with time. That at one stage, I never thought I'd get over Richie leaving me. That we humans are resilient creatures, even if we don't always feel it.

Today is bad. Today is awful in fact, but it is only today. I need to get through it, one step at a time, and then do it all over again tomorrow.

I sip my coffee and look out of the kitchen window towards the snow-covered hills and fields. It's still pretty dark out there, and that suits me. I'm in no mood to look at beauty and sunshine. I should probably go and find the nearest big city and sit at its grottiest bus stop, the kind full of litter and cigarette butts and vomit. That would suit my mood better.

I wonder how Gabriel is this morning. When I left him, he was grim-faced but determined. We didn't even hug goodbye, neither of us willing to risk what that might result in. I drove home upset, but at least I had the kids and Gary to cheer me up. He has nobody.

I imagine him alone in that house, and even though it looks a lot better than it did when I first arrived, it is still too big for one man by himself. The picture I paint in my mind is enough to make tears sting the back of my eyes, and I squeeze them away. He's not dead, I tell myself. He's still just a few miles down the road. I can still see him. Still visit Belle. Still carry on searching for the perfect rug for the living room.

That is something … but it doesn't feel like it's enough. It's not just the sex I'll miss; it's the companionship. The affection. The continued sense of amazement as I learn more about him, and more about myself.

Have we made a really stupid mistake? Have we let this all go too easily? I know it was him who suggested a break, but I went along with it. Should I have fought harder? Insisted we held off until we'd both calmed down before we made any decisions? Did he interpret my lack of resistance as me giving up on us?

There are too many questions, and not enough answers. I'm so confused and tired I barely know my own name, but I am starting to think we were too hasty. That I let him slip away without any real attempt at figuring things out. As soon as he said he wanted a break, a self-preservation siren went off in my head, and I ran for my emotional life.

I think that's partly because of what happened with Richie. With him, I held on to hope that he would come home, for way too long.

Every time I got a message from him, or heard a car outside, I'd have this little moment where my heart leapt and I thought things would go back to normal. One day, Sophie caught me staring out of the window at a passing Nissan Qashqai, the same type and colour as his, and said to me: 'Mum, give it up. I can't believe how long you've clung on to this marriage. They should make you the patron saint of lost causes.'

She was right, and even though I forgive myself that weakness now, I never wanted to experience it again. I never wanted to revisit that feeling that my wellbeing depended on somebody else's choices. So when Gabriel started to pull away, I let him. Even though my heart was breaking in two, I let him. I didn't want to beg, and I still think that maybe he's right—that we do need more time—but I certainly didn't articulate that to him. I just agreed, and left.

What if he thinks I don't want him? What if he's woken up this morning feeling exactly the same as me, with his own regrets and his own pain?

The more I think about it, the more it makes sense to go and see him. Even if it's just to talk things through properly, or to say a real goodbye. I can't stand the thought of leaving things like this, of pretending what we had didn't matter. It might be over, but that doesn't mean I'm ready to put it entirely behind me. What we had deserves more than that. *We* deserve more than that. We might not be able to salvage the whole relationship, but we can at least try and salvage the way it ends, and leave things on a more settled note between us. If it's ending, it should end well.

I feel so much better after this one-sided conversation with myself that I actually manage to eat my breakfast. I come up with a cunning plan: I will finish work at the café, and then drive over to see him. Okay, maybe it's not that cunning, but it is a plan.

I feel like a weight has been lifted from my shoulders, and I'm not sure if that's because I'm doing the right thing, or because even just the thought of being with him again makes me feel better. It could, of course, be both. Last night felt wrong, on so many levels, and I hate that. I hate the idea of us becoming strangers, people who bump into each other and feel awkward. I need to fix it, or at least try to.

Decision made, I regain some energy and a sense of purpose. I shower, and dress, and even put on a bit of make-up. Whatever happens, I tell myself, I'll be fine. Like Gloria so wisely says, I will survive.

I message the kids, telling them to look after Gary and not burn the house down, and grab my car keys. I'm still singing that stupidly catchy song as I walk to the hallway, and stop in surprise at the sight of a padded envelope lying on the mat.

I stare at it for a bit, like it might contain anthrax, then pick it up. I occasionally get post here, forwarded from home, but this just has my name scrawled on the front, and no stamp. It's been delivered by hand, and I suspect I know whose hand it was.

My fingers tremble a little as I tear it open, and a set of keys falls to the floor. I ignore them, and examine the letter that came with them. It's written in pencil, on sheets of that small notepad he carries with him. The one I first saw the night we went badger-watching, a million years ago. I bite my lip, and read.

Dear Max,

Just wanted to let you know I'm taking off for a bit. I'm sorry about yesterday. I was an idiot, and I wish it never happened. But I think I need to try and get my head straight, and I don't think I can do that when I'm around you. I know we said we'd still see each other as friends, but that's not going to work and we both know it.

I'm not sure how long I'll be gone for, or where I'm going, maybe back to France for a while. I'm arranging for someone to come and see to Belle every day, but I'm sure she'd still appreciate a visit from you; you were always her favourite person. I'm enclosing keys to the farmhouse, just in case. I'm sorry, and thanks for everything. Take care of yourself.

He has signed it simply with his name. He is not an XOXO kind of man, I know that, but I wish he was. One little kiss at the end might have helped.

I realise I am crying, and I fold the little pages up and shove them in my bag. I can hear sounds of movement upstairs, and I remind myself of my vow, that my kids will never have to deal with my emotional wreckage ever again. Anyway, I don't have time to break down. I have to go to work.

I wipe away the tears, and put on my coat, and face the world. Outside, it is dazzlingly white, so cold my eyelashes almost freeze. I march through the little path that leads to the green, and see Ruby and Rose out in the snow, Midgebo chasing them around.

They have their school uniforms on, but are bundled up in extra layers and wellies as they roll a big ball of snow around the grass.

'Max!' one of them shouts (I can't tell them apart), 'we're making the world's biggest snowman before Becca takes us to school. Dad says if it's big enough it might go in the Guinness Book of Records!'

'Which is stupid,' the other adds, 'because Guinness is just that black beer he drinks!'

They are so sweet, so funny. So untouched by adult life. I chat to them for a few minutes, wishing them luck, then drive to the café to meet their mother. I sit in the car park for a few moments first, gathering myself into a whole, refusing to do what I want to do and read that letter again. The contents won't have changed, and there's no point torturing myself about what might have been, or what I should have done differently. He's gone, and that's that.

I am determined to keep the act up, as much for my own benefit as anyone else's, and I'm grateful to have a job to keep me busy. It's a solace, a safe haven, the perfect distraction.

It's also, praise the lord, a bustling day in the Comfort Food Café. That's not always the case, but we get a coach load of senior citizens in on their way to Cornwall, all of them oohing and aahing about the decor and ordering a vast array of breakfast items. Making bacon sandwiches and pots of tea and buttering thick doorstep toast is way preferable to sitting around feeling sorry for myself, and also means it's easier to avoid Laura's probing gaze.

After the coach party, we have a steady stream of customers, and Cherie comes down to help out. I love watching her work, seeing her float around the room making everyone feel welcome and special. For such a big woman, she moves with such ease and grace. I want to be Cherie when I grow up.

Once the place is quieter, I keep myself busy with some cleaning. Today, I decide, is the perfect day to scrub the already pristine toilets. I do that, and I dust the book shelves, and I check the board games to make sure they have their all pieces. I find Buckaroo's plastic bundle of dynamite rammed inside the snakes and ladders, so it's a good job I did. I refill all the salt and pepper shakers, and check the ketchups, and then I gather up a bin bag and some rubber gloves.

'Where are you going now?' says Cherie, as I walk past. I realise that the café is now empty, and she is sitting with Laura at one of the tables sipping a coffee.

'Erm … I was going to shovel up dog poo from the field. It's easier when it's frozen.'

This is a universal truth known to all dog owners, but Cherie shakes her head at me, her silvery-grey plait wobbling.

'No, you're not going to do that, Max. We've been watching you run around like a blue-arsed fly for the last half-hour. There's nothing else that needs doing. Sit down.'

She says this in the kind of tone that you can't argue with, and I do as I'm told. Laura gets me a cappuccino, and I give them both a huge beaming smile over the steam. I am doing so well at this faking it business.

'That is the creepiest smile I've ever seen,' Laura says, shaking her head. 'You look like a possessed demon doll in a horror film. What's up? You've been weird all day, and we're worried about you.'

I look at their concerned faces, and remind myself that they are not my children. That I am allowed to appear vulnerable around them. That maybe I need to talk about all of this before I explode.

'I think,' I say quietly, 'that my life is a bit of a mess. In general. I think things might have gone tits up.'

'Everything seems to go a bit tits up when you're our age,' says Laura, gazing down at her chest. 'Apart from your actual tits. They just seem to go down. Can you be more specific?'

'Gabriel's left. He's gone to France, and I might never see him again, and he'll probably put the farmhouse up for sale! What if I'm looking on Rightmove one day and it's there, with its lovely sofa and the Brassica paint on the landing! What if someone else buys it? What will happen to Belle? And the badgers? And me? I keep telling myself to be more Gloria, but I just feel so bloody sad!'

The two of them exchange looks at this outburst, and Cherie says: 'I'll get the cake.'

Once she's back, I tell them both everything that has happened. They don't interrupt, they just sit and listen. It feels like a monumental relief to get it off my chest, even though I'm constantly crying or trying not to cry. I've eaten some of the apple pie, and drunk my coffee, and dumped my emotional load all over my friends' heads. I feel like I've gone on for hours, but they don't seem to mind.

Cherie reaches out and pats my hand gently, saying: 'Oh my love, I'm so sorry. What a palaver! What a bit of bad luck that he happened to see you and Richie, and make all the wrong assumptions!'

I nod, my lower lip still feeling a bit wobbly, and reply: 'It was bad luck. But … I don't know, Cherie, maybe it was for the best? It doesn't feel like that now, but there's obviously a lot of anger inside him. A lot of pain. It would probably have spilled over at some point or another, and I don't need more drama in my life. Maybe it's good it happened before things had gone too far. Before we were in too deep.'

'Sweetness,' she replies, an amused smile on her lips, 'I think it's a bit late for that.'

'What do you mean?'

'I mean you're already in pretty deep, aren't you? You're clearly head over heels in love with the man!'

I stare at her dumbly for a few seconds, and Laura adds, 'She's right, Max. You might be trying to fool yourself that it was still casual, but it's obviously not. Have you told him? That you love him?'

'Of course not!' I reply, exasperated. 'How could I, when I didn't even know? Why didn't you tell me earlier for God's sake?'

They both burst out laughing at this, and eventually, against all the odds, I have to join in. I really am ridiculous.

Are they right, I wonder? Am I in love with Gabriel? Of course I bloody am, I admit to myself. I've been ignoring what was right in front of my face because it was frightening, because I wasn't ready. Well, ready or not, it's happened, and I've realised it just as he's disappeared. Or maybe because he has, who knows?

'I suspect he feels the same way,' Laura says. 'Except he doesn't have helpful friends to point it out to him over apple pie. It's probably why he ran away; it all felt a bit too big. He thinks he's blown it, and he knows he's got issues, and he obviously couldn't stand the thought of being here and not being with you. You have to call him, and tell him you love him, and make him come home. It's the only option, Max.'

'It's not. I could move to Outer Mongolia, or join a convent, or volunteer for a drug trial where they erase your memory.'

'That's from a film, and it never works! Look, how did

you feel, when you read that letter? And also, why doesn't he have normal-sized paper?'

'It's a Gabriel thing. And I suppose I felt … devastated. The only thing that was keeping me upright was the thought of going to see him after work, and trying to fix us. And then I read it, and I didn't even have that. I feel awful, Laura. Just empty and scooped out and hollow. I know it'll pass. I know I won't actually die of a broken heart, but right now, it feels like it.'

I start to cry again, and Cherie comes to my side of the table and wraps me up in one of her trademark hugs. I sob on her shoulder, and she strokes my hair, and I let it all out. When I finally stop shuddering against her, I see that I've left streaks of damp mascara on her top.

'It's okay,' she says, following my eyes. 'Now we're even. I did the same to you on your first day here, didn't I? But look, love, Laura's right. If you don't at least try, you'll never forgive yourself. Take it from us two, because we know better than most: life is too short for missing out on love. You blink your eye and it's gone. Grab hold, and keep it safe, my darling girl, because you deserve it, and so does he.'

Chapter Nineteen

I know they mean well, and they might even be right, but I don't call Gabriel. It's a complicated thing, and after I spoke to them I gave it a lot of thought.

Firstly, he clearly doesn't want me to call him. There was no 'keep in touch' element to that letter, and phones work both ways. If he's not in contact, then that's because he doesn't want to be.

Secondly, they don't really understand. I hate thinking this, but it's true. This is something I could never say out loud, because it makes me sound like an awful human being, but their husbands died. That is terrible and tragic and I've seen the toll it's taken on them both.

But their husbands had no choice about that; they were torn from them by illness or accident. They didn't walk away willingly, after telling them they'd 'let themselves go'. Don't get me wrong, I don't wish that Richie was dead, and I am not in any way claiming that what I went through was worse than what they went through. Of course it wasn't. But it was different.

They've had to deal with grief and loss and suffering, building a new life without their loved ones. That is horrible, and my heart goes out to them. But they haven't faced the same circumstances as me, the rejection, the self-loathing, the long war of attrition. It's all left its mark, and it's not something I want to go through again. Whether I love Gabriel or not, I also need to love myself. And that means having some self-respect. I will not give another man the chance to tell me I'm not good enough.

This is all fine in theory, but back in the real world I still feel like crap, despite the copious amounts of Bakewell tart that Laura keeps baking for me. My comfort food isn't really doing the trick, but I appreciate the thought behind it.

What does do the trick is keeping as busy as I possibly can. It was a perfect storm when Richie left, and if I'd had my mum to take care of, or my job hadn't gone kaput, maybe I'd have coped better. Here, I have plenty to do. I am useful, and helpful, and can contribute to the community.

Work gets even busier once the schools break up for the holidays, with more people arriving for a Christmas break in our gorgeous little corner of the world. I extend my hours, and at my suggestion we start doing evening meals. It's a weird time to start, the week before Christmas, but Cherie leaps on the idea as soon as the words come out of my mouth. Maybe I'm not the only one who wants to keep busy. We agree to do it as a trial for two nights, and it's a sell-out both times.

It's also the Max and Cherie show, as Laura has commitments at home. Cherie came up with the menus, and we all helped prepare. Sophie and her friend Jess waited on the tables, and it was chaotic but a lot of fun. Cherie says she's definitely going to carry on with it, and is already planning for the week between Christmas and New Year, 'when nobody can remember what day it is and they're all sick of turkey'.

I've renewed the tenants' lease on the house in Solihull, and realise that I'm okay with leaving it behind. Part of me wanted to run home once things got hard, but I talked myself out of it. There is nothing there for me now. My life is here, even if Gabriel isn't.

I'm also giving more thought to my side hustle of doing up the Rockery cottages. Cherie seems serious about it, and on changeover day she walked me round them while they were being cleaned for the next guests. They're all charming in their own way, but the decor is on the tired side. Each one has a lot of potential, and I am brimming with ideas about what I might do if we decide to go ahead.

Sophie suggested, jokingly, that I should start my own YouTube channel called Max's Home Makeovers, and I shocked her by saying I might. I won't, of course—put a camera on me and I'm guaranteed to walk into a lamp post —but it was worth it just to see the look on her face.

I visit Katie and happy-cry when I hold her baby, and I do some Christmas shopping, and Auburn and Finn take me on a tour of Briarwood, the big old manor house where all the geniuses live. Most of them have gone home for

Christmas, but some remain, locked into their work. I don't understand most of it, but when one of their inventions changes the world I'll be able to say I was there at the beginning.

I visit Belle every other day and take her treats, and in her own disgruntled way she seems pleased to see me. I check out her stables and water troughs, and she's being taken care of. I never go inside the house, though; I just couldn't bear it. Couldn't bear to see it empty and quiet, haunted by the things I've done there, by the person I became there. By Gabriel.

I develop a knack of shutting down my brain every time I even think his name, and that works while I'm busy. It works while I have something to distract me. The problems come at night, when I'm lying in bed trying to sleep. Then, I am helpless, and it all comes rushing in, crushing me in a landslide of regret. I miss him so much it hurts. Everything I do in my oh-so-busy life, I want to tell him about. I want to show him the pictures of little ugly-gorgeous Oliver, and talk to him about Briarwood, and test out the evening menu on him.

Every night, I find myself writing him a message on my phone, telling him about my day, asking about his. Telling him that I love him. And every night, I delete it without pressing send.

I feel like part of me is missing, and I have phantom pain where Gabriel used to be. I hide it from the kids well enough that neither of them even asks how I am; they carry on being selfish and inconsiderate, which is exactly the way

I want it. I've told them he's gone away for Christmas and they've accepted that, plus it's not technically a lie. He has gone away; I've just no idea when he'll be back, or even if he will.

I am in pain, but I am in secret pain, and that is a strange kind of consolation. I just need to stay busy, keep myself occupied, never leave an empty moment where the sadness might swoop in and grab me.

The day before Christmas Eve is a Monday, and the café is closed. The weather is miserable—relentless rain and sleet battered the windows through the night—and I wake up to face a rare day that is so far unfilled. It makes me panic a little, and I lie in bed wracking my brains to come up with a mind-numbing task. All my gifts are bought and wrapped, the cottage is pristine, and I can't do any more work on it until the kitchen is done in the New Year.

I'm considering buying a wetsuit and asking Sam for an impromptu surf lesson when my phone pings on my bedside cabinet. As ever, I experience that little whoosh of hope. Much as I try, I can't quite kill it completely.

It's actually a message from Edie, and even seeing her name come up on my contacts makes me smile. She told me once she has to use a magnifying glass to see the keypad on her phone, but I suspect she was having me on. It's hard to tell with Edie; there's a lot of devilment in her.

> I found some pictures for Gabriel, but I haven't heard from him. Pop round if you have time, but don't worry if not.

She signs off with a string of emojis that show old people with walking sticks, and then a giant winky-smiley face.

I am up and out within half an hour, taking Gary with me. He's not best pleased and tries to sneak back inside once he realises it's raining, but if I'm not long at Edie's, I can use him as an excuse to go for a long walk. He looks up at me, as though he can read my mind, and I swear to God he narrows his eyes.

The single street of the village is busy, the butcher doing a roaring trade and the front of the florist's shop filled with poinsettia in pots and bouquets decorated with holly. I nip in and grab a bunch for Edie. Nobody ever goes anywhere empty-handed in Budbury, I've come to realise.

I see Auburn through the window of the pharmacy and give her a wave before I knock on Edie's door. I've never actually been inside her home, and it's charming. She lives in one of the tiny whitewashed terraces that line the road, and the front door opens right into the living room. She has old-fashioned lace antimacassars on the chair arms, and everything is made of chintz. There's a life-size cardboard figure of Anton du Beke from *Strictly* in one corner, his smiling face covered in bright red lipstick kisses. I don't ask.

I hand her the flowers, and she takes them in delight. I notice belatedly that there are already four other vases full of very similar bouquets, and realise I'm not the only one to have had that thought.

'Yours are my favourite,' she assures me, as she adds yet another vase to the collection. 'Tea, coffee? Tequila?'

I opt for coffee, but am curious as to whether she actually has the tequila or not. I wouldn't put it past her. Maybe it's the secret to her long life.

Once we're settled and Gary is curled up at my feet, she passes me a plain cardboard folder, and says: 'Took me a while, but once Gabriel asked me to look I was determined! I do like a challenge! I found them in the county archive in the end. When the little local newspaper we had went digital, they donated all their old photos. These are copies, so he's welcome to keep them.'

I open the folder, and find three pictures. Black and white, obviously, as they date back to the forties and fifties. One shows the street outside, and I am amazed at how little it's changed. The shops are different, and there are hardly any cars, but essentially it is the same. There's some kind of party going on, tables set up and people waving flags, bunting draped from house to house.

'That was Coronation Day,' Edie announces, smiling at the memory. 'We had a street party. And look, there they are —the Pumpwells.'

I follow her finger, and see a family sitting together at one of the tables. Mum and Dad look quite stern, but the teenagers are clearly having a ball, grinning and holding glasses in the air.

'That's Norman and Marjorie,' Edie tells me. 'I seem to recall Norman got quite drunk on scrumpy that day. He'd only have been young, and I think he ended up taken home in a wheelbarrow…'

The next one features the whole family standing

together by the side of a field, a display of vegetables in front and a big piece of machinery behind them. Again, the parents look dour, but I suppose these are people who had gone through through two world wars and lived a tough life on the land.

'That one was taken as part of an article about the "modern face of farming in Dorset",' she says. 'I've got a copy of that as well. They don't look very modern now, I know, but they were one of the first farms to have their own combine harvester. That was big news back in the day!'

The last photo is the one that really gets to me. Edie tells me it was taken as part of the same article, and it shows Norman and Marjorie standing outside the farmhouse. The extension on the side of the building was clearly new back then, but other than that, it looks the same.

Norman is tall, dark-haired and handsome in that 1950s way, maybe about sixteen at the time. He has his arm around Marjorie's shoulders, and they're both smiling for the camera. Marjorie herself is a stunner, with glamorous swept-up hair and a playful look that still shines through after all this time.

I stroke the picture, wondering what was going on in their heads when this was taken. They look happy, but were they? By that stage, was Marjorie's unwanted marriage already planned? Was Norman already dreaming of leaving to go to university? One moment, frozen in time, when they were so young the whole world must have felt like an adventure.

'It was a bit of a scandal when she eloped,' says Edie,

her face wrinkled in time. 'I didn't know them well, but I remember it happening. Back in those days there was a lot more pressure on young people to stay with their families, to carry on with the farming. It's not like that now, and I never know if that's a good thing or not. I suppose it depends on the young people. But Marjorie clearly never wanted what was mapped out for her.'

'Neither did Norman,' I reply. 'He wanted to be a doctor.'

'Did he really?' she says, sounding surprised. 'Well, I never knew that! Marjorie running away would have put the kibosh on that, I suppose. What a shame, for both of them. We never found out what had happened to her, but when Gabriel turned up out of the blue, it seemed like she'd at least gone off and had a nice life. I'd have told him all of this, Gabriel, but he never asked. All those times we sat here having a cuppa, he never once asked. I got the feeling he didn't want to know, and it wasn't my place to push.'

'That sounds like him,' I say, smiling gently. 'He probably would never have asked; it's just that we found some letters back at the farmhouse, from Majorie. He loved his grandmother and I think it made him curious.'

'I'm curious too. What did happen to her?'

'Well, she married the archaeologist, and lived happily ever after. She had a daughter, Gabriel's mum, who sadly died when he was only sixteen, but it sounds like she basically went on to have a long, full life. She died in 2021, when she was eighty-four.'

'Oh, so young!' says Edie sadly, and I bite back a laugh. I suppose from her perspective, it is young.

I gather up the pictures, and sit and chat with her for a little while longer. She tells me all about her nieces and their children, and shares her own memories of the Coronation Day street party, and it's all very pleasant. She doesn't require much in the way of encouragement, and I can see why Gabriel found her easy to be around: he could sit in his traditional stony silence and just listen to the anecdotes.

Eventually I thank her, and make my way outside. It's still raining, but it's less heavy. There's more snow forecast over the next few days, and the weather people on the telly are going into ecstasies about it being a white Christmas.

I call into the pharmacy, where Auburn is perched on a stool blowing into a lollipop in the shape of a whistle. She toots at me as I walk in, and tells me she's been rushed off her feet doing last-minute prescriptions all morning.

'Have you got any photos', I ask, 'of Mr Pumpwell? I know you were friends, and that he started coming to village events in his later years.'

'Reluctantly, and with a great deal of kicking and screaming, but yes. And I'm sure I'll have some on my phone.'

'Is there any way you could print them off for me? Pretty please?'

'Sure,' she says, giving a final whistle as she jumps off her stool. 'Are they a Christmas gift for Gabriel? And if I print them for you, will you tell me if he's a good kisser?'

I laugh, and also feel grateful that Cherie and Laura

haven't told anybody else what has happened. It's hard enough to deal with, without everybody knowing and feeling sorry for me.

I give her a definite maybe, and agree to call back later in the day to collect them.

After that I head to Applechurch, the next village down the coast from Budbury. In comparison, it's a bustling metropolis with several antique shops, two pubs, and a small supermarket. It doesn't have quite the same charm, but it does have what I need.

Once the rain clears properly, I take Gary for a walk along the clifftop paths for an hour. I've been doing a lot of walking recently, and it's pretty much the best thing in the world for a good, solid head-clearing. Even on a dull day like this the views are breathtaking, the rolling swell of the sea stretching out into infinity.

I've managed to fill in most of the day, and once I collect the prints from Auburn, I have a project in mind for the rest of it. Gabriel might not still be here, but his house is, and I've always wanted to be able to put some family photos up on those old stone walls. I might not have found the perfect rug, but I'd like to add the pictures. It will feel like the final touch, having Norman and Marjorie back home.

I go back to Hyacinth, where I find a group of Young People gathered around the dining room table playing Monopoly. There is much screeching and laughing, and I can see that Lizzie, Laura's daughter, is absolutely slaughtering them all. She has a huge pile of fake cash in front of her, and hotels on Mayfair. Go Lizzie.

'Where's your brother?' I ask.

'Dunno. I was nice, I promise, and I asked him to play. He said he was going to do something more interesting, like watch the kettle boil.'

I check the kitchen, just in case he meant that literally, but then head upstairs. I knock on his door, and find him lying on his bed wearing his headphones, staring at his phone.

'Can I use your desk?' I ask. Both the kids have small desks in their rooms allegedly for their studies, but Sophie's is set up with her PlayStation and if I move anything even a fraction of an inch, she will rain down hellfire.

When he shrugs, I take it as a yes and get set up. I found a really nice old frame in one of the shops in Applechurch, and I carefully dismantle it and insert the backing card. I smile as I look through Auburn's photos, seeing a variety of shots of the late Norman Pumpwell. He's very old on these, sitting in the café with a party hat on, looking like he'd prefer to be anywhere else in the world. It's hard to imagine him as that teenaged boy who got so drunk on scrumpy he had to be pushed home in a wheelbarrow.

There's one of him sitting in his kitchen, a 'Birthday Boy' banner decorated with little footballs up on the wall. He's almost smiling as he looks at the cake in front of him, and the background shows me exactly how much renovation work has been done on the room.

I compile a nice collage of all the different shots, with the old black and white one of him with Marjorie taking pride of place in the centre. When I'm done, I lean back in the chair and survey it. It's perfect, I think. Even if Gabriel never comes back to receive it, this will be my little gift to the farmhouse. To the memory of Norman and Marjorie.

'That's cool,' Ben says, lurking behind me. 'The group shot looks a bit like the Addams Family, though. Who are the younger ones?'

'That's Norman Pumpwell, Gabriel's great-uncle, and Marjorie, his grandmother. It's a long story, and a bit sad.'

'Right. I prefer them fast and happy. When's he coming back?'

'Who?'

'Santa Claus. Who do you think I mean? Gabriel.'

'Oh. I don't know.'

He stares at me, his eyes narrowed, and then gives me an unexpected and totally delightful hug.

'I hope it works out, Mum. He's nice, and he makes you happy. But if it doesn't work out … well, screw him, eh? It's his loss.'

I can't tell if he suspects there's something wrong or not, and I don't want to push the subject. I don't want to have to talk about it, because if I do, there's a strong chance my veneer will crack, and the real me—the nighttime me—will come spilling out. The photos have me teetering on the edge already.

'Damn right,' I say enthusiastically, wiping my hand across the glass of the frame. 'His loss.'

Chapter Twenty

I wake up at just after six on Christmas Day itself. It's still dark outside when I open my curtain, but the full moon is painting the fresh snow with a silver coat. I can see over to the green, and the cottages that surround it. Several already have lights shining from their windows, probably the ones that contain small children. Ruby and Rose probably never even went to sleep.

I might have considered staying warm and snug in bed for a bit longer, but my very first thought had been, *I wonder where Gabriel is waking up today?* Allowing myself to disappear down that rabbit hole wouldn't be very festive, so I'm up and about before I accidentally slip down it.

I get my first few coffees down me, and then wake the kids up. There is a chorus of groans and swearing as I do this, and Sophie actually tries to kick me. I am too nimble and dodge out of her way, singing 'Jingle Bells' at the top of my voice. Finally. It's revenge for all those years I was dragged out of bed at the crack of dawn to see if Santa had been.

They stagger down the stairs a little while later, and after a few gripes they soon get into the spirit of things. Gary goes first, opening his little doggie treat stocking. He tears at the wrapping paper and shakes it about ferociously in his mouth, like he's trying to kill it.

I get a nice framed photo of the three of us from them both, which I immediately put on the mantle, and the traditional selection of things that smell nice. They open their gifts—a combination of cunningly disguised cash, video games and books—and I make us all pancakes.

Ben has us in hysterics after he calls his dad, when he tells us that Valerie bought him a Botox gift voucher for Christmas, and the morning passes in enjoyable laziness. Ruby, Rose, and their cousin Little Edie knock for us at about eleven, to see if Ben and Sophie 'want to come out and play'.

They might technically be adults, but they're wrapped up and out of the door like a shot. Of course they want to play! I take Gary to join in, and I find every child who is staying at the Rockery already out there. There are snowball fights and games of tag and a couple of them are even playing badminton. Every time the shuttlecock plummets into the snow, one of the dogs tries to run away with it.

We have been invited to Laura's for Christmas dinner, and I make my way over to Black Rose to see if I can help. She shoos me out of the kitchen with a tea towel, and I end up on the squishy sofa with Cherie instead. There are far worse places to be.

The whole day passes off pleasantly enough, a blur of food and laughter and intermittent bad dog behaviour. Midgebo makes off with a mouthful of pigs in blankets, but the turkey remains safe.

'I left those on the edge of the table on purpose,' says Laura as she dishes up. 'He's not happy unless he's managed to steal something, and it is Christmas.'

After lunch, Matt takes all the children outside to run off some steam, and us ladies find ourselves gathered in the big living room with a bottle of Baileys and an impressive selection of party hats from crackers.

The TV is on with the sound muted, and we all sit sipping our drinks staring at the moving pictures of a Christmassy-looking ballet on the screen. The post-dinner slump has taken hold, and the coal fire is making me sleepy.

'It's *The Nutcracker*, isn't it?' says Cherie, pointing at the television. 'Look, there's the Sugar Plum Fairy.'

'I don't know,' Becca replies, watching intently. 'I always wish I was into stuff like this. I always wish I was a bit more cultured. Like, I know this is a ballet and is supposed to be enriching, but in reality I'm just staring at the men's willies in their tights.'

We all splutter with laughter at that comment, because I have a sneaking suspicion that we've all been doing the same. I look around the room, at the faces of these women who not so long ago were strangers. Now they're my friends, and I have finally found my tribe, all thanks to

Sophie deciding to reply to a random job advert she saw on the internet. I am grateful, but the gratitude doesn't quite drown out the sadness that lies beneath the surface.

As the women all play a game of choosing which of the dancers they'd snog in a hot tub, my mind inevitably wanders. To Gabriel, and where he is and what he's doing. I hope he's not alone, and didn't wake up in a sleeping bag. I think about Norman and Marjorie, and what Christmases were like on the Pumpwell farm. I'd guess 'not a lot of fun' from seeing photos of their parents.

I think about all the years I've been lucky enough to spend with my own children, and even about Richie. This time next December they'll have a new addition, maybe one that is wearing a Baby's First Christmas outfit. He won't be able to smile at it, though, because of all the Botox.

I think about my own mum, and the way she used to look forward to watching the *Eastenders* Christmas Day special. As her illness drew her life smaller, she made the most of every pleasure that came her way. She used to hum along to the theme tune and pretend she was playing the drums during the 'duh-duh-duh' dramatic bit. 'They'll never beat that one where Dirty Den gave Angie the divorce papers on Christmas Day,' she'd announce, every single year.

'Come on, Max, which one is yours?' Cherie asks, dragging me back to the here and now. I stare at the still-muted television, and randomly pick one of the dancers.

'You can't have him!' Laura bleats. 'Becca's already picked him!'

'That's okay,' says Becca, winking at me. 'I'm happy to share. Looks like there's plenty of him to go around!'

This brings on more laughter, and more Baileys being poured. I put my glass to one side and stand up. They all stare at me, and I realise it looks like I'm about to make an announcement, or do a performance. Maybe a little pirouette.

'I'm going to see Belle,' I tell them. 'I realise she's a donkey and doesn't know it's Christmas, but still.'

'Actually, as a donkey, her ancestors played a pivotal role in the nativity story,' Becca points out. 'You should ride around on her and pretend you're the Virgin Mary.'

Anyone trying to ride around on Belle is pretty sure to end up dead, I suspect, but I pretend I'm giving it some thought just to entertain her.

I thank Laura for the lovely day and make my goodbyes. I've only had a very small glass of Baileys, so I'm still okay to drive. I'm usually happy to get tipsy at Christmas, but today I refused all offers of wine, partly because I didn't want to risk becoming a morose drunk, and partly because I suspected I was always going to do this. I want to see my framed photo collage go home, where it belongs.

I grab what I need from the house, and check on the kids on my way to the car. Matt and Sam, Becca's boyfriend, have organised some kind of rugby game, and I see Sophie tackle Ben to the snow with a spectacular ankle grab. All is well with the world.

The drive there is quiet, the winding country lanes completely empty of the traditional tractors, and as I pull into the courtyard I toot my horn. No idea why, there is nobody here but Belle, but it's become an ingrained habit I suppose.

I've brought her some ginger biscuits, which donkeys love according to the internet. As I lean against the fence, she ambles towards me letting out a bray-scream. I love the pattern of her hoofs against the snow, and smile as she approaches. I lay a biscuit flat on the palm of my hand, and she hoovers it up. I scratch her ears, and she gives me such a gentle nuzzle I don't even worry for the safety of my ear lobes.

I go inside, and it is so cold I shiver. I suppose he must have turned everything off before he left, and the kitchen doesn't feel the same without the warmth of the Aga circulating. Nothing feels the same, I think, as I make my way through to the living room. The donkey jug is empty, and the curtains are closed, and there's a thin sheen of dust on the shelves. While I'm here, I might give it a little spruce up. If I do end up seeing it on Rightmove, I don't want it to look grubby.

He never did get around to buying a tree, and this place is the exact opposite of Laura's home. That was cluttered and draped in tinsel and fairy lights, every available surface covered in dancing snowmen and a wind-up festive Elvis that sings Blue Christmas in a tinny voice.

I hammer in the picture hooks, and thread through the string. After a few minutes getting it perfectly even, I sit down on the sofa and admire my handiwork.

It looks perfect, I think, displayed above the cast-iron

fire surround. I hope that Norman and Marjorie would be pleased, and even if Gabriel never sees it, it feels like the right thing to have done. Maybe I'm mad, bringing a Christmas gift for a house, but I don't care. This was their childhood home, and even though life tore them apart, they're back here together now.

I get out my phone, and take a picture of it. I compose a little message to Gabriel, and rewrite it several times.

> Norman and your grandmother are waiting for you.

> So am I. I love you. Happy Christmas.

This is normally the stage at which I press delete, but somehow, as I sit here in this empty house I poured so much heart and soul into, I can't quite bring myself to do it. I stare at the words, at the jumble of feeling behind them, and before I can change my mind I hit send.

After that, I stare numbly at my phone for about seven hours … or at least that's what it feels like, as I sit here bundled up in my hat and scarf. Every time the screen starts to fade as though it's going to shut down, I tap it again to keep it alive. And every time I do, I see exactly the same result: nothing.

I know there are a million rational reasons why he wouldn't reply straight away. He could be abroad, and in a different time zone. The signal here is patchy, so it might not even have gone. He could be asleep, or in the bath, or on a plane. He might just not have noticed it, as he is not a phone person and regularly lets it run out of charge. Like I say, a million reasons.

Or, a nasty little voice whispers in my head, maybe he just doesn't want to reply. Maybe he's ignoring me. Maybe reading those words, seeing that I love him, has pushed him over the edge and even as we speak, he's contacting an estate agent and arranging to get the place valued so he never has to come back again.

I stare at Marjorie and Norman, and say, 'I'm being stupid, aren't I? So what if he never replies. You never replied to Marjorie, did you, after all those letters? But you still loved her. At least I haven't left it too late, right? I've opened the door and it's up to him if he walks through it or not. Anyway. No point in crying over sent messages.'

Neither of them answer, and I tell myself to get a grip. That it's not the end of the world; it only feels like it.

As I gather my things and stand up to leave, I notice something that is out of place. Just from the corner of my eye, I spot a single paperback back left out on the little side table. I pick it up, discover that it's a James Patterson thriller. Maybe it's what he was reading before he left, and he forgot to take it with him.

I flick through it, a weird part of me wanting to touch something that he has touched, and the scrap of paper he was using as a bookmark flutters out. I am trying to put it back in the right place when I notice that it is a receipt from a service station in Dover, dated the day before. I stare at it, screwing up my eyes as I double- and triple-check the tiny typed numbers. No matter how many times I look, it still says December 24th.

I am instantly on high alert, looking round like a bloodhound. Is he here? Was he here? Where is he? Am I pleased, or scared, or now deeply embarrassed about the message I just sent?

I climb to my feet, seeing the room in a new light. There is no sign of the fire being lit, and the house is cold, but that means nothing. This is Gabriel we're talking about, a man who has so little regard for his own comfort that he lived on microwave meals for more than a year. The house has an old-fashioned water boiler that you can switch on and off as needed, and he may well have been here, used it, and left again.

I go into the kitchen, and open the fridge. The little light comes on, and inside I see a four-pack of Carlsberg and the kind of pie you get at a garage. I slam the door shut, and say 'Shit!' out loud. He's here … or at least he has been.

I shout his name just in case, but get no response. Cautiously I creep upstairs, realising that he could simply be asleep after a long journey. I check the bathroom, and the smell hits me. Lemon and basil. He's not only been here, he's had a bath. My heart is racing by this point, and as I approach his room, I have no idea what I want to find. Part of me even wants to run while I still have the chance.

I open the door a few inches, and see that he is not there. The blast of disappointment tells me that no matter how conflicted I feel, I was hoping he would be, hoping to see him there huddled beneath the duvet, or even in his old sleeping bag. I have no idea what I'd have done if he was, but I am disappointed.

The bed is neatly made, and his rucksack has been dumped next to it. I see a few crumpled up sheets of his stupidly small note paper scattered across the duvet, and can't resist smoothing them out and looking at them.

There are four, and each one starts with the same words: 'Dear Max.'

One gets as far as 'I hope you're well,' and another says 'I just wanted to say,' before annoyingly tailing off without any indication at all of what he actually wanted to say. The fact that he's discarded them obviously means he wasn't happy with his words, and I wonder if this is his version of what I've been doing, writing messages and then deleting them.

What was it that he wanted to 'just say'? That he was leaving forever? That he's coming home? That he's joining the bloody circus? This is too frustrating, and I head back downstairs, forcing myself to be calm and think logically—to think at all.

I glance through the window, see that it is almost dark. The badgers, I think. Maybe he's gone to see how his mammal friends are doing. I get a torch from the cupboard, and grab one of the fleeces that he's left hanging on the back of the door. It's cold out there, and I didn't expect a trek through woodland. I'll probably trip over a branch and turn into a human ice cube.

It's a tricky hike through the snow and windswept trees, and more than a little creepy. I've become much more used to the countryside sounds in the last few months, but my city brain keeps setting off alarms about mad axemen and muggers. It's also a complete waste, because when I reach the hide, there's no sign of him. Or the badgers for that matter.

I sigh in frustration and pick my way in reverse over the fallen branches and snow-covered tree roots, all the way back to where I started. I check the garage at the side of the house, and see that his Land Rover is gone but there are marks on the floor from his tyres. No tracks outside, because fresh snow has fallen in the last few hours. I feel like a detective, a really rubbish one.

Belle lets out a low bellow in the darkness as I emerge from the garage. She's like a guard donkey. Even the mad axemen and muggers would run for their lives if they heard that.

I'm freezing cold by this stage and can't feel any of my extremities. I get into my car and put the blowers on, holding my chilled fingers in front of the heat. Okay, I think, let's be rational. I almost laugh out loud at that point, because none of this is rational. I feel hyped up and wired and desperate. I need to see him, even if it's just so that he can tell me it's over. I've lived in limbo since he left, and I can't go on like this.

As I gaze out of the windscreen at the pitch-black night sky, another idea forms. What if he's gone to the hill fort to look at the stars? Didn't he say it was his favourite thinking place? And judging by those scrunched up sheets of tiny paper, he's definitely been doing some thinking.

I check my phone again, and see that nobody has messaged or called. Which means the kids are still alive, at least.

I sit there and chew at my lip for a few moments wondering what to do, then reach a decision. I've come this far, I might as well see it through. Of course, there's every possibility he's simply in the pub, or even hiding from me at the back of the barn. This will be the last place I try, I tell myself, as I pull out of the gate.

It's a hefty drive in the dark and the snow, and it's only thanks to directions from my phone that I find it at all. I end up parking in a different spot, the map-reading lady who lives inside the satnav assuring me I am at the right hill fort but on the other side. I feel uncertain as I gaze up at a white mass ahead of me, concerned that I will tackle Dorset's version of Mount Everest and then find out I'm in the wrong place, or he's not even there at all.

I pull my hat down as far as it can go, puff in some breath for later and switch the torch on. The path from this side of the hill is just as winding as the other, but maybe a little less steep. I pass a few people on my way up, obviously heading home, and exchange Christmas greetings. They probably think I'm mad, and they may just be right. After that, it's just me and the grazing sheep looking at me curiously before they scatter.

When I'm almost at the top, I stop and look up. I look at that sky, at that dazzling landscape of stars, and sigh at how beautiful it is. I tell myself that whatever happens, those stars will still be there, and so will I. I've been so wrapped up in my quest that it is good to stand still for a moment, to try and let some of the calm up there in the heavens soak into my soul.

I carry on with my climb, and am exhausted by the time I reach the plateau. It's strangely bright up here, the moonlight and the glimmer of the stars reflecting from the flat white sheen of the snow. It's surreal, like walking through the Aurora Borealis.

I gaze around, scanning the area and doing a sweep with my torch. I'm about to give up when I spot someone, on the far side of the hill. I freeze solid for a moment, suddenly unable to move. It might not even be him—but then again, it might. And if it is, what am I going to say to him? I've been concentrating so much on finding him that I managed to leave myself unprepared for this part.

I've been acting a role since the day he put that letter through my door. I've been faking it, for the kids, my friends, even for myself. I've been pretending I am okay when I'm not okay at all. I know I will survive without him, but I don't want to just survive—I want to live. I want to be with him, to hold him and touch him and laugh with him. I want to accept him with all his flaws, and for him to do the same with me. I want it all, and even though I might not get it, I have to try. I realise that Cherie was right: life is too short for missing out on love. He might reject me, but I have to at least give him the chance, and not do the rejecting for him.

I set off, my boots crunching on the snow, filled with adrenaline and hope and dread in equal measures. Flurries of snowflakes fall around me and on me, but I don't even feel them.

As I get nearer, the figure stands up, and I know immediately that is him. He spots me, and starts to run in my direction. I run as well, feeling like I'm flying as I stumble and trip, desperate to reach him. I drop the torch and don't stop to retrieve it, leaving it casting an eerie gleam along the hilltop.

We reach the mid-way point, and I don't speak; I just throw my arms around him. Seeing him again is like a physical relief, the sudden lifting of a weight. All my emotional aches and pains clear away as soon as our bodies touch.

He grabs hold of me, pulls me tight, almost lifts me off my feet. My hands link behind his neck, and I snuggle into his chest. Everything is right with the world, at least for these few seconds. I smell the lemon and basil, and feel his heart beating fast beneath my cheek, and know that I was right to do this, whatever happens next.

'Max,' he mutters, squeezing me so hard I lose my breath, 'I was just coming to find you. I got back in the early hours, and didn't want to intrude on your Christmas. Then your message landed, and I decided I didn't care.'

I look up at him, the moonlight shining on his beautiful face, his hair tumbling out from beneath his beanie hat. I reach up, run my fingers along his cheekbone, and say: 'You could never intrude. You're part of me, Gabriel. I've missed you so much.'

'Me too. I went to see my dad, then was heading for

France. I made it as far as Calais and then got on the next ferry back. I realised I was miserable without you, and I don't want to be miserable anymore. I was running away, and I've been doing that for too long. I can't run away from myself, and I don't want to run away from you. You're the only thing in my life that makes sense. I love you too, Max, and if you want me, I promise I'll never leave again. I know I'm a mess, and I know I'm not easy, but if you want me, I'm yours.'

'I want you,' I reply without hesitation. 'I want your mess. I want everything about you. I know there will be problems, but aren't there always? You're a human being, not an android, and whatever problems there are, we can face them together. I love you, Gabriel, all of you.'

We stand and stare at each other for what seems like forever. I can't get enough of looking at his face, of touching him to make sure he is real. To make sure that he is actually here, on this moonlit hill, holding me close.

A big, fat snowflake lands right on the tip of my nose, and he laughs as he wipes it gently away. He lifts my chin so I am gazing up at him, and his eyes are shining.

'Shall we go home?' he says simply.

'I already am,' I reply.

He smiles, and his lips touch mine. We kiss like we have never kissed before, wrapped up in our blanket made entirely of stars.

Epilogue

Spring

It is April, and it is glorious. Sunshine pours from the sky; the trees are fresh and green, and the whole landscape around us is lush with new life.

The badgers have produced three more cubs, and we spend hours together watching them play, small bundles of fur tumbling around the woodland.

We have moved into the farmhouse, and settled into the rhythms of life together. Sophie will be heading to Cardiff for university in September, but for now, she seems happy here with her friends and her little job at the café.

Laura is already looking for a replacement, because I have sadly had to resign from my job there. I still help out when they need it, but I am concentrating on my new enterprise. The Rockery is a work-in-progress, and I have sold the house in Birmingham.

Gabriel and I are combining our skills, and have bought our first project together: a run-down cottage further down the coast that comes complete with spectacular sea views, rising damp and yet another avocado bath suite. Between us we have everything we need to transform it into a beautiful home, and I am so excited about it. I am finally living my Rightmove dream.

Today, it is my birthday, and we are hosting a party. Gabriel has been predictably gruff about it, and still feels uncomfortable when his territory is invaded. He's here, though, looking all sexy and Heathcliff as he tries to make small talk with our guests. Every now and then he catches me staring at him across the room, and gives me The Look. The one that makes my insides melt.

He surprised us both in the New Year by deciding to see a counsellor. Once a week, he disappears off in the Land Rover to talk to a complete stranger about his feelings. It is literally the most un-Gabriel-like thing I could ever have imagined, but it seems to be helping. There is a gradual sense of lightening in him, of pressures lifting. Clouds clearing. I am proud of him, and tell him so at every possible opportunity.

It's not changed him completely, though, and I know he was secretly reluctant to throw open the doors of his home to the entire Budbury collective … but he did it anyway. The house is looking beautiful, and I finally found that perfect rug. Norman and Marjorie look down from the mantlepiece, and more pictures have been added, especially of Belle, with her new friend, Beast.

Beast is a younger male, and incredibly submissive by nature. Matt helped us find him at a rescue centre, and despite his name, he is actually very handsome. He doesn't seem to mind Belle bossing him around, and she has certainly mellowed since he arrived. They're a bonded pair, just like me and Gabriel.

I find Laura standing by the fence to the paddock, a carrot in her hand and a nervous look on her face.

'I'm worried Belle will bite my hand off, and that would make baking a lot more tricky,' she says.

'It's always a possibility. I'll distract her, you do Beast instead.'

She laughs as we feed the donkeys, then turns to look back at the house. The garden around us is starting to blossom, and the wildflower meadow is beginning to show signs of colour. There is chatter and laughter coming from inside, and the serenade of birdsong hovering in the background.

'It's gorgeous,' she says. 'The house. It's like you've brought it back to life.'

'That's exactly what we aimed to do,' I reply smiling. 'And in the process, we accidentally brought each other back to life as well.'

'I know. It's magical, isn't it? I was thinking that the other day, when I was drafting up an advert looking for someone to replace Sophie. I wonder who we'll get next, and what will happen with them?'

'I have no idea, but I'd guess something special. Thank

you … for everything. For talking me into this. For knowing it was right for me before even I did.'

'You're welcome, all part of the Comfort Food Café service. Right, I need to start wrangling the girls and get home. They're probably still sitting in silence in the kitchen.'

Ruby and Rose are desperate to see the badger cubs, but after we explained that they had to be completely quiet if they did, they've been proving they're capable of doing that by refusing to speak ever since they got here.

She disappears off into the house, and passes Gabriel on his way out to find me. Belle brays at him in warning, and he keeps his distance. She's not mellowed *that* much.

'It's gone well, hasn't it?' he says, sounding surprised as he drops a kiss on my forehead. 'I never thought I'd have a birthday party here.'

'Well, now you have. Another milestone. Are you okay? I know it doesn't come naturally to you, having them here.'

'No, it doesn't … but I have a secret coping mechanism.'

He slides his hands around my waist, and tugs me into him. I squeal a little, delighted, and ask, 'What is it?'

'When I'm in a room full of people and I'm feeling uncomfortable, I just find you. When I look at you, everyone else disappears. They're just background noise. You're the only person I need. I love you, birthday girl.'

Acknowledgments

I can't tell you how much I enjoyed writing this book. Being back in Budbury and at the Comfort Food Cafe felt like coming home, and I hope you enjoyed Max and Gabriel's story. It came from the heart, and I think they both really deserved their happy ending.

Real life, of course, is never so simple – including my own. Losing myself in the Cafe community was a privilege, and one I couldn't have enjoyed without a lot of support at home. Thank you as ever to my family – especially my children, Keir, Daniel and Louisa.

I am lucky enough to have friends just as good as those in this book. There are too many to list (see, told you I was lucky!), but a few to mention in particular are Sandra Shennan (for the morning beach walks and sanity saving chats), Paula Woosey, Pamela Hoey, Ade Blackburn, Karen Murphy and Helen Shaw.

Thanks also to fellow writers and fantastic pals Milly Johnson, Jane Costello, Miranda Dickinson, Clare Williams and Rachael Tinniswood. This is a strange job and it would be even stranger without this gang to talk to. I'd also like to thank the super supportive bloggers and reviewers who spread the word about my stories, especially the Friendly

Book Community on Facebook, which totally lives up to its name.

Coming back to Budbury also means I got to work with the brilliant Charlotte Ledger, my editor and friend, as well as Bonnie Macleod and the team at One More Chapter – thank you for all your help. Behind the scenes, big thanks to my agent Hayley Steed and Mina Yakinya at Janklow & Nesbit. I might have written the book, but these people helped put it into your hands.

I'd love for you to stay in touch – please join me on my Facebook page, or sign up to my newsletter. I don't send out too many, I promise!

YOUR NUMBER ONE STOP

ONE MORE CHAPTER

FOR PAGETURNING BOOKS

The author and One More Chapter would like to thank everyone who contributed to the publication of this story...

Analytics
James Brackin
Abigail Fryer
Maria Osa

Audio
Fionnuala Barrett
Ciara Briggs

Contracts
Sasha Duszynska
Lewis

Design
Lucy Bennett
Fiona Greenway
Liane Payne
Dean Russell

Digital Sales
Lydia Grainge
Hannah Lismore
Emily Scorer

Editorial
Arsalan Isa
Charlotte Ledger
Federica Leonardis
Bonnie Macleod
Janet Marie Adkins
Ajebowale Roberts
Jennie Rothwell

Harper360
Emily Gerbner
Jean Marie Kelly
emma sullivan
Sophia Wilhelm

International Sales
Peter Borcsok
Bethan Moore

Marketing & Publicity
Chloe Cummings
Emma Petfield

Operations
Melissa Okusanya
Hannah Stamp

Production
Denis Manson
Simon Moore
Francesca Tuzzeo

Rights
Vasiliki Machaira
Rachel McCarron
Hany Sheikh
Mohamed
Zoe Shine

The HarperCollins Distribution Team

The HarperCollins Finance & Royalties Team

The HarperCollins Legal Team

The HarperCollins Technology Team

Trade Marketing
Ben Hurd

UK Sales
Laura Carpenter
Isabel Coburn
Jay Cochrane
Sabina Lewis
Holly Martin
Erin White
Harriet Williams
Leah Woods

And every other essential link in the chain from delivery drivers to booksellers to librarians and beyond!

The Comfort Food Café is perched on a windswept clifftop at what feels like the edge of the world, serving up the most delicious cream teas

For tourists and locals alike, the ramshackle cafe overlooking the beach is a beacon of laughter, companionship, and security – a place like no other.

A place that offers friendship as a daily special, and where a hearty welcome is always on the menu.

Available in paperback, eBook, and audio!

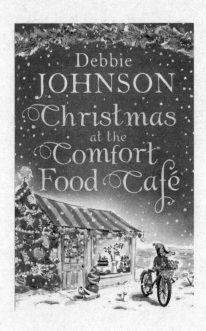

Becca Fletcher has always hated Christmas but she has her reasons for being Little Miss Grinch…

Now, though, she can't avoid her version of ho-ho-hell – because she's travelling to the Comfort Food Café to spend the festive season with her sister Laura and her family. She's expecting all kinds of very merry torture.

Little does Becca know that the café is like no other place on earth. Perched on a snow-covered hill, it's a place where her Christmas miracle really could happen – if only she can let it…

Available in paperback, eBook, and audio!

Welcome to the cosy Comfort Food Café, where there's kindness in every cup of hot chocolate and the menu is sprinkled with love and happiness...

Moving to the little village of Budbury, Zoe hopes the crisp Dorset sea breeze and gentle pace of life will be a fresh start for her and her goddaughter, Martha.

Luckily for them both, the friendly community at the café provide listening ears, sage advice, shoulders to cry on, and some truly excellent carrot cake...

Available in paperback, eBook, and audio!

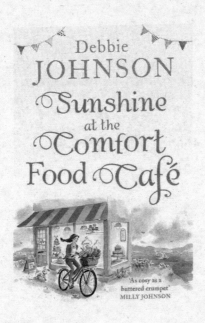

Debbie
JOHNSON
Sunshine
at the
Comfort
Food Café

'As cosy as a
buttered crumpet'
MILLY JOHNSON

*My name is Willow Longville. I live in a village called Budbury
on the stunning Dorset coast with my mum Lynnie, who
sometimes forgets who I am. I'm a waitress at the Comfort Food
Café, which is really so much more than a café … it's my home.*

For Willow, the ramshackle café overlooking the beach,
together with its warm-hearted community, offers
friendship as a daily special and always has a hearty
welcome on the menu. But when a handsome stranger
blows in on a warm spring breeze, Willow soon realises that
her quiet country life will be changed forever.

Available in paperback, eBook, and audio!

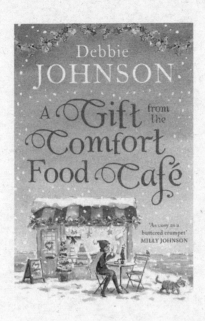

Return to Budbury for a Christmas to remember...

Christmas has never been Katie Seddon's favourite time of year. Whilst everyone else shares memories of families coming together and festive number ones, the soundtrack to Katie's childhood wasn't quite so merry.

But since she moved to the village of Budbury on the gorgeous Dorset coast, Katie and her baby son have found a new family. A family who have been brought together by life's unexpected roads and the healing magic of a slice of cake and a cupful of kindness at the Comfort Food Café.

Available in paperback, eBook, and audio!

Wedding bells ring out as the Comfort Food Café and its cosy community are gearing up for a big celebration...

But Auburn Longville doesn't have time for that! Between caring for her poorly mum and running the local pharmacy, life is busy enough – and it's about to get busier. Chaos arrives in the form of a figure from her past putting her quaint village life and new relationship with gorgeous Finn Jensen in jeopardy.

Settle in for a slice of wedding cake at the Comfort Food Café – a place where nobody ever wants to leave.

Available in paperback, eBook, and audio!

YOUR NUMBER ONE STOP

ONE MORE CHAPTER

FOR PAGETURNING BOOKS

One More Chapter is an
award-winning global
division of HarperCollins.

Sign up to our newsletter to get our
latest eBook deals and stay up to date
with our weekly Book Club!
<u>Subscribe here.</u>

Meet the team at
<u>www.onemorechapter.com</u>

Follow us!

 <u>@OneMoreChapter_</u>
 <u>@OneMoreChapter</u>
 <u>@onemorechapterhc</u>

Do you write unputdownable fiction?
We love to hear from new voices.
Find out how to submit your novel at
<u>www.onemorechapter.com/submissions</u>